Am I delirious? Am I dying after all?

Breathing slowly and deeply, Roy took stock. Nope. Not delirious. There *was* a woman in bed with him. He could feel the warmth of her breath on his skin, the dove-soft tickle of her hair. With the utmost care, he turned his head. A deliciously feminine scent drifted to his nostrils. Ignoring the shooting pains rocketing through his skull, he tensed his face and neck muscles and aimed his eyes downward.

A vision of tumbled blond met his gaze—winter grass touched with sunshine.

He thought, *My God, it's my angel. I didn't dream her.*

She's real.

Dear Reader,

Welcome to the New Year—and to another month of fabulous reading. We've got a lineup of books you won't be able to resist, starting with the latest CAVANAUGH JUSTICE title from RITA® Award winner Marie Ferrarella. *Dangerous Disguise* takes an undercover hero, adds a tempting heroine, then mixes them up with a Mob money-laundering operation run out of a restaurant. It's a recipe for irresistibility.

Undercover Mistress is the latest STARRS OF THE WEST title from multi-RITA® Award-winning author Kathleen Creighton. A desperate rescue leads to an unlikely alliance between a soap opera actress who's nowhere near as ditsy as everyone assumes and a federal agent who's finally discovered he has a heart. In *Close to the Edge*, Kylie Brant takes a bayou-born private detective and his high-society boss, then forces them onto a case where "hands off" turns at last into "hands on." In Susan Vaughan's *Code Name: Fiancée,* when agent Vanessa Wade has to pose as the fiancée of wealthy Nick Markos, it's all for the sake of national security. Or is it? Desire writer Michelle Celmer joins the Intimate Moments roster with *Running on Empty*, an amnesia story that starts at the local discount store and ends up…in bed. Finally, Barbara Phinney makes her second appearance in the line with *Necessary Secrets*, introducing a pregnant heroine and a sexy cop—but everyone's got secrets to hide.

Enjoy them all, then come back next month for more of the best and most exciting romantic reading around.

Yours,

Leslie Wainger

Leslie J. Wainger
Executive Editor

Please address questions and book requests to:
Silhouette Reader Service
U.S.: 3010 Walden Ave., P.O. Box 1325, Buffalo, NY 14269
Canadian: P.O. Box 609, Fort Erie, Ont. L2A 5X3

Undercover Mistress
KATHLEEN CREIGHTON

INTIMATE MOMENTS™

Published by Silhouette Books

America's Publisher of Contemporary Romance

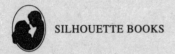 **SILHOUETTE BOOKS**

ISBN 0-373-27410-6

UNDERCOVER MISTRESS

Copyright © 2005 by Kathleen Creighton-Fuchs

This edition published by arrangement with Harlequin Books S.A.

® and TM are trademarks of Harlequin Books S.A., used under license.
Trademarks indicated with ® are registered in the United States Patent
and Trademark Office, the Canadian Trade Marks Office and in other
countries.

Visit Silhouette Books at www.eHarlequin.com

Printed in U.S.A.

Books by Kathleen Creighton

KATHLEEN CREIGHTON

has roots deep in the California soil but has relocated to South Carolina. As a child, she enjoyed listening to old-timers' tales, and her fascination with the past only deepened as she grew older. Today, she says she is interested in everything—art, music, gardening, zoology, anthropology and history, but people are at the top of her list. She also has a lifelong passion for writing, and now combines her two loves in romance novels.

Chapter 1

Celia Cross was of the opinion that if you had to suffer from insomnia, there couldn't be a better place for it than Malibu.

On those clear nights when she found herself wide-awake at three in the morning, there was the moon path beckoning just beyond her beach house windows, stretching off across the sea like a highway to China. And though she lacked the courage to follow the lure of that glittering path, there were still the seemingly unending expanses of beach to explore at a pace of her own choosing. At three in the morning, there was only the whispering surf for company, and little likelihood of any human presence, friendly or otherwise, happening by to intrude on her solitude.

At the same time, there was just enough of a civilized presence in the dark hulks and occasional lights from the beachfront houses of the rich and famous to reassure her she wasn't entirely alone. And on nights like this one, when the fog lay thick as cotton batting along the water's edge, enveloping her in its cocoon of cold silence, it was easy to imagine what it might feel like to be the last human soul alive on earth.

With or without fog, Celia never felt nervous about walking or running alone on the beach in the wee hours of the morning. To be truthful, nowadays there wasn't much of anything—anything that walked, swam, slithered or flew, anyway—she did fear, though she had a sense that fact hadn't pleased the therapist when she'd told him during the first months after the accident.

"Why do you think that is?" the doctor had asked probingly in the annoying manner of psychotherapists. Celia had replied with something flip and meaningless because, in the annoying way psychotherapists had of sometimes illuminating unwelcome truths, deep down she'd known the real answer: *Maybe I'm not afraid of anything because I really don't give a damn.*

Then she thought, mentally smacking herself like a misbehaving puppy, *Bad girl. Bad thoughts.*

Pushing back the hood of her sweatshirt, she broke into a determined run, veering onto the sheet of firm wet sand left by the retreating tide. A moment later, though, limited visibility forced her back to a walk to keep from tripping over the piles of rubbery kelp that littered the sand. There was more of it than usual tonight, dredged up from the undersea forests just offshore by some tropical storm way off in the Pacific. There'd been big surf earlier in the week.

An especially large clump of debris loomed ahead of her in the fog, and she angled her path to go around it. Only a few yards still separated her from the mass when she halted suddenly, and her heartbeat quickened. Had it been a trick of her eyes, her vivid imagination? Or had something in that tangled pile *moved?*

She stood motionless, shivers of excitement cascading through her as her eyes strained to penetrate the darkness and fog. Thoughts of sick or injured sea lions crossed her mind—people did find them on these beaches now and then, though she herself had never been so lucky. She'd heard, too, of beachcombers finding pelicans or sea gulls tangled in fishing line, and even dolphins and whales beached on the sand.

What if it is *something alive…sick…hurt? What do I do?*

Here she was, alone on a beach at three in the morning, and she didn't have her cell phone with her. How stupid was that?

She didn't recall her brain telling them to, but her feet were moving again, carrying her toward that dark and shapeless mass. Nervous but curious, wishing she had, at the very least, a flashlight, she leaned cautiously closer, peering into the pile. Okay, there was a whole lot of kelp—the smell of it was sharp and raw in her nostrils. And…oh well, shoot, it was only driftwood after all—a big piece, gnarled and misshapen, like the trees from an enchanted forest. Was that all it had been? Just a piece of *driftwood?* With a hiss that was half relief, half disappointment, she straightened, laughing silently at herself and her overwrought imagination.

But—about to move on, once again she froze. Okay, no doubt about it. A branch of that "driftwood" had definitely *moved.*

She bent closer to examine it, holding her breath, poised to leap back out of danger at a split-second's notice—and that was when she heard it, barely audible above the hiss and sigh of the surf. A sound. *A low sound, like a moan.*

She sucked back a gasp, and again without conscious decision, found that her hand was moving…reaching toward…whatever it was that was buried in all that debris. Nervously, she pulled it back. *Chicken, Celia!* Shifting, she edged herself closer, then put out her hand again—slowly, this time, and carefully…until she touched—*Oh, ick!* Her fingers had touched…*something.* Something cold and clammy. And smooth. It felt like…*skin.* Not scales or feathers or fur, but skin. *Human skin.*

Horror washed over her, as shocking, as breathtaking as if one of the waves curling onto the sand a few feet away had crashed over her head. She opened her mouth to scream, but the sound that emerged was more like a whimper. *Oh God, oh God, oh God, it's a body—a human body. Oh God.*

Okay, but not a *dead* body. She'd seen it move—hadn't she? She'd heard a groan. *She had.* Could something that cold, that still, possibly be *alive?*

Whimpering to herself, Celia tore with her hands at the masses of kelp until she was kneeling close beside the inert shape. Her hands explored, gingerly at first, and then, having so far encountered nothing particularly gruesome, with more confidence. Her search revealed a head covered with short, damp hair, a jaw rough with beard stubble. *Okay, obviously a man.*

She put her fingers against the side of his neck just below the jaw, the way she'd seen it done countless times on movie and TV screens—the way she'd even done it on camera herself once or twice, come to think of it. She searched for a pulse—and went clammy with a weird combination of relief and panic when she found one.

At least he's alive!

Oh God. He's alive.

Which meant it was now up to her to see he stayed that way. *What do I do now?*

Call 911, obviously.

Except she didn't have her cell phone with her. Which meant she was going to have to leave the guy lying here on the sand and run back to her house to call for help. But what if he died while she was gone? What if he was badly hurt, bleeding to death even now?

"Badly hurt" was probably a given, considering he was lying face down and unconscious. Other than that… Quelling panic, she proceeded with her inventory. He seemed to be naked from the waist up; below that were sodden trousers—no, shorts—and below that, bony masculine legs that, as far as she could tell— relentlessly squashing horrifying images of shark attack victims—were intact. No shoes or socks, which, she supposed, wasn't surprising, given the fact he'd almost certainly just come out of the ocean.

She ran her hands over a back dense with muscle—she could feel the indentation of spine between hard, rounded ridges, heavily crusted with sand. Moving her hands outward from there, she felt a rib cage…shoulder blades…all well-padded with that resilient, though frigid, muscle. Her hands slipped down the sides of the torso—and recoiled. Cold horror sliced through her.

Simultaneously, the man uttered a sound, something between a gasp and a groan.

"Oh God," Celia said in a breathy squeak, "I'm so sorry." Shaking, she held up her hand in the darkness, trying to see what it was on her fingers. Something sticky. Sandy and sticky. But of course, even in the dark and the fog, even without seeing it, she knew what it was. What it had to be. She touched the man's back and whispered it again. "I'm sorry...I'm so sorry."

So, clearly, the man *was* injured. *And* bleeding. There was no way around it—she was going to have to go for help. But to leave him lying here like this—alone...so still...so cold...

Impulsively, she pulled off her sweatshirt and laid it across his naked back. As she tucked the hood around his neck, she leaned close to whisper brokenly in his ear. "Hold on, okay? You're going to be all right. I'm going to get help. I'll be right back—I promise. Don't die, okay? I'll be right back."

She crouched, leg muscles tensed like a runner in starting blocks, but instead of rising, she sucked in air and froze once more. Something had clamped around her wrist, something cold and hard as steel. But it wasn't steel. It was human flesh. *A hand.* A whisper, faint as wind-driven sand, stirred across her cheek.

"Please...help...me."

Something—an emotion completely unknown to her—trembled through her chest. Tears—of nervousness? excitement? relief?—sprang from her eyes. "Yes, yes—I will, I'll get you some help. I will." She was babbling, half weeping. "I have to go, now, okay? But I'll be back, I promise—" Again, she tried to rise.

Where the poor man got the strength, she couldn't imagine, but his grip on her wrist tightened, holding her where she was. Beneath the sweatshirt she'd placed over them, the powerful shoulders bunched and succeeded in lifting his head barely an inch off the sand. His voice rose in volume to a raspy croak. "Don't...call...police."

"No, of course not," Celia babbled, thinking only to soothe him. "You need an ambulance. Paramedics—"

"No!" The croak became a cry of desperation. "Don't…tell… *anyone.* Nobody…can know. They…can't…know. *Promise.*"

The grip on Celia's wrist became painful. "Okay, okay, I *promise,*" she gasped. "No police—okay?"

"Promise…" The word sighed away into a whisper as his grip relaxed and his head dropped back onto the sand.

O-kay, she thought, shaken. What was *that* all about? She sat back on her heels, rubbing her wrist and chewing on her lip. *No cops? They can't know? Can't know what?*

Obviously, the man was delirious—out of his head. Obviously, she had to call 911, because if she didn't, the guy was going to die right here on the beach. She had no choice.

She ran a hand over her face and let out a breath that was almost a groan. Okay, maybe she'd been in television *way* too long, but dramatic scenarios of every sort were running on fast-forward through her mind. Why would somebody in this kind of shape not want the police involved, unless they had good reason not to? Was this guy some kind of criminal? Was he running from the police? What if the police were the ones who'd shot him?

Celia, get a grip. You don't even know that's a gunshot wound.

But…somehow she did. A bullet, or maybe a knife—anyway, she *knew* that wound in the man's side, the wound her fingers had touched, was the result of violence—human, not animal— and that it had been deliberate, not accidental. And sure, the man lying helpless in the kelp might be a dangerous criminal, but something told her he wasn't.

And if he isn't a criminal?

More scenarios sped across the video screen in her mind. What if he truly was in mortal danger, but for some reason couldn't risk letting the cops know about it? Soap operas and television dramas and action movies were full of stories about good guys with good reasons not to involve the police. Just because those particular stories were fiction didn't mean it couldn't happen in real life. Well, it *didn't.*

She cleared her throat and gingerly touched the man's shoulder. "Hey, listen—can you walk?" She waited, but there was no answer, not even a moan.

"*O-kay,* I'll take that as a no." Swearing under her breath, she pushed herself to her feet. Muscles and bones only recently healed screamed in protest, and she took a moment to placate them with some hurried shakes and stretches before, with a worried look back at the still, dark lump on the sand, she set off back the way she'd come. After the first few plodding steps, she broke into a run.

It wasn't all that far to her place—perhaps a hundred yards or so, though it seemed like a mile. Her legs were on fire and she had a stitch in her side by the time she left wet, packed sand to angle uphill across the soft, deep powder toward the carriage lanterns she'd left burning on the deck to light her way home in the fog. The lamps gave off a weird coppery glow that was more eerie than welcoming, and Celia couldn't suppress a shiver as she thought of the man she'd left lying back there on the beach and the words he'd spoken in a raspy whisper, like death: *Don't tell anyone…they can't know.*

At the bottom of the wooden steps she hesitated, put one foot on the first step, then hesitated some more. *Don't…tell…anyone.* Well, dammit, she had to tell *someone.* She sure as hell couldn't do this alone.

She didn't consciously make the decision. But one second, she was standing there, about to go up the steps and into her house where there was a telephone and all sorts of trained help only a three-push-button call away, because that was what any sane person would do. And the next, she was doing an about-face, and jogging past her own deck and turning into the narrow canyon between the shadowy forests of wooden pilings that supported her deck and the one next door. She clattered up her neighbor's steps and onto his deck and then she was pounding on his sliding glass door with her fist; it was too late to change her mind.

She waited, listening to the competing rhythms of the surf and her thumping heartbeat. *Come on, Doc...come on...*

She cupped her hands around her eyes and peered through the glass, and she could see a light from somewhere throwing furniture shadows across a woven grass carpet. *Dammit, Cavendish, I know you're in there.* He had to be—at three in the morning, where else would he go? And most likely asleep—or dead-to-the-world drunk—she thought, as she pounded again, then grasped hold of the handle and jerked it hard, prepared to go in and roust him physically, if necessary.

She was only mildly surprised when the door slid open a foot or so; Malibu Colony people were notoriously careless about locking their ocean-front doors.

She stuck her head through the crack and called hoarsely, "Hey, Doc—you awake? Doc—"

She broke off as a short, stocky bathrobe-clad figure shuffled into view, carrying a wine bottle and a glowing cigarette in one hand and turning on lights with the other as he came toward her.

Jowly cheeks covered with a quarter of an inch of reddish-gray stubble creased in a wry grin when he saw Celia.

"Shoulda known it'd be you—my lovely fellow insomniac," he drawled in a British accented voice that, thankfully, was only a little slurred. He pulled the door wider and flicked his cigarette in the general direction of the water. "Come in, sweetheart, come in. Join me in a glass." He held up the bottle and frowned at it. "Oh, hell—this bottle's pretty well killed. But, there's more where it came from."

"Thanks—not now—I can't." She spoke rapidly, breathlessly, as she caught hold of his sleeve and began to pull him across the deck. "Come quick—you have to help me. I need you. *Hurry!*"

Hauling back against the tow like a balky mule, her neighbor managed to slow her down enough to extricate himself from her clutches. As he huffily adjusted his bathrobe over his barrel chest, he peered at her in the lamp-lit murk, taking in her bare arms and torso, which, at the moment was covered only by a stretch-cotton sports bra.

"You've actually been out in this crap? Oh, *don't* tell me— what'd you do, find a beached seal? You don't want to mess with those things, sweetheart, they can bite your arm off. Come on in here and call animal control. Better yet," he added, doing a lurching about-face and heading back toward the doorway, "wait for morning."

"Not a seal," Celia gasped, grabbing again at his arm. "It's a man."

He halted, staring at her along his shoulder as if he weren't sure he'd heard her right. Shadows made the bags under his eyes seem even larger than usual. "A what?"

She nodded rapidly. "He's hurt. Badly, I think. I need—"

"Oh, Lord. Celia." His face seemed to crumple like a deflating bag. He closed his eyes and lifted the wine bottle to press it against his forehead. "For God's sake, leave me out of it. Call nine-eleven. You know I can't—"

"That's just it. He doesn't want cops or paramedics. He was insistent about that. Frantic, actually…"

Peter Cavendish, known to his Malibu neighbors as Doc— and to most of the rest of the world as the physician responsible for prescribing the drugs that had led to several well-publicized addictions and one tragic overdose, now permanently stripped of his license to practice medicine—heaved a sigh that was heavily mixed with swearing. He opened his eyes and leveled a glare at her. "I don't believe this. You know what that means, don't you? Means the guy's got to be either crazy or crooked."

"But what if he's not?" Celia said stubbornly. "Come on, Doc, I figured if anybody'd understand about not wanting to get the cops involved…"

"Sure. Right." Doc gave another sigh, this one of resignation. "You know this is blackmail, don't you? Okay, *okay.* I'll have a look at the bloke. But I'm warning you—if he looks like he's in any danger of dying right away, we're calling nine-eleven and leaving me out of it. Understand?"

Light-headed with relief, Celia nodded.

Pausing long enough to stuff the wine bottle into a potted bird of paradise plant, Cavendish followed her down the steps.

"How far away is this guy?" he asked when he caught up with her. Hobbling awkwardly as his bare feet made contact with shells or rocks buried in the sand, he hissed a sibilant obscenity and added, with a sideways glance at Celia's feet, "How can you stand to jog barefooted?"

"I have eyes in my feet. And," she panted, "it beats getting sand in your shoes. It's not that far—only seems like it because of the fog. There. See?" She pointed as, at that moment, an obliging air current parted the fog like a curtain, revealing several piles of kelp ahead on the smooth slope of wet sand. Including the one that was larger and bulkier than all the rest.

When she saw it, her heart gave a sickening lurch and fear rose in her throat. *Oh, please, let him be alive,* she thought as she broke into a run. *I can't be responsible for another death—I can't.*

The man was lying where she'd left him—*exactly* as she'd left him; he didn't appear to have moved at all. Chilled and shaking, Celia dropped to her knees beside him and pressed her fingers against the side of his neck. Against flesh that seemed to bear no more signs of life than molded plastic. She held her breath and then, deafened by her own heartbeat, groaned in anguish, "Oh, God, I can't find a pulse."

"I'd be greatly astonished if you did, in that particular spot," Doc said acidly, taking her by the arms and moving her to one side. He dropped heavily to one knee beside the body and put his fingers just—she'd have sworn—where hers had been. After a moment, he nodded to himself as if satisfied by what he'd felt, and Celia let out the breath she'd been holding.

Crouched in the reeking kelp, she watched the doctor's hands move quickly and confidently over the man's body, following much the same path hers had taken so timidly a short while ago.

"The only wound I could find is on his side, there—on the right," she said when she was sure she could speak without squeaking.

Doc nodded brusquely and lifted one side of the sweatshirt Celia had spread across the man's back. After a moment he muttered, as if to himself, "Okay...this appears to be a gunshot wound...small entrance, by the feel of it. Can't seem to find the exit. Give me a hand here—I want you to help me roll him. Take his hips...just like that."

Thrilled to be doing something helpful, Celia hitched forward, put her hands where the doctor told her to and braced herself.

"Okay, nice and easy now." Taking the man by the shoulders he gently, carefully turned him. "That's good. Great. Now, let's see. Ah, yes. Here it is—see? Huh—damned odd place for an exit wound..."

Though she tried, Celia couldn't see much of anything in the foggy darkness. She shivered, conscious for the first time of the chill and the damp, and the fact that she was wearing shorts and a sports bra and nothing else. Hugging herself to keep her teeth from chattering, she said, "How bad is it?"

The former doctor grunted and sat back on his heels. "Well, I suppose the good news is, it's—as they say on television—a through-and-through. And, quite amazingly, the bullet—or whatever—doesn't seem to have hit anything vital. On the other hand, he's bound to have lost a good bit of blood, and floating around in the Pacific for God knows how long hasn't done him any good, either. To put it in terms you'd understand, he's weak from blood loss, suffering from hypothermia, probably in shock, any one of which ought to have killed him and still could. The man needs to be in a hospital, love. Now. Yesterday." He lurched to his feet with another grunt and a groan. "You need to call—"

"No!" Celia was on her feet, too, reaching across the unconscious man's body to clutch at the sleeve of the doctor's robe. "*No.* I promised him. I *promised.* Look, we can—" She looked around wildly. "Okay. Here's what we do. We carry him back to my place. You don't have to do anything—just help me get him there, that's all. I'll...I'll take full responsibility. You can show me what to do—you don't have to touch him. Nobody will have to know—"

"Celia, darling. Sweetheart. I don't know how to break this to you, but you're not a doctor. Even if you did used to play one on TV."

"A nurse," Celia snapped. "I was a *nurse,* not a doctor." Realizing that wasn't exactly a plus, she added hurriedly, "Anyway, you said the bullet didn't hit anything vital. Seems to me it ought to be pretty well cleaned out, after soaking in salt water for who knows how long. Salt's good, right? And you can get me some bandages, can't you? Some antibiotics?" She gripped his arm and shook it. "Come *on,* Doc—dammit, help me! Please."

For a long five-count he continued to resist, swearing softly but vehemently. Then, shaking out of her grasp, muttering about the impossibility of saying no to a half-naked woman, he bent over and thrust his hands under the unconscious man's shoulders. "All right—I know I'm going to regret this. But it's for damn sure not doing him any good lying here whilst we argue about it. Don't just stand there, pick up his feet."

Celia hurried to comply, but discovered it was easier to say than do. Picking up his feet failed to raise the man's butt so much as an inch off the sand. Finally, she managed to achieve her desired purpose by planting herself between his legs and hooking her arms just above the knees, then hoisting them up high enough to rest on the top curve of her hips.

"Good...Lord," Doc gasped as they staggered back up the beach with their burden, "the guy's *heavy*—must weigh one-eighty, at least."

Celia, still trying to keep the middle third of the man's body from dragging on the sand, had her jaws clenched tightly shut and didn't reply. Clearly, carrying a grown man's deadweight, even for two people, was a lot harder than they made it look on TV. She also decided she must have seriously underestimated the distance between her house and that pile of driftwood and kelp.

Surely, no NFL team ever labored longer or harder to traverse a hundred yards of ground.

Still, somehow, after stopping several times on the way to grab, breathlessly cursing, at painful gulps of cold, astringent sea air, Celia caught sight of the carriage lanterns' rusty glow through the fog. Doc, she noted, was wheezing alarmingly as he hitched himself backward up the steps leading to her deck.

"You okay?" she asked, gritting her teeth and sweating rivers in spite of the cold. "You know…it's gonna kind of…defeat the purpose…if after all this…I have to…call 911…for *you.*"

"Don't worry about me," Doc grunted. "Just…wouldya try not to crack the guy's backbone on these damn steps? Are you *looking* for a lawsuit?"

Celia snorted—and was appalled when the snort turned into laughter. Where *that* had come from, she had no idea—stress reaction, she supposed. Here she was carrying half of a man's deadweight—*oh, bad word choice, Celia!*—in her arms, for God's sake. A seriously wounded man, moreover, and God only knew how he'd gotten that way. What she really wanted to do right then was collapse on those steps and give in to a colossal fit of the shakes.

But, of course, she couldn't. Wouldn't. Not now. Not yet. She clamped her teeth together and set her jaw and from some unknown storehouse found strength to take one…more…step.

Then, miraculously, they were in Celia's living room. In a half crouch, managing to maintain her hold on the man's legs, she reached behind her to pull the sliding door shut, and all at once it was warm and dry and still. The surf thunder became a distant whisper beyond the glass and the fog.

"Where do you want him?" Doc's question was a gasp.

Celia didn't answer. The lights she'd left on in the room were low and soft, but they were enough to give her a good look, her first clear look, at what she'd been carrying so blithely, so casually. Something clenched inside her, and her body went cold from the inside out.

She whispered soundlessly, "Oh, my God…"

Out there in the dark and the fog, he'd been only…well, a *body*. A human being, obviously. A man, sure—but anonymous. Impersonal. Even not quite real. But now…oh God, now he had a face. An arresting face, even by the standards Celia was accustomed to—Hollywood standards—with strong bones and symmetrical features. Awake and healthy, she thought, he'd probably be a very handsome man. Though matted with sand, she could tell his hair was dark, and so was the beard stubble that covered his chin and jaws and nicely chiseled upper lip. Dark lashes made crescent shadows on his cheeks. She wondered what color his eyes would be.

The hair on his body was dark, too, and frosted with sand…clotted with sand that was mixed with something darker in two places—one low on his side, the other, larger and less evenly defined, high on his chest, above the bulge of pectoral muscle and below the collar bone. His skin must be deeply tanned, she thought, for his deathlike pallor to have turned it such a dreadful shade of gray.

He was a person. A badly hurt person. A person even she could see was in real danger of ceasing to be one, *forever.*

"Celia, love…" Doc prompted. There was a note of desperation in his voice.

She shook herself. "Yeah, well…I suppose…" She hesitated, chewing her lip while she tried to think. Dammit, there really was no choice. "My bedroom—"

"No way I'm climbing those stairs. Perhaps the couch? It's going to be the floor, if you don't make up your mind *quick.*"

"My bedroom's downstairs," Celia said shortly, nodding toward the hallway beyond the stairs. "The den-slash-guestroom's upstairs now. I had to move after the accident." Her lips twitched wryly. "Tough to climb stairs with two broken legs."

"Ah. Yes. Right. Okay, fine. Lead the way."

The doctor shuffled sideways, Celia changed places with him in a clumsy do-si-do, and together they managed to maneuver the unconscious and increasingly cumbersome body down the hallway and into the room that at one time had served her as an office, library, memorabilia storage closet and guest room. Now, the queen-size adjustable bed she'd had installed after the accident occupied a great deal of it, along with a comfortable leather armchair that had belonged to her father, a huge plasma screen TV set, and the bookcases and glass-fronted cabinets that held the things that were most precious to her—books and photographs, of course, her three Daytime Emmys, and the assortment of odds and ends, ranging from priceless to quaint to totally silly, sent or brought back to her from movie locations all over the world by her legendary parents. Only the desk and the computer, which she'd never used much anyway, had been banished.

Now, Celia hoisted her burden's sagging midsection onto the armchair, draped his legs over the wide, curved arm and left Doc to hold up his half while she hurried to turn on lamps, remove the assortment of throw pillows and fold back the lavender velvet comforter that covered her bed.

Resisting a nervous and completely uncharacteristic housewifely impulse to tug and tuck and straighten, Celia turned and regarded the limp form draped across the chair. "I don't know, do you think we should try to get some of the sand off of him first?" Now that the man was actually in her room, she was beginning to have serious doubts, cold-crawly-under-the-skin, leadweight-in-the-stomach doubts, about what she'd just done.

Doc gave her a withering look. "Dear heart, if we don't get the poor fellow warmed up and some fluids into him and that wound tended to *now,* sand is going to be the least of your worries. Come, come—pick up your end and let's get him into that bed—and do try not to jostle him any more than you have already. Don't want to get that wound bleeding again. Assuming he's got any blood left in him…"

Sand…and blood. In my bed. Great. Letting out her breath in a determined gust and steeling herself against an unreasonable and queasy reluctance to touch that chilled flesh again, she thrust her arms under the man's legs. Which she couldn't help but notice were bony and muscular, with not an ounce of fat on them, and moderately adorned with coarse dark hair. Quite nice legs, actually; under different circumstances she'd even have said they were attractive.

"Celia…love—"

"Okay, okay." She braced herself and lifted, took two shuffling steps with her ungainly burden, heaved, lifted and dropped it. Then she straightened and stood staring down at the incredible sight before her: the dusky-skinned, sand-encrusted, battered and bruised body of a man, sprawled on her clean white delicately violet-sprigged sheets.

Doc Cavendish, unimpressed by the strangeness of the vision, shoved her briskly out of the way and bent over the injured man, lifting an eyelid, feeling for a pulse. Throwing her a glance over his shoulder, he snapped, "Bleeding seems to have stopped. Hypothermia's the most critical condition. More blankets—electric, if you have one. Heating pads. Hot water bottles. Failing that, you might soak some bath towels in hot water, wring them out and bring them to me. *Now*—chop-chop!"

Celia's heart was pounding, her insides quivering with a strange excitement as she hobbled up the stairs, snatched blankets and comforters from the linen closet there, then carried the pile down the stairs to her room where she dumped it on the armchair. In the downstairs bathroom, across a narrow hallway from the room she'd taken over as her bedroom, she grabbed an armload of towels and, from under the sink, the flat rubber hot water bottle she'd brought home with her from the hospital and never used again. She ran the water scalding hot and filled the bottle, then dumped the towels in the shower and left the water running over them. They were beginning to send up billows of steam as she ducked back across the hall.

Out of breath, she watched Doc slide the rubber bottle inside the cocoon of blankets that now encased the unconscious man. "Shall I…I don't know, boil some water?"

He gave her a sardonic look as he straightened. "He's not a lobster, dear heart. Warm will do. Plain water, tea, bouillon, chicken soup, I don't care—just get as much warm liquid into him as you can whilst I go and fetch my doctor stuff."

Celia whirled to stare at his retreating back with alarm. "But—but…you're not going to just…*leave* me here with him! What shall I do if he…if he—"

"If he dies?" Doc looked back at her, his jowly cheeks creased in a weary smile. "I'd be greatly surprised if he did, considering what he's already survived. Don't worry—I'll be back in a jiff." And he was gone.

With a frustrated whimper and one last wild look at the blanket mound on the bed, Celia headed for the kitchen, where, like the character she'd played for so long on one of the world's most popular daytime soaps, she proceeded to follow the doctor's orders. *"Nurse Suzanne, another unit of O-neg—STAT!"*

And, she fervently reflected as she filled a mug with hot water, dropped in a couple of bouillon cubes and set it in the microwave, she'd give just about anything right now for a few of those units of O-neg, not to mention the actual skills and training to know what to do with them.

Back in the den, she placed the mug of steaming broth on the nightstand, then took a deep breath and sat down gingerly on the edge of the bed. The mound of blankets beside her remained still as a corpse, and when she touched it, felt cold as one, too. *Oh, God…I don't want to do this!*

Okay—she'd asked for this. It had been her idea to bring the guy here, right?

She hitched herself around until she was braced by the pillows piled against the headboard—carved mahogany, hand-carved in someplace exotic, India, maybe, she'd forgotten exactly where—that had been her mother's. With a considerable amount of wriggling around, she managed to get herself wedged behind the unconscious man's shoulders so that his head was propped on her chest.

His head…on her chest. Cold, damp, sand-crusted hair pressed against her bare skin…her bra…her breasts.

Suppressing a shudder and closing off that part of her mind, she stretched out her arm, groped for and found the mug. Carefully, she lifted it—and nearly let it slip from her fingers when she felt a moan vibrate through the man's body. It seemed to penetrate through his skin and straight into hers.

She froze, quivering inside. She could feel her heart hammering against the cold, muscular back, feel the weight of that back pressing sand grit into her skin. His head rolled on her shoulder, sending new shock waves through her. She heard the faintest of whispers and, bending her head close to his lips, once again felt that stirring of air across her cheek.

"It's all right," she managed to say in a broken, gasping voice. "You're safe now."

"Max…"

"Yes, yes…it's okay," she murmured, soothing him while her mind was shrieking, *Who the hell is Max?* "Don't try to talk—"

"Max…*Max!*" She could feel powerful muscles tense as he struggled to lift his head. A terrible shudder racked his body. Words like ground gravel strained to escape from jaws gone rigid as stone. "It's…boats, Max. Could kill…millions. *Don't tell anyone. They can't know!*"

Fear rushed through Celia like a blast of cold wind.

Chapter 2

One month earlier:

"Boats…" Roy Starr dropped the word like a lead weight into the silence as he stared across the vastness of the city that slumbered beneath an indigo blanket bejeweled with a billion points of light. Out there where the lights ended lay the Port of Los Angeles, one of the largest, busiest seaports in the world. Every year, millions of tons of cargo moved in and out of the harbor, on uncounted thousands of ships.

The man beside him, shorter by half a head and slighter by fifty pounds, aimed his gaze in the same direction and nodded. "According to the chatter, that's where the next attack's gonna come from. Not by air this time. By boat. What's that line from… whoever it was—'One if by land…two if by sea…'"

"Longfellow—'Paul Revere's Ride,'" Roy said absently. He'd been raised by a Georgia schoolteacher, so he knew those kinds of things. He glanced at his handler, the man he knew only as Max, and frowned. "They been able to narrow the target any?"

There was the hiss of an exhalation as Max pivoted and leaned his backside against the fender of his car. "Most likely west coast. That's all they'll say at the moment. Likely timed for the Christmas or New Year's holiday, for maximum impact. We've stepped up security on the main ports of entry—Seattle, Portland, San Francisco, Los Angeles—checking all container ships from point of departure on, screening for radiation, and so on. We feel we've got the big ones covered pretty well."

"Then…"

"It's not the big ones we're worried about." Max paused. "You saw that segment on *60 Minutes* a while back?"

Roy nodded, his lips twisting in a smile without much humor to it. "Yeah, I wish they'd quit giving the terrorists ideas."

Max snorted. "I doubt there's anything they could come up with Al-Qaeda hasn't already thought of. This one, though…" He paused again, and Roy wondered whether it had been his imagination or whether a shiver had just passed through the man's body. "Think about it—how many small-boat harbors do you suppose there are between San Diego and Santa Barbara? How many private fishing boats…yachts…sailboats? Wouldn't take a very big one to carry a biological or chemical agent into a marina. With the right wind conditions…" His voice trailed off.

Roy nodded, fighting a wave of nausea. In Los Angeles, unless there was a storm moving down from the Gulf of Alaska, or the Santa Anas were blowing, the prevailing breeze blew from the west, straight in off the Pacific. It wouldn't take much of one to carry a killing cloud into the basin, where eight million innocent souls lived and worked…and slept. "Jeez," he said.

After a long, cold silence, he took a breath. "You must have a lead, or you wouldn't have called me."

Max straightened up and nodded. "Not sure you'd call it a lead. One name keeps popping up more often than it should. Abdul Abbas al-Fayad—know him?"

Roy frowned. "Sounds sort of familiar. Where've I—"

"He's been on the watch list for a while, but you'd probably know him from the tabloids. Made the news a few years back when he bought a mansion in Bel Air from some old-time famous movie star, then proceeded to annoy the hell out of his neighbors when he turned the place into a cross between the *Playboy* mansion and something out of the *Arabian Nights.*"

"Oh, hell yeah, I remember—painted all the naked statues so they were anatomically correct, didn't he? Something like that?"

Max nodded, his lips twitching in a smile without amusement. "Outraged his royal relatives back home, too—not exactly the accepted role model for an Arab crown prince, I guess. They disowned him—not that it slowed him down any. Abby—as he's called—is a billionaire in his own right."

Roy made a derisive sound. "The guy's hardly a terrorist. He's a playboy. And a nut."

"A playboy…" said Max, and paused meaningfully before adding, "…with a *boat.*"

"Ah."

"A helluva *big* boat. One of those megayachts—the *Bibi Lilith,* which I'm told translates as 'Lady of the Night'—I swear to God. Do you suppose he knows what that means in English? Anyway, the damn thing looks like the *Queen Mary.* Over three hundred feet long and luxury all the way. Twenty guest cabins in addition to the main stateroom, *and* a crew of thirty."

"Uh-huh," said Roy, in a neutral tone.

Max gave him a sideways look. "Don't you skipper a fishing boat? Something like that?"

"Yeah, I do," Roy said, thinking, with a sudden sharp twist of longing, of his beach house on Florida's Gulf Coast, and his boat, the *Gulf Starr,* which was currently in the capable hands of his best friend and business partner, Scott Cavanaugh. Scott had recently and unexpectedly become his brother-in-law, too, thanks to his recent marriage to Roy's sister, Joy—something he was still having some trouble getting his mind around.

"What'd you do, get me on this boat's crew?" He was think-ing this assignment might have a definite upside, in spite of the grim nature of its purpose.

"Wish we could, believe me. Problem with that is, you'd have to infiltrate the guy's inner circle, and they're a close-knit, sus-picious bunch—mostly related, and even that doesn't mean they trust each other. Even if we could manage to pull it off, it would take time—a whole lot more than we've got." Max was gazing at the distant harbor lights again. There was another pause, and then: "Your dad used to own a big rig, right?"

Wary, now, wondering what Max was getting around to ask-ing of him, Roy nodded. "That's right."

Max let out a breath. "I hope to God he taught you your way around a diesel engine."

"I've turned a wrench or two in my time," Roy said. He didn't mention the fact that his father had died too soon to have taught him much of anything, and that what he knew about diesels he'd mostly learned from his brother, Jimmy Joe. That, and trial and error.

Except, there wasn't going to be any room for error here. In his current line of work, an error most likely meant people—a lot of people—were going to die.

"So, you're thinking about…what, sabotaging an engine?"

Max's teeth flashed bluish white in the artificial light. "Can you think of a better way to get you on board? They call for a mechanic—"

Roy shook his head. "Tough to jimmy up a diesel—at least, bad enough to need a technician to fix it."

Max gave him a long look. "I know you'll think of some-thing," he said as he turned back to the vista.

There was a long silence. Then Roy asked, in a voice so care-ful it could have been mistaken for indifference, "Any plans to raise the alert level?"

Max's reply was a puff of air too muted to be called a snort. "Again? Unless we have something specific to tell 'em, who's gonna pay attention?" He turned abruptly and tapped Roy's chest with an index finger. "We need surveillance on that boat. We need something specific. If Abby…" His voice trailed off. He shook his head, once more scanning the sea of lights.

"Even if we knew for certain, what good would it do to tell *them?* Look at 'em down there. Ten million people. What do you think they'd do if they knew a cloud of death was heading their way? Can you imagine it? *Jeez…*"

For a long moment there was silence, and the balmy Southern California autumn night seemed to grow colder. Then Max said softly, "Whatever it takes, we have to keep a lid on this thing. Let's find out where this is coming from, but for God's sake, don't let it get out we're even *close* to looking at this guy. Abby's a media magnet even under normal circumstances—surrounds himself with the biggest names in showbiz and politics. If even a hint of this were to hit the media…" He caught his breath, then growled, "They can't know. Understand? *Nobody…can know.*"

When the shivering started, Celia did the only thing she knew how to do: She wrapped her arms around the injured man's body and held him, rocking him like a baby and whispering, "It's okay…it's okay…I've got you…shh…I've got you."

"Ah, those maternal instincts," Doc said in his dry, ironic way as he came into the room. He was carrying a scuffed leather bag which he placed on the armchair next to the bed. "Can't keep 'em buried forever, can you, love?"

"He was *shivering*," Celia snapped, glaring up at him. She felt a bit foolish, now that her backup had returned, although perhaps rather in need of some soothing and mothering herself, after what she'd just heard. Except *her* chills, her shivering, were all hidden inside.

Don't tell anyone. Nobody…can know.

Who in the world is *this guy? Babbling about bombs and death and luxury yachts…*

Oh, God, what have I gotten myself into? Why didn't I do the sensible thing and call the cops when I had the chance?

She still could, she supposed, only how was she going to explain what the guy was doing *here,* in her house? *In her bed?*

She was once more acutely aware of the weight of the cold, hard body pressing against her, the grittiness of sand, the sharp, sea smell of his hair. He was muttering unintelligibly through pale lavender-colored lips that barely seemed to move, and shivering less violently, now, in fitful bursts. Was that a good thing or a bad thing?

"Has he said anything that might tell us who he is?" Doc casually asked, glancing at the man's face as he bent over him, his fingers monitoring pulse beats.

Celia shook her head. "Nothing I can make out," she lied, repressing a shudder. And then, reconsidering a little, "He keeps talking about somebody named Max."

"Hmm…" Doc folded down the top edge of the blankets and frowned at the ragged wound high on the man's chest. Even from her position, wedged behind the injured man's broad shoulder, Celia could see that the crater was glistening with new, red blood. "Friend, family…lover?"

"I don't think so," she whispered. The cold hollow place inside her had just gotten bigger.

Okay, Max, this was my bright idea…I hope to God it works.

Silently cursing the circumstances that had him clinging to the hull of a superluxury yacht in the cold, dark Pacific, Roy rode the gentle swell outside the marina's breakwater and listened to the mutter of voices far above his head. The security guards were making their rounds…right on schedule. He'd clocked them three full rotations and they hadn't varied their routine. *This* time he was going in.

The voices faded, blending into the shush and sigh of the waves. Roy glanced at the greenish numbers on the face of the chronometer on his wrist and patted the waterproof packet taped to his chest inside his wet suit. The packet contained a chip roughly the size and shape of a postage stamp, and it would be his job to install it in the motherboard of the computer panel that controlled and monitored the yacht's three big—and, according to their schematics, virtually indestructible—diesel engines. According to the yacht manufacturer's blueprints he'd committed to memory, the computer was located in the central control room, essentially a locked vault deep in the bowels of the yacht, near the engine room.

Amazing, he thought, that such a tiny thing could bring those engines to a standstill. Even better, the cause of the problem would be almost impossible for anyone but a technician to detect. Any call for such a technician would, of course, be intercepted by Max, who would immediately dispatch—who else?—Momma Betty Starr's little boy, Roy, who would then have convenient access to virtually every nook and cranny of the *Bibi Lilith.* If any WMDs of any kind were being transported in this yacht, he'd find them.

Unhooking a device that resembled a medium-size firearm from his belt, he aimed it upward and pulled the trigger. A thin smile of satisfaction curved his lips when he heard a soft *thunk* from somewhere on the deck above his head.

Moments later, he was ascending rapidly and silently, hand over hand, toward the starless, milky sky.

Piece o'cake.

"That's about all I can do for him," Doc said, closing his medical bag with a snap. "The rest is up to him—and you, I suppose. Keep those warm towels coming, and do try again to get some hot liquids into him."

"What about all that stuff he was saying? Do you think…" Celia frowned at the fitfully quaking mound of blankets on her bed. "Maybe we should…"

The doctor made a dismissive sound. "He's delirious—that'd be the hypothermia talking." His lips curved in a sour smile. "Sounded rather like the plot of an Arnold Schwartzenegger movie, didn't it? I wouldn't worry about it, dear heart. Worry about getting him warmed up." He stifled a yawn as he turned.

Celia gave a yelp of dismay. "You're not leaving me!"

He sank into the armchair with a grunt and a sigh. "Thanks, love, much as I'd prefer my own bed, I'd rather not have another death on my conscience if I can possibly avoid it. Forgive me, though, if I close my eyes for a bit…and wake me if he does anything interesting, will you? Besides mumble and shake, I mean…" Doc's voice trailed off.

Celia's gaze returned to the gaunt, gray face on her violet-sprigged pillow. It was an arresting face, she thought, the bones strong and rugged without being coarse, the stubble of beard, slightly arched eyebrows and comma of hair on his forehead almost black against his dusky skin. His nose appeared swollen, and had a definite bump on the bridge. She wondered again what color his eyes were.

He looks like a pirate, she thought. *Okay, a very sick pirate.*

Another shiver rippled through her. The cold radiating from the blanket-wrapped body seemed to be seeping into hers. *No…I don't want another death on my conscience, either.*

Reclaiming her seat on the edge of the mattress, she shifted and maneuvered herself until the man's upper body was once again propped almost upright against her. "Okay…" she murmured as she picked up the mug of chicken broth, "let's try this again."

Once more, the man's head rolled on her chest and she felt the faint stirring of words against her cheek.

"Shh," she whispered, with a catch in her voice. "It's all right. Don't try to talk."

But his lips moved again, and her heart quickened as she leaned closer in order to hear.

"Piece o'cake," the man said.

It should have been.

He'd been monitoring the *Bibi Lilith* for over thirty-six hours, and he knew the security guards' routine backward and forward, to the second. He'd made it all the way to the control room, even got the damn door unlocked without a hitch. Then, either his luck ran out or his intel let him down. Maybe both.

Who could have foreseen on this particular night one of the guards would just happen to get hold of some bad shrimp, or an intestinal bug—who knew what it was that sent him, at that precise moment, in search of a vacant crew's head?

The guy came out of nowhere—Roy rounded the corner and there he was. And in that narrow passageway, there was no place for him to hide. Trapped like a deer in a hunter's headlights.

Lord knows, things couldn't have looked more hopeless for Momma Starr's baby boy than they did at that moment. But life was precious to him—he hadn't realized how precious until he'd realized he wasn't giving his up without one helluva fight.

In that moment, instinct took over. Instinct…and then some pretty intense combat training, thanks to which, in the first chaotic moments, he very nearly succeeded in making his escape. He'd taken out the first guy and was heading for the deck, but seconds later the narrow passageway had filled to bursting with security guards, all of them *big*. And heavily armed. And, it seemed, all of them bent on pounding him into a lifeless bloody pulp. He could feel his body being buffeted by blows from all sides, though oddly enough, with all the adrenaline pumping through him, he felt almost no pain.

Then, suddenly, he felt nothing at all.

"Doc," Celia sobbed, "help me—I don't know what to do! Oh God—what's happening? Is he dying?"

Doc's face, as he bent over the injured man, was close to hers. She saw one bloodshot eye flick her way, then narrow in a frown as he straightened. "Just unconscious, at the moment."

"He was shivering and mumbling, then all of a sudden he just went…like that." She was ashamed, now, of her panic. "So…*still.* I thought…" She'd thought he'd died on her, that's what she'd thought. Literally. And how awful would *that* be!

"Take your clothes off," Doc said.

Celia stared at him. "What?"

"I said, take off your clothes. Now. We've got to get him warm. If we don't, I'm not giving any odds on him making it. Without thermal wraps and IV fluids, and given his size and the difficulty involved in getting him into a shower or bathtub, the best way I know of to do that is the old-fashioned way—skin to skin. And *I'm* sure as hell not going to be the one to cuddle up to him. This was your idea. Come on, love—up you get."

"I'm not taking off *everything,*" Celia said, glaring at the doctor as she eased herself out from under the injured man's limp body. "I'm keeping my underpants on, and that's final."

Doc grunted impatiently. "If you feel you must. Just hurry up, will you?"

"Turn around."

"Dear girl, might I remind you that I am a doctor?"

"Not anymore," Celia said darkly, standing her ground.

Doc rolled his eyes, but obediently turned his back. With fingers that felt stiff and uncoordinated, she unbuttoned and unzipped her shorts, shook them down to her ankles and stepped out of them. She stood for a moment chewing on her lips. Then, throwing a nervous glance over her shoulder at Doc's rigid back, she peeled off the damp and sandy sports bra and dropped it on top of the shorts.

Her breasts shivered and her nipples puckered as she lifted the edge of the quilt and perched gingerly on the edge of the mattress. Taking a deep breath and sucking in her stomach in a futile effort to avoid making contact with his body, she arranged herself alongside the injured man.

"Okay, now what?" Although she wasn't cold herself—not really—her teeth insisted on chattering. She tensed her jaws to make them stop doing that.

"Snuggle up to him, darling. Wrap your arms and legs around him. Do I really have to explain it to you?" Doc sounded amused.

Oh...God. Every nerve ending in her skin rebelled at the touch of that clammy body. That hard, unfamiliar masculine body.

She gasped. "He's *naked*."

"What did you expect? Would you rather I'd left those sandy wet drawers on him? Don't be such a prude. Anyhow, I doubt he even knows you're there." Doc was leaning across her, lifting and pushing at the man's loglike form. "Here—scoot in and wrap yourself around his backside. That's the ticket…as close as you can get. Skin to skin, dear. I shouldn't have to tell you how, should I? Touch him everywhere you can." And he pulled the comforters tightly around her, tucking them in behind her so that she was trapped…cocooned inside the bundle with the unconscious stranger.

Celia closed her eyes and counted the rapid thumping of her heartbeats. Her face was pressed between cold, gritty shoulder blades. She didn't know what to do with her hands. Her palms, stiffly flattened over his rib cage, measured the faint, slow tick of his pulse. Her tightened nipples hurt where they mashed against hard muscle. Shivers cascaded through her body in waves. Between them she muttered brokenly, "Okay…what…now?"

"Now?" Doc exhaled in a gust as he sank once more into the armchair. "I don't know, dear heart. Hope and pray you're the hot-blooded type, I suppose."

Roy became aware of the pain first, a dull throbbing ache in his head, his belly, his back—in fact, in just about every part of him. That soon led to the realization that he was cold and uncomfortable on top of the pain, and only a little additional mental exercise told him the reason: he was lying on his side on a hard slick surface—the deck of a ship? Yes, and—he was wearing only a pair of shorts—what had happened to his wet suit? Additionally, there was a piece of duct tape over his mouth, and his wrists were bound together behind his back—also with duct tape. The deck beneath his cheek was vibrating, a deep, throbbing thrum, and a cold, damp wind was stirring across his naked skin.

He remembered now. He was on board the megayacht *Bibi Lilith*. And, apparently, the yacht was no longer riding at anchor just outside the marina. She was now under way, heading at full speed out to sea.

Careful to move nothing else, he opened his eyes. *Still dark.* Apparently not much time had elapsed since he'd been caught trying to plant a Trojan horse chip in the engine control computer.

The chip. Where's the damned chip?

They'd stripped him down to his shorts, and the packet had been tucked inside his wet suit. They'd found it—had to have found it. And were probably at that very moment trying to figure out what it was and what he'd intended to do with it. It was, he reasoned, probably the only reason they hadn't killed him yet. They'd want to know what damage he'd done, who had sent him, how much he knew. His heart thumped and his skin crawled at the thought of the means they might be planning to employ to extract that information from him before they killed him and threw his body overboard.

Overboard. Well, hell. That was the reason the yacht was heading out to sea. They'd want to be in deep water when they dumped him.

It took only a few seconds for his senses to gather all this information, and for his brain to process it. After that, his brain wasted a good bit more time skittering around trying to figure a way out of the situation he was in. The only thing that activity produced was the conclusion that his prospects weren't good. He was alone on this mission, without backup, vastly outnumbered, and what weapons or means of calling for help he'd had were on his belt, which had been removed from him along with his wet suit.

Looking on the bright side, he was alive, at least for the moment. And, they hadn't gone too far offshore yet. The lights of L.A. were still visible out there, rising and falling on the horizon. If he could make it to the water, he might have a chance. A small one, for sure, but it beat the hell out of anything that could happen to him if he stayed on this boat.

I have to make it to the water....

He moved experimentally and heard a mutter of voices respond immediately from somewhere nearby but beyond his line of vision. The voices were speaking something other than English. *Arabic? Persian?*

He heard the scuff of footsteps, and a dark shape bent over him. He moaned, again as an experiment, and was rewarded with a vicious kick in the ribs for his trouble. Another voice spoke, and Roy felt himself jerked roughly to his feet. The tape was ripped cruelly from his mouth.

He stood swaying, licking his stinging lips as the dark shapes closed in around him. *Now? Shall I make a move now?* His mind calculated the distance to the railing. *Too far!* Besides which, his legs still felt wobbly and his head was swimming. He'd never make it alive.

While he was making that assessment, the line of dark shapes directly in front of Roy broke apart, and another shape moved into the gap. This man, obviously the one in charge, lifted a hand and drew long and deeply on a cigarette, briefly and faintly illuminating hawklike, angular features—good-looking in a dark-browed and bearded sort of way. I'll know him, Roy thought. *If I live to see him again, I'll know him.*

"Who do you work for?" The words coming at him from out of the darkness were spits of sound—short and sharp, but deadly, like the sounds a gun makes when it has been equipped with a silencer. "Why are you here?"

"I don't...work for anybody...except myself," Roy said, with what he hoped were convincingly weak-sounding coughs. "Figured...a yacht like this...there's gotta be something worth stealing—"

A fist thudded without warning into his stomach. He doubled over, retching feebly. Lights ricocheted inside his skull.

"Wrong answer," the staccato voice said calmly. "If you wanted to steal you would have been upstairs, in the salon, or the staterooms. What were you doing outside the control room? Answer me correctly this time, or the next thing to hit your stomach will be a bullet."

Roy considered his options and kept his mouth shut.

His interrogator shrugged as he drew once more on his cigarette, then tossed it over the railing. Roy watched the reddish spark arc downward and out of sight, like a short-lived shooting star.

"It doesn't matter," the interrogator said in his curiously passionless voice. "I know who you are. You are an agent of the United States government. You are trespassing on this yacht. The computer chip you were carrying with you will be analyzed and your intentions will be discovered. But in any case, whatever you were sent to do, you have failed. Whatever else you may have left behind, it will be found." He gestured to the other shapes. "Take care of him."

Roy's heart lurched as he heard the unmistakable jangle of heavy chain from somewhere close behind him. *Whatever I do, I can't let them put that chain on me.*

Still clinging to the guise of casual and inept thief, Roy whined, "Wait! What—what are you doing? Hold on a minute! *Jeez!* What's with you guys? What ever happened to calling the cops?"

The interrogator paused to look back, and a light from somewhere on the yacht's upper decks caught and illuminated his smile. "Police ask too many questions." The voice now sounded almost gentle. "This is much simpler. Cleaner. Nothing of you will ever be found…no evidence. Fewer questions." He turned to continue on his way.

Roy shook away the nearest of his captors and lurched toward the interrogator, calling out, "Wait—dammit!" as if he were bent on pleading his case, arguing for his life.

It was a desperate gamble, but the deception gave him the split second he needed. For that split second his captors froze expectantly, and he surged past them on a wave of pure adrenaline, veering instead toward the ship's railing.

The railing loomed ahead of him, an impossible distance away. He focused on it and ran…no, dove for it—his legs didn't seem to touch the deck. An awkward half crouch was all he could manage with his hands secured behind his back. As he lurched forward, he heard angry exclamations from behind him. Then shouts. He plowed on, every nerve in his body humming, every muscle spasming in expectation of the brutal slam of bullets into his flesh.

The railing was *there,* right in front of him. He struck it hard, then arched and twisted his torso up and over, and he was falling, falling free through the darkness. From far, far away, he heard the crackle of gunfire, the zing of bullets slicing past him, the hiss and spit as they hit the water.

He felt a searing, burning sensation slam into his side and knife through his chest and had time for only one thought: *Oh, hell, I'm hit!*

The black Pacific swell rose up to swallow him.

The cold...

Roy had never been so cold. Being a Southern boy, born and bred, Lord, how he *hated* to be cold.

But, at least he was alive, and at the moment, being cold was the least of his worries. For starters, he was alone in a vast, dark ocean, although maybe the alone part wasn't altogether a bad thing, considering the company he'd just left. At first, he'd feared his erstwhile captors might turn the yacht around and come to search for him to finish him off—maybe even launch one of the outboards. The moment of euphoria he'd felt when he'd realized they weren't going to do that was short. Clearly, his would-be killers were confident the sea could be counted on to complete what they'd started. They didn't even consider it worth their trouble to make certain.

Taking stock of his current circumstances, he could see their point. He was shot and bleeding profusely, miles from shore, in an ocean full of sharks. With his hands taped together. Behind him. It was, he thought, one of those *Perils of Pauline* cliffhanger moments, where it looked as if things couldn't possibly get any worse.

Except that, in those old movie serials, rescue always came at the beginning of the next episode. He was pretty sure nothing like that was going to happen here. In his case, things definitely *could* get worse.

Fighting back panic, Roy floated on his back and rested. While he rested, he took stock of his situation. And, in those first few minutes, the best he could do was draw courage from small victories.

Number one, I'm alive.

That was a biggie. And, he was no longer being hunted, at least by anything human. And, while the water was god-awful cold, that was a good thing, too, it seemed to him, in that it appeared to help numb the pain of the bullet wound in his side.

Or chest? Side? Both? And if that's the case, why am I still alive?

Oddly, though, he didn't feel as if anything vital had been damaged. *The blood...* He didn't like to think about that blood.

Normally a fly-by-the-seat-of-the-pants kind of guy, now Roy forced himself to think methodically. To prioritize. *First things first. One thing at a time. Think about sharks, for instance, only if and when they show up.*

In the meantime, if he was going to swim to shore—and that did seem to be his only hope for survival—he was going to need the use of his arms. So, the taped wrists were obviously his first priority.

It turned out to be easier than he'd expected. His captors, clearly never intending the bonds to have to hold him for very long, had made the mistake of taping his wrists overlapping each other in opposite directions, leaving him enough slack in his joints and muscles so that, in his semiweightless state, it was possible for him to contort his body and maneuver his feet through the closed circle of his arms. Once he had his hands in front of him, his teeth made relatively short work of the tape. Now his arms were free—another victory.

But it was one he'd paid a high price for.

Intent on his task, he'd closed his mind to the pain in his chest and side, and to the fact that way too much of his blood was leaking out of his body. Now, rising and falling with the swell, he fought waves of nausea and dizziness, of the invading chill and weakness. Once again he floated, looking up at the milky sky…resting, and struggling, now, to keep his tenuous grip on consciousness.

He lost track of time. *Stay awake…keep moving…stay alive.* That was his existence now. That, and the rise and fall of the ocean beneath him, like the respirations of a giant living being. From the top of each swell, he could find a measure of encouragement in the line of lights along the shore, never seeming to move closer, but still there…always there…a beacon and a hope. Then…down he'd plunge into the trough…and he was alone again with the darkness and the cold.

Chapter 3

The man was stirring again. And muttering. Not the wild litany of horror Celia had listened to with chilled fascination for most of the night, but a single word, repeated with choked and pitiful desperation:

"Cold...c-cold..."

"I know..." she whispered against his back, tightening her arms around him, her hands unthinkingly stroking. "Shh...it's okay...it's okay..."

"C-cold." He turned suddenly, reaching for her.

She gave a gasp as his arms came around her, folding her against his naked body in a shockingly intimate embrace. Her face was trapped now in the hollowed curve of neck and jaw, held there by the weight of a bony masculine chin, her lips pressed against a tickling thread of pulse. "Doc!" she squeaked in panic. "Doc—*help!*"

The loud snores coming from the direction of the armchair continued unabated.

Oh, God. What now? She squeezed her eyes shut and held herself still, holding even her breath. *Okay...okay. Don't panic. He's unconscious. Delirious. This is okay. You're fine.*

Willing herself to the discipline of slow, deep breaths, she felt calm gradually overtake her. And with the quieting of her own mind and body, became aware that the man was shaking again. Not the terrible, racking shudders of hypothermia, but something gentler, and oddly *rhythmic.* She held herself utterly still, listening...and came to a stunning but inescapable realization: *the man was crying.*

Incredible, but yes, it was true. Though still less than fully conscious, the man in her arms was silently weeping.

The feeling that came over Celia then was unlike anything she'd ever known, an emotion she could neither name nor describe. It awoke from somewhere deep inside her, rippled through her chest and shivered over every inch of her skin. She felt almost frighteningly fierce and primitive and powerful...and at the same time incredibly soft and gentle and nurturing.

"So...*cold,*" the man whispered.

"I know..." Celia answered, her throat husky with the new emotions, "I know...but it's okay...you're safe...I've got you."

In that moment, in some strange way, she felt he belonged to her.

When the first slithery *something* brushed his skin, he felt it like the sting of a whip. Fresh adrenaline slammed into his exhausted body. His mind shrieked, *Shark!* Every muscle, nerve and sinew braced for the jolt of teeth tearing into his flesh.

Instead, there it was again—that light, slithery touch, almost like a caress. Like cold, clammy fingers drawn flirtatiously along his torso...his arms...his legs. Sick with horror, it was several long seconds before the truth penetrated his tired brain: Not sharks. Nor any kind of fish, in fact.

It was seaweed.

It came to him that he must have drifted into one of the vast beds of giant kelp that lie off the coast of Southern California.

But what did that mean for his chances of survival? He knew next to nothing about kelp, his entire experience limited to the rubbery tangles he'd seen washed up on the beaches, smelling of brine and dead sea creatures. *Good thing or bad thing?*

In the end, he supposed, it probably didn't matter much, one way or the other. He was so cold…so weak…and still so far from the lights. *So far…*

Keep moving…stay awake…stay alive…

Something bumped him. Definitely something big, this time. Something heavy. Definitely not seaweed.

He struck at it weakly, still fighting for life, out of raw instinct, to his last living breath. *Take that, shark!*

But whatever it was didn't seem at all impressed by his futile gesture of defiance. It didn't bother to move away from him. It didn't move in for the kill, either. It merely dipped sluggishly into the flattened slick between waving fronds of kelp, then surfaced and nudged him again. And again. As if, he thought, it was trying to get his attention.

Vaguely annoyed—*Either finish me or get the hell out of my way, damn you!*—Roy pushed at the object again. Again it dipped and bobbed, in what seemed to him almost like a friendly invitation. And on the very edges of consciousness, his reason flashed the word: *driftwood.*

Instinctively, without even knowing why, with the last remnants of his strength and will, he grasped the floating log and hitched himself onto its gnarled length. Clinging to it, he gave in once more to the darkness and the cold.

It wasn't as bad as he'd thought it would be, dying. Rather a relief, in fact, after the cold and the pain and the constant, unrelenting struggle to *keep swimming…keep moving…stay alive.*

He couldn't very well be expected to keep moving, keep swimming, could he, when he couldn't feel his arms and legs. Couldn't feel much of anything, in fact. He seemed to recall knowing this was because his body was concentrating its remaining resources, bringing everything into its core to keep the vital organs alive. Soon, even those would quit functioning. Heart or brain...which would be the last to go? His heart, probably. He could already feel his brain shutting down—at least, he assumed that was what was happening, since he was having such weird fantasies—pictures and sounds and sensations that made no sense to him. Voices—strangers' voices. One in particular, a woman's, crooning to him as if he were a child. A little baby. He found it unexpectedly comforting.

He dreamed a face to go with the voice—an angel's, naturally. This angel, though, had a body like a *Playboy* centerfold, which was definitely something they hadn't told him about in Sunday School. The angel snuggled her voluptuous body next to his, warming him. Soothing him with her voice...warming him with her body.

Yeah, he thought, this dying business isn't so bad...

Resurrection, though, was *hell.*

Protesting, he came rocketing up out of black oblivion and into a blinding, thundering artillery barrage of *pain.* Pain was *everywhere.* It pounded behind his eyeballs and stabbed the muscles of his arms and legs like a thousand tiny, vicious knives. It seared through his chest and yawned cold and empty in the pit of his belly. His skin burned. His *molars* ached. He hurt so badly he retched, which was not only humiliating, it made everything hurt more than ever. The urge to throw up was incredibly strong, and it was only because he couldn't stand any more of that pain that he managed to fight it back down.

At first, he thought he wanted to go back to the nice darkness and stay there, even if the darkness was death. Then he thought maybe he *had* died, that those Sunday School teachers years ago had been right about where he was destined to end up.

The notion scared him enough so he dared to open his eyes, and that was when he figured out he was most likely alive after all. At least, he was unless the hereafter looked a lot like somebody's den, and God or the devil was a chubby guy wearing a purple silk bathrobe, sound asleep in a big ugly armchair and snoring like a buzz saw with his mouth wide open.

Reassured, Roy gave in to the lead weights attached to his eyelids and let them sink down...down.

A moment later they fluttered up again. His heart beat a wild tattoo against his ribs. *What the hell? Am I delirious? Dying after all?*

Breathing slowly and deeply, he took stock. *Nope. Not delirious.* There *was* a woman in bed with him. He could feel the humid warmth of her breath on his skin, the dove-soft tickle of her hair. Her arm lay draped like a strap across his torso, and one of her legs had overlapped and slipped intimately between his. With the utmost care, he turned his head. A deliciously feminine scent drifted to his nostrils. Ignoring the shooting pains rocketing through his skull, he tensed his face and neck muscles and aimed his eyes downward. A vision of tumbled blond met his gaze—winter grass touched with sunshine.

He thought, *My God, it's my angel. I didn't dream her. She's real.*

The body snuggled against him tensed, suddenly. The cloud of blond hair parted, and he found himself gazing into a single wide-awake eye—an eye of the clearest, most vivid blue he'd ever seen. The eye, surrounded by thick, sooty lashes, stared back at him—for about two seconds. Then, with a flurry of movement that reminded him of an uncoiling spring, the arm, the leg, the eye, and all the various body parts that went with them, separated themselves from him and retracted into a blanket-wrapped bundle. The bundle was topped by a face befitting an angel, an oval flushed with the loveliest shade of pink, like the insides of some seashells, and dominated by two of those smudgy blue eyes.

"You're awake." The words, breathless and husky, issued from lips so lush and full that, gazing at them, he felt twinges at the back of his throat, as if he'd just caught the scent of something delicious, like bacon frying or bread baking. And that, more than anything, finally convinced him he truly was, against all odds, alive.

"Lord, I hope so," he murmured. But the sound he'd intended, the voice he'd expected, wasn't there. Instead, he heard only a stickery whisper.

To his bemusement, the eyes gazing down into his grew luminous and shimmery. "Oh—God. Oh, God, *you're awake.*" A hand emerged from the blanket mound, wavered toward him, then stopped. "Wait-wait—it's okay. It's okay." Her voice was trembling, though there seemed to be a note of laughter in it, too. "Don't move, okay? *Doc!*" She threw that over her shoulder, in the general direction of the sleeping man in the armchair. "Hey! Doc! Wake up! He's awake. He's alive. He's *okay.*"

Alive? Okay? Doc? Where in the hell am I?

He couldn't bring himself to ask, because *Where am I?* sounded too much like a bad movie script. And as for whether he was okay, he had some serious doubts on that score. He'd never felt less okay in his life.

He hissed in a breath when he felt something cold touch his skin. Another barrage of shooting pains assailed him as he forced his eyes to focus on the shape bending over him. A hand was doing something under the heap of blankets that covered him to his chin. A masculine hand. Recognizing both the chubby man from the armchair and the stethoscope dangling from his ears, he thought, *How 'bout that—he really is a doctor.*

But this isn't a hospital I'm in.

At least, he'd sure as hell never *heard* of any hospital putting a naked woman in a patient's bed.

Wait a minute! Why am I not in a hospital? Who the hell are these people?

The mystery of that, and the mental energy required to solve it, became too much for him. Overwhelmed by pain, weakness and other physical discomforts, only one thing seemed of vital importance to him now.

"Thirsty…"

The man called Doc nodded curtly and retracted the stethoscope from under the covers. As he straightened he lifted his eyebrows at the blanket-wrapped bundle perched next to Roy. "I think we're ready for that broth now, Celia, dear."

Roy watched in mute fascination as the head atop the bundle made a slight but definitely negative motion, and every strand of that blond hair seemed to dance and coil as though it had a separate life of its own.

The doc looked startled, but before he could say anything, the woman's lips tightened and her blue eyes narrowed to flinty chips. "Close your eyes," she said in a voice to match the look.

The doctor, with a much-put-upon sigh, did as he was told. The woman shifted her glare to Roy. "You, too."

In that moment, gazing into those incredible eyes, all he could think about was how close he'd been to never looking upon a woman's body—naked or otherwise—ever again, and his mind said, *No way.*

The doc said, "Celia, love…"

For a long, unmeasurable moment she stared back at Roy. Then, with a muttered, "Oh, for heaven's sake," she got up off the bed with a flounce, throwing down the blanket.

There followed a profound and respectful silence as the two men—she couldn't *seriously* have expected the doc to keep *his* eyes closed, could she?—watched her leave the room…blond hair bouncing on a smooth, gently curving back…tapering to a rounded bottom not so much covered as nicely framed by wisps of pale blue fabric…anchoring a pair of long, well-muscled legs.

When she was gone, the silence extended for another second or two before the doctor cleared his throat. Roy said, "Your wife?" in a careful voice that sifted from his throat like sand.

The reply was a sharp bark of laughter, and then, in a British accent, "Dear boy, not even in my *wildest* dreams."

"Ah," Roy said, and fell silent, pondering the fact that he felt less weak and pitiful than he had only minutes before. Sex, he thought—the male imperative—was evidently a more powerful life force than he'd ever imagined.

"I dreamed she was an angel," he said after a moment, in his new, scratchy whisper of a voice.

"An angel?" The doc seemed to find that amusing. "Hardly. Though, I am quite certain you owe her your life." He peeled back the blankets in an offering sort of way.

Avidly interested in seeing what had been uncovered, Roy tried to raise his head to look at himself. Then he thought better of it and lifted an exploring hand instead, wincing when his fingers encountered a heavy layer of gauze and tape. Well, he'd suspected as much. "I'm shot, right?"

The doctor nodded. Roy closed his eyes and exhaled carefully. "How bad?" *And why am I here and not in a hospital?*

"Through and through, my boy." The doc's voice had perked up several notches, as if plugged into a new source of energy. "You were lucky. Looks to me like the bullet entered *here—*" Roy felt a light touch, low on his side "—and my guess is, it grazed the first couple of ribs and fractured them, but was deflected enough that it then plowed up through chest muscle, and…came out *here.*" The hand brushed the bandages high on Roy's pectoral, then described a line in the air that barely missed his jaw and earlobe. "Continuing on the same trajectory… Damned odd trajectory, that is…I can't…quite figure out—unless you were *above,* and the shooter was…"

Roy opened one eye and saw the doctor making wild gestures and contorting his purple-robed body while he tried to reconstruct the shooting scenario. He stopped when he saw Roy watching him and lifted one bristly eyebrow. "I don't suppose you'd care to tell us, uh…"

"Sorry," Roy mumbled, closing his eyes, "can't help you there. Don't remember much."

"Ah. No. I suppose not." The doc drew a disappointed-sounding breath. "Well, then. Can you at least tell us who you are? Your name? Is there someone we can notify?"

Roy didn't reply. In spite of his racing heart and a desperate and overwhelming sense of urgency, he knew he couldn't fight anymore, knew he couldn't have lifted a finger right then to save his own life. But weak as he was, his survival instincts were still strong, and at the moment there was no way in hell he was telling anybody anything. *Not until I know who you people are, and what in the hell I'm doing here!*

It wasn't much of a stretch for him to pretend exhaustion and slip back into slumber.

Celia stopped off in the bathroom across the hall long enough to put on a bathrobe, and while she was at it, splash some water on her face and drag a brush through her hair. While she was doing that, she stared at her reflection in the mirror above the sink, at the watercolor wash of pink on her skin, at the mark on one cheek left by a crease in the pillowcase, and felt her body grow warm inside the lightweight robe. No matter what, she thought, I can always manage to *look* good.

Though, why should she care whether she did or not, when it was only Doc and some half-dead stranger?

Stranger. As the word flashed through her mind she felt a *lifting* beneath her ribs, a sudden surge of excitement, anticipation and an indefinable yearning. What does this *mean?* she wondered as she swept down the hall, the ends of her robe separating and flapping in the breeze she made. *All that stuff he talked about. Is it true? What does all of it mean...for me?*

Entering the kitchen, Celia checked in surprise when she saw, across the serving island and the creamy-carpeted living room, beyond the expanse of glass framed by the curtains she'd forgotten to draw the night before, the Pacific Ocean glittering in the morning sunshine like a vast field of molten gold. A glance at the clock above the stove told her it was early for the fog to have burned off, a sure sign a Santa Ana or another storm was on its way. She felt a shivering in her scalp and down the back of her neck, as if the wind had stirred the fine hairs there.

Once again, she went through the motions of getting a mug out of the cupboard, filling it with water and two cubes of bouillon and setting it in the microwave. While it was heating, she arranged a spoon and a napkin on a tray, and put a kettle on the stove to heat more water for tea. All the while she was doing that, her mind was replaying every word the stranger had spoken during the long dark night. She was used to memorizing pages and pages of script at a time, and she remembered every horrifying, improbable detail.

Could it possibly be true? In the middle of the night, in the fog, it had been easy to get caught up in fantastic scenarios. It had seemed, as Doc had suggested, rather like watching a movie thriller on DVD. Today, with the sun shining, and the injured man awake and lucid in her bed…

What if it's true?

The tray in front of her blurred. She saw instead a pair of eyes…the wounded stranger's eyes. She'd wondered what color they'd be. Hadn't expected them to be so dark. Dark…like unsweetened chocolate. Like coffee. Something strong and heady and not at all sweet. They seem to her impenetrable, like the night. Full of danger. Full of secrets…

The *ding* of the microwave's timer scattered her musings like so many sparrows. She snatched the steaming mug out of the oven and was placing it on the tray when the tea kettle went off like a factory whistle, startling her. She swore under her breath as she licked scalding bouillon from one hand and grabbed at the shrieking kettle with the other—efficiency in the kitchen had never been her strong suit. Boiling water was, in fact, about the limit of her expertise and for the next several minutes she was forced to concentrate on the task at hand, clamping down on the strange excitement simmering inside her as she got out tea bags and another mug, poured hot water and added a sugar bowl to the assortment on the tray.

But as she carried the tray down the hallway to her bedroom, she felt a warmth in her cheeks and a quickening in her pulse, a fire in her belly that could only be one thing: desire.

Not the usual kind of desire—Celia couldn't remember the

last time anyone had kindled *those* particular fires in her. No, this was the kind of yearning, burning desire of her actor's soul that consumed her whenever she got her hands on a really great script, one that had a really great part in it for *her*. The kind of part she'd give her very soul to play. *There's a part in this for me, I know there is.*

She could feel the tension the moment she walked into her bedroom. The way it feels, she thought, when you walk in on a conversation right after somebody's dropped a big bombshell. There was Doc, standing with his hands in his bathrobe pockets, frowning down at the man in Celia's bed. The man himself had his eyes closed, and his face was like a death mask.

She halted inside the door, both shoulders and tray sagging with disappointment. "Don't tell me. He's out cold again?"

"So it would seem," Doc said, with a particular lilt in his normally dry British voice that Celia happened to know meant he wasn't pleased.

"So…you haven't found out anything? What about a name?"

Looking frankly frustrated, Doc shook his head.

Celia settled herself on the edge of the bed with the tray on her lap. Head tilted, she studied the rugged, unresponsive features. Fascinated in spite of herself, she noted scrapes and hollows, shadows of bruises that had escaped her notice before.

They worked you over good, didn't they?

She remembered the strange and overwhelming protectiveness and sense of ownership that had come over her in the night, and felt an unsettling desire to touch those shadowed places…

"Well, then," Doc said grumpily, "since he seems in no danger of kicking off right away, I think I'll leave him in your nurturing hands. I'll leave you some painkillers—the OTC kind, of course," he added dryly. "As for antibiotics, even if I had any, I'd be a bit leery of giving him those, in case he might be allergic. Infection's going to be the main thing to watch out for, and if that wound starts showing signs of it, I'm afraid you're going to have to get him to a hospital whether he wants it or not.

Aside from that, he just needs time to recover from the hypothermia and blood loss—time, and plenty of rest and nutrients, fluids and so on. Which I'm quite sure you are capable of providing."

He scrubbed a hand over his face as he turned and made for the door. For the first time since they'd carried the stranger into her house, Celia felt a pang of guilt. Doc had been a good friend to her in her darkest hours and, come to think of it, had been through quite a lot of darkness himself.

"Doc—thanks," she said softly. "For…everything. I appreciate it—I really do."

"No problem." He dredged up one of his bitter smiles. "I'm afraid I don't do all-nighters as well as I once did. So—I'm off to bed. I don't think you will, but if you need me for anything, anything at all—give me a ring." He gave a wave and left her.

Celia brought her gaze back to the man in the bed—and felt a small jolt, like a zap of electricity, when she saw the eyes that had been closed before were now open. Watching her. *Eyes…like the night…full of danger…full of secrets.*

"So," she said in a light and breathy voice, while her heart thumped in contrabass, "you're awake after all."

"More or less." His voice reminded her of blowing sand, while his eyes clung, hard and cold as limpets, to her face.

Tearing hers away, Celia aimed them instead at the tray in her lap. "Do you think you could eat something? Doc says you need to. You have lost a lot of blood."

"Maybe…water…"

"Broth," she countered, giving her head a determined shake as she picked up the mug and spoon. "It's mostly water. Plus, it's warm. Here—open up." She leaned toward him, humming inside with a curious high, a mixture of excitement and anticipation, confidence and…not exactly *fear*—more like stage fright. *Like opening night on Broadway—if I should ever be so lucky.*

The man's brow furrowed in a frown of reluctant acquiescence. She clamped her teeth on her lower lip, holding back the tumult of her feelings as she watched the parched lips open…followed the spoon's unsteady path toward them…saw the spoon hover…the lips purse…sip…and the amber liquid disappear.

She heard his soft sigh and responded with a single bright bubble of laughter. "See? That wasn't so bad. Have some more."

He didn't answer, not with words, but the eyes that flicked toward her held a spark she hadn't seen there before and his lips, before they opened to accept the spoon, seemed to carry at least the promise of a smile.

"I thought you were going to die, you know," she said in a conversational way as she watched the spoon make its journey from the mug to his mouth and back.

"Yeah, me, too." The voice was sandy, still, but seemed to her to be getting stronger.

"Well, I'm very glad you didn't."

"Yeah, me, too."

She laughed again. "I'm sure. Really, though. I don't know what I'd have done if you'd died. I'd sure have had some 'splainin' to do. Doc and me both."

"Yeah?" He let his head relax back against the pillows, as if the effort of swallowing had exhausted him, though his eyes still studied her warily from under lowered lashes, like some wild thing watching from shadowed woods. "Why's that?"

"For bringing you here, obviously. Instead of—"

"Where, exactly, is here?" His voice, less whispery, less sandy, now, had a gruff and growly quality that made Celia's own throat feel in need of clearing.

"My house, of course," she said, pausing the spoon just shy of its target. "My bedroom. Actually, that's my bed you're in."

"How?" He growled the question, then watched her with narrowed eyes as he opened his mouth like an impatient nestling for the tardy spoonful.

"We carried you," Celia said as she delivered it, watching her hand to avoid meeting his eyes. "Doc and I did. Let me tell you, you weren't exactly light, either."

"Umh." It was his only comment, since a trickle of broth was making its way down his chin.

Unthinkingly, Celia snatched up the napkin from the tray and dabbed at it...and in the next instant her hand was slowing... pausing...as a strange little frisson of awareness raced across her skin. She felt frozen in time and place, unable to move her hand, the napkin or her eyes away from the place where it touched his mouth and chin.

The lips moved, forming a single word. "Why?"

She jerked, cleared her throat, and dropped the napkin back on the tray. "Why what?"

He spoke slowly, separating each word. "Why...bring... me...*here?*"

She shrugged. Her hand shook slightly as she picked up the spoon again. She could feel those eyes... *Black coffee or chocolate...not at all sweet...* "It was the closest place."

He accepted a spoonful of broth, licked his lips, then murmured, "Why not a hospital? You didn't call paramedics?"

Celia took a breath, placed the spoon and mug on the tray. She felt herself bracing as if to meet a physical force. "You asked me not to," she said finally. "Begged me...actually."

She thought, as a shiver of nameless excitement raced through her: *Here's where it begins.*

Chapter 4

"I've answered your questions," she said, lifting her chin. "I think it's time you answered some of mine. It's only fair."

The thought flashed into Roy's mind: *Now it begins.*

Her dilated eyes, black pools surrounded by narrow rings of blue, stared into his. Mentally bracing himself for the lies he was about to tell, he tilted his head toward her, ignoring the thundering pain that small movement induced. "Fire away. *Although,*" he added as her lips were parting, before she could speak, "I have to tell you, I don't remember much. About what happened to me…how I got here. Or there—where you found me. In fact, nothing actually."

"Nothing at all?" She watched him, her gaze slanted and narrow with disbelief.

He found it unexpectedly exhausting, fighting the thrall of those eyes. He leaned his head back on the pillows and in self-defense, closed his. "Not a thing. Sorry."

"How 'bout your name? Do you remember that?"

Her tone was sardonic, but from underneath his lashes he saw that her lips had tilted up at the corners in an oddly demure little smile. Something stirred deep down in his belly, making him think once again how glad he was to be alive and able to appreciate the wonder of a beautiful woman. Warmed by that, he chuckled and gave in. "That I can do. It's Roy. Roy Starr."

"Roy..." She tilted her head and touched her tongue to her lips, as if tasting the word. The stirring in his belly became a drumbeat. "You have an accent. I'm thinking...Georgia?"

He gave a huff of laughter and closed his eyes. "You have a good ear," he murmured, thinking he'd better get himself under better control, that he was going to have to watch his step with this lady, whoever she was. Apparently not much got by her.

"Yes." She said it, not in a smug way at all, just stating a fact, then added, "You pretty much have to, in my business."

"Oh yeah? What's that?"

"I'm an actress."

"Huh. Shoulda guessed."

"Why?"

He'd had his eyes closed, drifting closer than he'd realized to the edges of sleep, so he wasn't prepared for the defensive, almost belligerent tone in which she shot that back at him. Which was maybe why he let his guard down for a moment, just long enough to tell her the God's honest truth.

"Because you're so damn beautiful," he said in a slurred voice, opening his eyes and looking straight into hers. "I figure, anybody looks like you has got to be."

And she surprised him again, this time giving a little shake of her head and looking away for a moment, with a twist of that expressive mouth of hers that wasn't a smile. If he had to guess, he'd have said the look was disappointment, but given his state of exhaustion and track record at reading the lady so far, he wasn't ready to bet on it.

"So," she persisted after a moment, bringing her eyes back to him, "are you?"

"Am I what?"

"Are you from Georgia?"

His lips curved in a smile of surrender and his eyes drifted closed once more. "Born 'n raised. Florida, now…"

He was so damn tired. Hell, he figured he had a right to be. He'd come closer to dying last night than he ever hoped to and lived to tell about it, and the last thing he felt like doing was answering questions. *Anybody's* questions, but particularly not those of a beautiful woman who seemed to be following some mysterious agenda of her own.

As if aware of his thoughts, the woman in question adopted a voice with a coy and disarming lilt. "And, what brings you all the way to Malibu, California?"

As a Southern boy born and bred, Roy was accustomed to that particular feminine tactic. He wanted to laugh, but the attempt took more energy than he had to expend. When the laugh turned into a cough, he was jolted with reminders of the pain in his throat and his chest and too many other places to count. He thought, *Serves me right, getting sidetracked by a pretty face.*

"Truth is," he muttered with a frown of effort, "I was s'posed to see a man about a boat."

"A *boat.*"

And he was glad he happened to be looking at her then, because if he hadn't been, he'd never have caught that flicker of…*something* in her eyes. Something sharp and wary, something that made his battered body summon, from God knew where, enough adrenaline to banish, for just a moment, the fog of exhaustion from his brain.

Riding the wave, he produced a smile he meant to be disarming—charming, too, if he could hope for that much. "Yeah, I run a charter fishing boat business down there on the Gulf—my partner and I do. He's my brother-in-law, too, as of a couple months ago. We just have the one boat, but we were thinking about expanding—getting another boat. Fellow out here had one for sale, so I came out to take a look at it. That's what I was doing…at least, I think…" The adrenaline crested and subsided. Back in the trough, he let his eyes drift closed. His forehead furrowed, and he didn't have to feign exhaustion and frustration…much. "*Damn.* Can't…remember."

"This man you were supposed to see." Her voice sounded stubborn, which took away a lot of its lilt and most of its charm. "His name wouldn't happen to be Max, would it?"

He felt his insides go cold. *How does she know that? How could she possibly know about Max? What else does she know?*

This time, his exhausted brain, unable to give him answers to those questions, did the next best thing it could do for him, under the circumstances. It brought down the curtain.

No! No, damn you, don't you dare! Celia silently protested as she watched the haggard face on the pillows go slack with sleep. Her curiosity was a burning ball in her stomach, but what could she do? She was pretty sure the guy wasn't faking this…sleep or unconsciousness or whatever it was, and she was equally sure Doc wouldn't be pleased if he knew she'd been grilling his patient while he was still in a weak and vulnerable state. But she had so many questions!

Vulnerable…

She probably wasn't ever going to get a chance like this again. Taking a calming breath, she placed the mug and spoon on the tray and the tray on the floor. Then, straightening, she sat and once again intently, minutely studied the battered face so incongruously framed in a delicate pattern of violets.

Is he handsome? She remembered she'd thought he might be, at first. And although at the moment it was difficult to see why, given the beard and the bruises, the battered nose and dry, cracked lips, she still thought he'd be more than presentable, under the right circumstances—cleaned up, spruced up, properly groomed, the wild and scruffy look tamed in *GQ* haircut and clothes.

But handsome? She disliked the word—it had always seemed

to her the masculine equivalent of *pretty,* meaning something pleasant to look at but not terribly interesting. Celia was accustomed to handsome and pretty people. She'd been surrounded by them all her life and linked romantically with a few. More than a few, actually. Way more. Anyway, handsome faces held no great fascination for her. So, what was it about *this* man's face that commanded her interest? More than commanded—she couldn't seem to tear her eyes away.

He said his name is Roy. Roy Starr.

A nice enough name, but in Celia's opinion it didn't suit him. It had a gentle, heroic, good-guy quality—like Roy Rogers, maybe?—that didn't seem to match up with the dark, battered face on the pillow. All that face needed, she thought, was a scar on one cheek and a cutlass clenched between the teeth, and he'd be the perfect pirate. Straight from central casting.

But, how did she even know if Roy Starr was his real name? What if he'd lied about that? And about being from Florida and owning a charter fishing boat business and all the rest of it?

Easy enough to check. She bent to pick up the tray and, after a moment's consideration, set the cup of tea on the nightstand, then rose and carried the tray into the kitchen. She left it on the counter and climbed the stairs—slowly, as had become her recent habit, but for a change not even noticing the tug of muscles and tendons on newly knitted bones.

Upstairs in the master bedroom she almost never used now, she seated herself at the large executive-type desk that sat before the sliding glass balcony doors like an island in a sea of sunshine. The morning sun coming through the glass highlighted the layer of dust on the desktop, and when she took the plastic cover off the computer, swirls of tiny particles danced into the light. She removed a stack of scripts from the chair and placed them on the floor, setting free a new flight of those tiny, joyous motes. A long-ago memory flashed into her mind: as a child, she'd imagined they were fairies and had tried, enthralled, to capture them in her hands.

She sat in the chair and powered on the computer. While she waited impatiently for the computer to work its way through the process of booting up, she tried to remember the last time she'd turned the thing on. It had been a while—she considered the computer, more particularly the Internet, just one more source of public intrusion into the cocoon of privacy she'd built around herself during the past year.

She could barely remember which icon to click to connect with the Internet but after a couple of false starts, managed to get online. She remembered watching something on one of the TV news magazine shows about something called Google—and, yes, there the word was, in big multicolored letters right up near the top of the Home Page, next to a box like a tiny blank movie screen.

She thought for a moment, then typed in the words, *Roy Starr fishing charters Florida* in the box. Feeling clever and venturesome, she clicked with a flourish on Search Web, then sat back to wait for results.

An instant later she jerked upright. The computer screen had already flashed back a blue bar with the words, *Searched the Web for Roy Starr Fishing Charters Florida. Results 1-10 of about 115,786. Search took 0.18 seconds.*

She gave a huff of astonishment and whispered, "Wow." Then, clamping her teeth on her lower lip, she leaned forward and began to read through the entries on the screen.

A few minutes later she was triumphantly connected to a Web site for STARR CHARTERS, and gazing at a picture of a rather ungainly-looking white boat afloat on impossibly blue water. Plainly visible on the boat's bow were the words, *Gulf Starr.* Below the picture, the company's name and logo were featured artistically, along with mailing and e-mail addresses and an 800 telephone number. Below that were the words, *Roy Starr and Scott Cavanaugh, captains—experienced, trustworthy, professional.*

There were links to other pages and other pictures—a good many of them. It took some time, but Celia visited and studied

them all. Most of the photographs featured happy sunburned
fishermen displaying their catch, but several afforded glimpses
of the crew, as well. The one most often shown was a big, burly
man with honey-brown hair cut short in a distinctly military
style. The brother-in-law, obviously. He looked to be in his mid-
forties, and had a nice smile—a very nice smile, Celia decided,
the kind that made the man wearing it look as if he might actually *be* trustworthy and professional.

The same could hardly be said of the *other* man in the photographs. This one had a lean and untamed look, with a whisker
shadow and longish dark hair that flirted with the wind. And, far
from inviting trust and confidence, *his* smile held a hint—just a
delicious shivery touch—of wickedness.

So he was telling the truth—about this, at least, Celia thought,
shaking off the shivers—though her heart went tripping on in
double-time, oblivious to her will. *But it doesn't explain how he
came to be shot and washed up half-dead on my beach.*

It didn't explain the nightmare babbling about boats and
bombs and millions of people dying. It didn't explain about a luxury yacht called *Lady Of The Night.* And who was *Max?*

Since the answers to her questions didn't seem likely to mag-
ically appear on the computer screen she was staring at, she
turned it off, huffed a frustrated breath and went downstairs.

In her bedroom, the stranger—Roy Starr, alleged charter boat
captain from Florida—slept on, his breathing raspy and rhythmic, not *quite* a snore. Celia tiptoed past him to her dresser, then
to the closet, gathering clothes and clean underwear. From the
bathroom she collected makeup and toiletries, and then, arms
full, trudged back up the stairs, pleased once again to note that
her legs barely protested.

The master bathroom felt chilly and unfamiliar to her when
she first entered it—hard to believe it had been almost a year
since she'd used it last. In some ways, she thought, a very long
year…and in others, the night of the accident seemed like only
last week. *Like yesterday.*

Nausea twisted coldly in her belly. She slammed the door on those memories and turned on the water in the shower.

She unbelted her robe and let it fall, as was her habit, in a heap on the floor, and as she did that the thought flashed into her mind: *Ohmigod, I'll have to call Mercy!*

Normally, the robe would stay where it had fallen until Mercy the cleaning lady or one of her helpers picked it up and either put it in the laundry hamper, or, if it was the day for it, in the washing machine. But, of course, the cleaning service was going to have to be cancelled, at least temporarily, since it would be hard to explain to Mercy and her girls the presence of a wounded stranger in her bed.

It occurred to Celia for the first time, as she stepped into the shower, that the man downstairs was likely going to change her life more than a little. Last night, what she'd done—getting Doc to help her, picking him up, bringing him here—she'd done in the dark and fog and loneliness of a sleepless night. *The wee hours of the morning.* People did crazy things in the wee hours of the morning—ask anybody! It hadn't occurred to her then what it was going to *mean,* practically speaking. Such as the fact that, apparently, she was now going to have to do her own cleaning.

And *cooking!* What about that? Celia did *not* cook. She'd never learned how to cook, and it was a bit late to start now. Before the accident, she'd seldom eaten a meal at home, if you didn't count breakfast—which she didn't. As far as she was concerned, mowing down yogurt, fruit and coffee while barely conscious wasn't really *eating.* During the past year she'd discovered the wonders of the local market's deli and meat sections, and why, with all the ready-to-serve gourmet stuff available, would anybody ever *need* to cook?

Now, it appeared, she was going to be shopping—and preparing meals—for two. At least for a while. *As long as it takes him to get back on his feet. How long might that be?*

Her fingers, following the trail of soap over the familiar contours of her own body, paused and lingered, feeling the still-alien ridges of scar tissue that wandered drunkely across her lower abdomen. A spasm shook her, something akin to grief.

I thought I was over that.

Closing her eyes, she put her head back and let the warm water sluice over her, carrying away the soap and the last of the sand that had been transferred from the stranger's body to hers in the course of the night. That strange, unbelievable night, while she'd held him and given him her warmth, and with her body—*this body*—had probably saved his life. This body, that had once been a source of pride—even arrogance?—to her, and which she could hardly bear to look at, even now.

And his body…lithe and lean in the photographs…young and tan and unmarred…

With her eyes closed and the water pouring over her face she saw it again the way she'd first seen it last night—bruised and crusted with sand, and the ragged hole high on his chest where a bullet had burst through. Like her, he'd carry a scar there, for the rest of his life.

In a thoughtful mood, a calmer mood, Celia turned off the water and reached for a towel. She dried and dressed in jeans, T-shirt and sandals, tied her wet hair up in a haphazard ponytail and put on a baseball cap over it. This was her grocery-shopping outfit. Celia knew how to dress if she wanted to be noticed, and once upon a time she'd enjoyed playing the celebrity…loved the attention, the adulation. Now, the thought of being recognized in public made her sick to her stomach. Dressed like this, she was almost guaranteed not to be recognized by anyone among the hoards of surf bums and sun worshippers that swarmed over Malibu in all seasons of the year.

Pausing only to add the finishing touch—a pair of sunglasses, no makeup—she went downstairs to look in on the sleeping stranger one more time. Then she went outside, locking the house behind her, and got into the modest American-made SUV she'd bought last summer when she'd finally gotten the doctors' okay to drive again. She was still getting used to it—it seemed tall and ungainly after her beloved Mercedes roadster, which she'd turned into a twisted mass of metal on the Pacific Coast Highway just over a year ago. The fact was, she was still getting used to driving at all and wondering if the day was ever going to come when she could get behind the wheel of a car without feeling that cold clenching of fear in her stomach.

This morning, mentally focusing on the task ahead of her the way she'd once prepared for a particularly challenging scene, she fought down the fear, backed the SUV carefully out of her driveway and headed slowly up the narrow winding street toward the Pacific Coast Highway.

Roy dreamed he was being chased. He dreamed of running, running, running, with his lungs on fire and his breath coming in tearing gasps. Then suddenly he wasn't running, he was swimming, but his lungs were still on fire.

Sharks. Sharks were chasing him, so he couldn't stop swimming, but his chest hurt so badly he was pretty sure he was going to die from that, anyhow. Hell of a choice—get eaten by sharks or have his chest explode. Since it was an impossible choice to make, he woke up.

He discovered that he was lying in a bed under a mountain of comforters, in a tangle of damp sheets, drenched in sweat and shivering with cold. And his chest was still on fire.

But no sharks.

Yeah, he remembered now. He'd been shot. He'd escaped from the yacht *Bibi Lilith* by diving overboard into the Pacific Ocean, but he'd been shot in the process and somehow, by some miracle, he'd wound up here. A gorgeous blonde and a chubby little guy named Doc had brought him here and put him in this bed, and for some strange reason hadn't called the cops or the paramedics to come and deal with him.

And the blonde had asked him about Max.

Max! I have to get hold of Max. Have to let him know... Let him know I blew the mission. Screwed up. Failed...

The house seemed profoundly quiet. He thought about calling out for someone to come and help him, but his head was pounding and his mouth felt like the Sahara Desert. He closed his eyes and gritted his teeth and managed to hitch himself up onto the pile of pillows behind him. The pain in his chest seemed to ease some, so he lay still for a minute or two, resting up for the next big step. He didn't know how he was going to manage it, but somehow or other he was going to have to get himself to a bathroom.

While he was trying to psych himself up for the ordeal, he let his gaze travel around the room, getting a good look at the place he'd come to, trying to get a fix on the kind of people into whose clutches he seemed to have fallen. An actress and a doctor? An odd couple, for sure—but no, the doc had said they weren't a couple. Roy was pretty sure he remembered that much.

The first thing that struck him about the room he was in was that it didn't look like a bedroom—at least, not the kind of bedroom he'd have associated with a gorgeous single woman. The walls were mostly covered with bookcases, the built-in kind, custom-made and expensive, from real wood finished in warm honey tones, some with leaded glass doors. Where the bookcases weren't, the walls were paneled with the same golden wood, and hung with framed photographs and movie posters, though not of the blonde, as he might have expected. These looked like old-style Hollywood. Many were black-and-white, and the people in them, a man and a woman, looked familiar to him, though he couldn't immediately think of their names.

The shelves and glass cabinets held books, a lot of them, but other things, too. An intriguing assortment of things, from what looked to Roy like just about every corner of the world: a kachina doll, a lacquered box painted with brightly colored birds, an elephant carved from something that looked like real jade. There was a stuffed bear that looked old, and one of those Russian dolls made of wood that have dolls inside of dolls, each one smaller than the one before, and a model sailboat, and a zebra, exquisitely carved from dark wood.

On one shelf high up near the top, there was a row of golden statuettes he'd seen before, though only in pictures. The three in the middle were of an off-balance female figure holding up an open sphere. Flanking these like bookends were two pairs of statuettes most likely everybody on the planet would recognize—a sleek but rather stiffly posed bald guy named Oscar.

Roy breathed a soft, soundless whistle and thought, *Wow, she said she was an actress, but she didn't say she was famous!* And he wondered why, if she'd won all those awards, he didn't know who she was.

Celia, love…

The name popped into his memory along with images of a sleek and voluptuous curve of back and bottom and long, graceful legs walking away from him, and hunger-juices miraculously pooling at the back of his throat…

Doc called her Celia. Celia what? Didn't ring any bells.

Summoning his strength and will, Roy pushed back the mountain of comforters and struggled to a sitting position on the edge of the bed, legs over the side, feet tingling on the carpeted floor. His head swam and nausea threatened, the pain in his head and chest, and all his joints and muscles—hell, even in his *teeth*— was so bad he wasn't sure he was going to be able to keep from passing out. And he was so damn *thirsty.*

As he rocked himself slowly, waiting for the dizziness to pass, he noticed a ceramic mug sitting on the nightstand. It was nearly full of a brownish liquid of some kind, and it didn't take much in the way of common sense to tell him it had been left there for him to drink. He picked it up and was shocked to discover how much strength it took to do that. Though his hands shook, he managed to get it to his lips. He sniffed, then tasted it. *Ugh.* Tea, tepid and unsweetened. But wet.

He drank it down clumsily, slurping and wheezing like a two-year-old, thanking God there wasn't anybody to see him.

By the time he'd emptied the mug and returned it to the nightstand, he felt as beat as if he'd run a marathon. His body weighed a ton, and all he wanted to do was give in to the forces of gravity…keel over into that nice soft bed and sleep for about a week. But there was all that tea he'd drunk, making it that much more imperative he haul his battered carcass to the nearest bathroom, no matter what it took.

Roy had always considered himself a pretty tough kind of a guy, with guts and willpower enough to get him through just about anything, something he considered he'd just finished proving, in case there was anybody who might have doubted it before. But damned if he wasn't ready to admit that midnight swim in the Pacific—after getting beaten half to death and shot besides—was *nothing*—a walk in the park—compared to what he was fixing to do now, which was drag himself a few yards across a room and one small hallway into a bathroom.

He did it, though. He got himself to where he needed to be, but by the time he'd finished his business, he was pretty sure he wasn't going to make it back. Still, he tried and kept on trying, even while the cold, clammy walls were closing in and the darkness poured like ink into his field of vision. The last thing he remembered was centering himself on the rectangle of the bathroom doorway and lurching for it, as if it were the gate to paradise and about to slam shut in his face.

Celia was humming a song from *Chicago*—and wasn't *that* a role she'd have given her soul to play—as she pulled the SUV into her driveway and turned off the motor. Who would have guessed picking out stuff to eat could be so much fun?

It had been a long time since she'd felt this motivated about going anywhere or doing anything. It came to her that she felt like she once had when she was starting a new role, learning a new script, getting into a new character. Eager, energized, excited. She felt…*alive.*

She was still singing and added a little hip bump for emphasis as she opened the back door and gathered up as many plastic grocery bags as she could carry. Juggling them into one hand long enough to unlock her front door, she went in and nudged the door shut behind her with one foot, then quickstepped across the entryway and into the kitchen, remembering to switch to under-the-breath humming in case her "patient" was still sleeping.

She lifted the grocery bags onto the counter and dropped her sunglasses and baseball cap beside them. Then, smiling to herself, warm with that lovely feeling she could only identify as excitement, she went to check on the man she still thought of as her stranger.

She turned into the hallway beyond the stairs, and it was an unmeasurable moment before her brain registered the object that lay across the far end of it, like a shadow stretching from the bathroom doorway toward the bedroom. Eagerness and reflexes continued to move her feet toward it, her smile lingering, bewildered, on her lips, even though her heart seemed already to have stopped beating.

Then, as the shock finally hit her, she uttered a horrified, "Ohmigod…" and hurled herself the remaining length of the hallway to drop to her knees beside the body that was sprawled, motionless, on the floor.

Chapter 5

Babbling, "Oh God, oh God," Celia pressed shaking fingers to the side of the man's neck.

Then, remembering how little success she'd had finding a pulse the last time she'd tried that, she clutched his shoulders and shook him instead. And all the while she was shaking him, her mind was screaming: *Damn you—Roy Rogers, or Blackbeard, whatever your name is—wake up! Don't you dare die on me now—don't you dare!*

She heard a groan and went limp with relief. She even allowed herself to feel a bit silly, now, for thinking the worst. He wasn't dead—of course he wasn't. It was obvious what had happened—he'd tried to get up to go to the bathroom and had fainted. The idiot.

The man on the floor stirred. He lifted his head, then one hand. Touched a spot in the center of his forehead and uttered a puzzled but distinct, *"Ow."*

"You fainted," Celia said flatly, relief making her cranky.

His eyes jerked toward her, as if he'd only just realized she was there—which was about the same moment it occurred to her that he was stark naked.

With studied unconcern, concentrating on keeping her eyes focused on his face, she ploughed on. "What were you trying to do, kill yourself? After all I went through to save your life?"

His brow furrowed. In a slurred voice, barely audible, he mumbled, "Had to…needed…the bathroom."

She made a scolding sound. "You couldn't wait for me to get back? What were you thinking? You could have hurt yourself."

Teeth flashed white in his beard-shadowed face, and her heart gave a queer little bump. It was unexpected, the first time she'd seen him smile. "Imagine that," he said in his soft, sandy whisper, and her skin shivered as if a breeze had brushed over it, but in places no breeze could have touched.

"Yeah, well." She coughed and shifted around so that her eyes wouldn't be so tempted to stray along the lean, dusky length of him. "Anyway, now I have to get you back into bed somehow, don't I? Can you get up? I suppose I can get Doc…"

This is déjà vu all over again, she thought, envisioning herself thumping up the stairs to Doc's deck and pounding on his sliding glass door. She really hated to have to do that—Doc was almost certainly asleep, now, making up for the night he'd lost.

"Naw…I can make it. Gimme a hand…" The man was struggling to sit up, one leg flexing, his body bowing and abdominal muscles tightening, one hand going to his ribs to support his injury as his lips drew back from his teeth in an unconscious grimace of pain.

Celia gave up trying not to look at his body. As she scrambled to her feet and moved around behind him to give him what help and support she could, she was thinking he reminded her of classical statues and Renaissance paintings of tortured saints—lean, sinewy and battered, but with an elegance of line and proportion more often found in those old masters' works than in life. He seemed completely unselfconscious about his nakedness, too, which could have meant either that the man had no natural

modesty at all or else had forgotten all about the fact that he
wasn't wearing clothes. Or maybe, Celia thought, he was just too
sick to care.

It was a sobering thought, and it helped to cool the heat in her
face and dampen, though not completely banish, the drumlike
pulse that had begun to throb in her belly.

She was sweating by the time she got him up on his feet and
across the few yards of carpeted floor to the bed. He was shivering, noisily and violently, like a small child who'd played too
long in the snow. The old-library-paste look of his complexion
alarmed her. What will I do, she wondered, if he faints again?

She stood beside the bed gazing down at him, huddled with
his eyes closed under the comforters she'd tucked tightly around
him. She thought he looked worse now than he had when she'd
first carried him in from the beach. He definitely seemed more
pitiful than piratical, the swashbuckling thrust of beard-stubbled
jaw and chin overshadowed by waving locks of dark hair plas-
tered to his sweat-beaded forehead, where a mouse-sized lump
was already blossoming. His eyes were blackened—from the injury to his nose, probably—and the skin below his lashes had a
bruised and delicate look. Seeing that, she felt something twinge
deep inside and drew a quick, startled breath.

I should get him something to eat, she thought, remembering
Doc's last orders. Food—that would be good.

She cleared her throat and watched the eyelashes flutter with
the struggle to lift. Dark eyes, frowning vaguely, focused on her
face. "Um," she said, folding her arms across her front to contain
the odd little current that had begun to vibrate in her chest, "do
you think you can…I mean, can I get you something to eat? Doc
said you need to eat. And fluids." She added accusingly, as if it
had been his fault entirely, "You lost a lot of blood, you know."

Roy found he wanted to smile, if only he had the strength; she
said it as if she were mad at him, glaring at him as fiercely as a
woman who looked as angelic as this one possibly could.
Meekly, he muttered, "S'more of that broth would be good."

"Huh," she said, in a lifting, surprised kind of way, "I'm amazed you even remember that. Okay—be right back." She pointed at him as she turned, fierce again. "Don't go to sleep, you hear me? I'll be *right...back.*"

"Yes, ma'am," Roy said in his best, well-raised Southern. Then he must have dozed off anyway, because it seemed only a moment before she was back with a tray, nudging him with her hip to make a place for herself on the edge of the mattress.

He batted at the quilts and tried to hitch himself up on the pillows, annoyed with himself for not having done that while he was alone and she wasn't there to see him struggle. When she set the tray on the floor and leaned over him to help him sit up, her nearness, her fragrance made his heart bang with a force that seemed too much for the frail shell that contained it.

He'd never felt like this before, and it dismayed him. His hunger, thirst and weakness seemed to have combined into a vulnerability so unknown to him and so appalling he had to try to deny it. He glared at her with hot eyes and barked, "*I can do it,*" in a voice that was plainly fraught with pain and nausea.

"Fine," she said with a coolness that shamed him, and placed the tray across his quilt-draped lap.

Then, what could he do but sit and stare at the steaming mug while the hunger and thirst pooled at the back of his throat, feeling like a grounded eagle gazing at a mouse just beyond reach of his talons. Shaking in waves, he remembered the mess he'd made with the tea.

"Guess maybe you'd better do it," he mumbled, grudging and chastened. "I'd most likely spill half of it."

She picked up the mug and spoon without saying a word, and he couldn't bring himself to look at her face to see if there was a smile of triumph on her lips or lurking in her eyes. He focused instead on the spoon, watching as she lifted it first to her own mouth to test its temperature before offering it to him. She did that so casually, so naturally it didn't occur to him until later what an intimate act it was.

The broth was the best thing he'd ever tasted. It both warmed him and made him feel stronger, and when, after several spoonfuls, the worst of the shivering seemed to have stopped, he said in a humble tone, "You're pretty good at this. You sure you're not a nurse?"

Concentrating on her task, she replied absently, "No, I only play one on TV."

"No kidding?" His eyes flicked to her face, making him jerk just enough to dislodge a few drips of broth from the brimful spoon. Before when that had happened he'd felt embarrassed and ashamed; now he barely noticed. "What," he asked as he lifted a hand to swipe at his chin, "are you on some kind of series?"

"Sort of," She was leaning over to reach for something—a napkin—on the nightstand, and he couldn't see her face. He gazed instead at her ear, the back side of it, the curve of the hairline, the random wisps of blond hair that had escaped from her ponytail. It struck him how very young and innocent, even sweet, that part of her seemed.

Distracted, he asked, more bluntly than he'd intended, "So… who are you?" Then, because he thought that might sound a little rude, tried to amend it. "I mean…what's your name? Should I—"

"Celia Cross."

"Celia…" *Celia, love…* He tested the name on his tongue, and thought, *I remember that.* Not that it meant any more to him now than it had when he'd first heard Doc say it. "Are you somebody I should…recognize?" Because he didn't.

She threw him an amused look, not quite a smile. "Probably not. The show I'm on is a soap."

"Pardon me?"

"A soap opera—or, as we in the business prefer to say, daytime drama. It's called *Doctors and Lovers.*" The amused look twitched into irony. "I play one of the latter. Who also happens to be a nurse—Suzanne Sullivan, in case you're interested. Head surgical nurse at Rosewood Medical Center, Rosewood, Ohio." Something—a shadow—took the light from her eyes as she lifted the mug of broth once more.

Intrigued by that unfathomable look, he shook his head, ignoring the proffered spoon. His hunger for answers, for knowledge was more compelling. "Aren't those daytime soaps pretty much a year-round, everyday thing? So what are you, on vacation or something?"

"Something like that."

She drew a catching breath, the way people do when they want to start on a fresh tack. Her lips smiled, though her eyes still avoided his. "Hey—I've been grocery shopping. Let me know when you feel ready for something besides broth, because I got so much good stuff." The center of her forehead furrowed charmingly. "At least, it *looks* like it would be good. I've never tried the pot roast—I'm sort of a semivegetarian…"

"*Sort* of…a *semi*vegetarian. That like being semipregnant?"

"Yeah, well…" She hitched up one shoulder and her smile deepened, producing an unexpected dimple as her gaze doggedly followed the spoon's path. "Meaning, I almost never eat red meat but I'm not a fanatic about it."

He accepted the spoonful of broth, then lifted his hand and caught hers before she could lower it again. She made a soft breath sound and the smile vanished. Her startled gaze lifted and slammed into his.

"Why are you doing this?" he asked in a harsh and garbled voice. It was something he'd asked her before, though the urgent need to know the answer seemed to have come upon him only now, in a devastating rush, like a rogue wave.

"You were on the beach," she said with a shrug, edgy and evasive, veiling her eyes once more. "I found you. What was I supposed to do, leave you there?"

"No—no, don't give me that. Anybody else would have called somebody. Cops…paramedics…"

She was ready for him now; her face had composed itself into the cool perfection of porcelain. "Then it's a good thing anybody else didn't find you, isn't it?"

His hand tightened over hers, and it felt small within his grasp—small, but unexpectedly substantial. Not soft, not helpless, but strong, the way small female creatures are strong in defense of their offspring. "Why didn't you?"

Her gaze lifted…locked with his. "You begged me not to."

"You said that before. Doesn't explain it. Not even a little bit." He couldn't explain the tension, or how he knew the battle being waged between them had little to do with the questions asked or answers given. But as the struggle went on in unblinking silence, he had a strange feeling the way she answered him now was going to be important to him down the road in ways he couldn't begin to understand.

After what felt like a very long time, she seemed to deflate, not in a defeated way, just a softening. She eased her hand from his grasp and he let it go, but with an odd sense of having relinquished some long-sought-after treasure.

She sat back and returned the mug and spoon to the tray in her lap, reestablishing subtle barriers between them. "I'm not sure I *can* explain it. Not…in a way you'd understand."

"Try me."

Her glance flicked at him—a brief flare-up of defiance. Then, letting go of a breath, she shifted the tray onto the mattress beside her and reached up to pull the fastening from her hair, giving her head a little shake as the sun-shot masses slithered and tumbled onto her shoulders. His throat tightened as a cloud of scent enveloped him…a delicately sweet fragrance that made him think, incomprehensibly, of weddings.

"I suppose I have to, or you'll just think I'm a nutcase," she said as she combed her hair back from her face with her fingers. She gave an airy laugh, though it seemed to him it was mostly pretense, lacking in ease and confidence. "I guess…well, part of it is—and I guess this won't come as a great shock to you, given my profession—but I have a pretty vivid imagination."

He gave a snort of surprise. "Imagination!" He didn't know why it surprised him. Maybe because it sounded like the truth when he'd expected all the build up to be the prelude to a lie.

"So, when I came upon this…*body*—you—lying on the beach, in the middle of the night, in the fog, and you'd obviously been hurt and then washed up there, like…like so much *driftwood*…that's what I thought, at first. I almost ran on by, but then…you moved. At least, I *thought*…but as I said, I have an imagination. What if I hadn't stopped? Can you imagine—"

"Just get on with it," Roy muttered, impatient with her tangents, which began again to seem to him like pretense. A distraction, nothing more.

"You obviously have no sense of drama," she scolded, in a tone more teasing than grumpy. But he noticed her eyes weren't laughing when she continued, "Well, anyway…there you were, unconscious, and so *cold*…and when I put my shirt over you—"

"Your *shirt?*"

The watermark frown appeared in the center of her forehead. "Well…yeah, it was all I had. I was out jogging. A jacket would have been too warm. So, I took off my shirt—"

"Thank you," he said huskily, remembering the terribleness of the cold. The pain of it. "For that."

"You're welcome." Was it *his* imagination, or had the color on her cheeks deepened? She hesitated, then glared at him in an annoyed sort of way. "*Anyway,* you said, 'Don't call police. Don't tell anyone. Nobody can know.'"

"Oh, come on." The way she'd imitated his voice—pitch, inflection, accent and all—unnerved him. It hit him then—really hit him—that she was, after all, an actress. And judging from those statuettes on the bookshelves, a damn good one.

"Those were your exact words. Believe me, if there's one thing I'm good at, it's memorizing dialogue." She sniffed and looked away. "You made me promise. What was I supposed to do?"

Roy didn't know how to answer that and didn't try.

After a moment, she gave a little shrug and her eyes, when

they came back to him, seemed to have grown darker. The rippled watermark frown gave them a confused look as she murmured, "I know, I know. Most people would have thought you were just being incoherent and called 911 anyway. But like I said, I have this imagination—maybe it's the business I'm in—but at the time, under those circumstances, I could think of all sorts of reasons why somebody might ask such a thing. And then..."

"And then...?" Roy prompted when she looked away again, and his heart beat faster with the thought that she might not give him the answers he wanted.

But, she did turn back to him, and this time there was no mistaking the darkness in her eyes. He was no psychologist, but he was pretty sure he knew genuine pain when he saw it. She drew a quick, shallow breath and said softly, "I sort of know what it's like, wanting to keep things...private."

Again made impatient by the fear she might not continue, he waited only a moment before he prompted, "I thought actors—"

"I haven't worked in over a year." She said it in a quiet, bitter voice. And then the words came at him in a rush, as if she'd taken the lid off one of those joke cans with the coiled-up springs disguised as snakes inside them. "I had an accident on the Pacific Coast Highway. I'd been shooting a guest appearance on another show, which was a great opportunity for me, and I didn't want to pass it up, even though I knew it would be hard, keeping up with my obligations on *Doctors...* Anyway, I was on my way home—it was Friday, after a long week of shooting, and I...I guess I must have fallen asleep. I don't remember it, but they tell me my car crossed the center line and hit another car head-on. I got two broken legs and a ruptured spleen out of it, so I guess you could say I was lucky. There was only one person in the other car—a forty-year-old woman. She was killed."

This time when she fell silent, Roy didn't urge her on. After a moment she gave another of those falsely airy laughs and fingered the hair back behind her ears—a self-conscious gesture that seemed uncharacteristic of her. "Naturally, the first thing everybody thought was that I was drunk or strung out on drugs. *I wasn't,*" she said with stiff-lipped, angry emphasis, "but that didn't keep the story—the speculation, the rumors, or whatever you want to call it—from making the rounds of the media. It was *everywhere*—the newspapers, and not just the tabloids, I'm talking the *L.A. Times,* TV news, magazine shows, talk shows—even the Internet. There were reporters, photographers, paparazzi— even in the hospital. It was…awful. I don't know if you can imagine…" She looked away, her throat working.

"Anyway," she concluded dryly, "I've had enough sensational publicity to last me a lifetime, so when you said, 'No cops,' that sounded fine with me."

She swiveled to pick up the tray, then rose, and irrational twinges of impending loss flashed through him at the thought of her going. He was groping for something to say that would keep her there longer without making him sound too infantile and pathetic, clearing his throat and trying to hitch himself higher on the pillows, when a red-hot poker buried itself in his chest. As air gusted from his lungs, as he was falling backward· into a whirling vortex of pain and dizziness, he heard her voice asking if he was all right. He heard the rattle of crockery, felt the mattress beside him dip as she sat on it. Felt her hand touch his forehead with surprising gentleness. The thought flashed through his mind: *That's one sure way to keep her from leaving.* He almost wanted to laugh, but it would have hurt too much.

"Damn," he said without unclenching his teeth. "Hurts."

"Doc left you some painkillers. Do you want—"

"Yeah…that'd help."

"How many? Doc said—"

"About…eight."

"Yeah, right. How 'bout two?"

He heard the rattle of pills in a plastic bottle. A moment later, he felt her hand slide under his neck, and that felt so good to him he wished he could think of a reason for her to leave it right there.

Something brushed his lips. "Here—open up."

He opened his eyes as he took the pills she gave him and found that her face was so close to his he could have counted her lashes—if he could have focused his eyes, that is. He could smell that sweet fragrance, feel the swirl of her breath on his skin. His lips tingled where her fingers touched them. Then the smooth coolness of china was there instead, and he was swallowing pills and tepid, bitter tea, his eyes were closing again, weakness and weariness flowing through him along with a regret as acute as pain.

"Where're you going?" Could that pitiful sound have come from *him?*

Her voice seemed to come from far away, so maybe he imagined the odd little catch in it. "I have to put the groceries away. But I'll be right back. Is there, um, something else you need?"

Answers! That's what I need...more answers. Against his better judgment, he lifted his head off the pillow so he could look at her. "One...thing..."

"Yes?" She took a step toward him, her image blurring and shimmery in his unreliable vision.

"Doc. What's his story? You told me why you did what you did. Doesn't explain him."

She folded her arms across herself in a quick, defensive motion. Even with the shimmer he could see her shrug. "Doc's my next-door neighbor. And my friend. I needed help—I couldn't very well move you all alone." She paused, and when he didn't say anything, abruptly unwrapped herself and went on with an air of surrender, "I went to him because I knew he'd probably do what I asked. Because I knew he has an even better reason than I do for not wanting to involve the authorities. Okay?"

Roy felt a chill go down his spine; once again, he was wondering what the hell kind of people he'd fallen in with. There was a deadly stillness inside him as he calmly said, "Oh, yeah? What reasons are those?"

Again, and for a longer time, she hesitated. Then she said flatly, "He lost his license to practice medicine. How and why is his story to tell. Let's just say that these days, like me, he likes to keep a low profile. Lucky for you—that's why you're here, instead of in a hospital trying to explain that gunshot wound to a bunch of police officers."

A smile flickered like a faulty lightbulb. "Also, unfortunately for you, maybe, it's why you only get ibuprofen for your pain instead of something stronger." She turned to go, then checked and looked back. Her smile was softer now and maybe sadder, too. "He was a good doctor, once," she said, and left him.

Alone, Roy slowly lowered his aching head to the pillows and closed his eyes. He was thinking, *What have I gotten myself into? Wounded soap stars and defrocked—was that the word?—doctors...* On the other hand, this was California, which everybody knew was the nut capital of the world. What did he expect?

I have to call Max, he thought. *He'll get me out of this crazy place. Probably get me some painkillers that work, too. I should have asked her for a phone.*

Why hadn't he, when he'd had the chance?

There'd been distractions, of course, other things going on, not the least of which was, he'd passed out cold on the bathroom floor. Lucky he hadn't cracked his skull. Or maybe he had—from the size and tenderness of the mouse on his forehead and the way his head was pounding, it felt like a distinct possibility. But there was something else, too, something he hadn't forgotten, but which had slipped to the back of his mind.

His name wouldn't happen to be Max, would it?

How could she know about Max?

The question clamored in his brain like an alarm bell. He knew he needed to answer it, had to do something about it, but...he was too weak, too tired, and his head hurt too much. There was nothing he could do about Max right now—nothing he could do about anything, really.

Except...sleep.

"I'm worried about him," Celia said. It was hard to tear her gaze away from the flushed face on the pillow in order to look at the man standing next to her, but she managed it. "I think he has a fever."

"I think it's safe to say he very likely does," Doc agreed, frowning judiciously down at his patient. Together, they watched the man mutter and mumble, eyes glaring, fierce and unfocused, at nothing. After a moment, he lifted his eyebrows and drew a considering breath. "Although, that's not necessarily a bad thing, you know. Fever is nature's antibiotic, after all, and, under the circumstances, the only one we have at our disposal." He glanced over at her, then quickly away, but not before she saw her own concern mirrored in his decidedly bloodshot eyes. "Keep a close watch on him, give him plenty of fluids, keep his head cool. If he's still feverish in the morning, well…I guess we'll have to think of something, won't we."

Celia listened to Doc's footsteps cross the room and fade away. *We both know what that "something" is, don't we?*

If the man didn't get better soon…if infection set in…they'd have to take him to a hospital. There really would be no choice. But how would they ever explain the gunshot wound? Her whole body grew cold when she thought about the questions…the cops…the publicity…the reporters…the photographers…the rumors, the speculation. Not to mention that she and Doc were probably going to be facing criminal charges.

The man in the bed muttered something she couldn't understand. His eyes were closed, now, and his skin had the unmistakable ruddy, velvety look of fever. Drawing a catching breath, Celia reached for the dish towel that was soaking in a panful of cold water on the floor near her feet. She squeezed out most of the water, folded the towel and laid it gently across her patient's forehead. *Nurse Suzanne couldn't do it better,* she thought, the irony of that almost making her smile.

Except, following a script, playing at being a nurse in a television daytime drama had never made her feel like this—the squeezing sensation in her chest…the tap-tapping pulse in her stomach. And she was quite sure real nurses would never allow themselves to feel this fierce protectiveness…this fervent sense that the man she was tending in some way belonged to her.

That she was responsible for him.

"I'm not going to let you die," she whispered, as emotion filled her throat and speaking aloud became impossible. "No matter what it takes, I won't let you die."

The only response was more incoherent muttering. And then, suddenly and distinctly, "Don'…go…'way."

"Don't worry," Celia said, her voice brusque and blurred. She brushed at her nose with the back of her hand and reached once more for the towel. "I'm not going anywhere."

Roy woke with the sense of having escaped from the clutches of a nightmare, except he couldn't for the life of him remember what it had been about. He knew he was lying on his side, and that he felt empty and damp. And chilly—he shivered in small pitiful fits.

But at the same time, he felt *light*. Almost…*happy*. Reluctant to open his eyes, for a time he drifted, battered but relieved, like the survivor of a raging flood washed up in quiet shallows, glad to have come safely through it, whatever *it* was.

Gradually, though, it came to him that he was going to have to do something about the various discomforts intruding on that strange, contradictory sense of well-being. Clammy sheets, for one thing. For another, the fact that he was so damn thirsty. Obviously, if he was going to do something about those things, he was going to have to open his eyes.

It took more effort than he thought he remembered from all the other times he'd done it, but he got the job done. Then for a minute or two, he thought he must still be dreaming—either that, or there was something seriously wrong with his vision. He blinked a couple of times and tried to focus, and when that didn't make things clearer, closed one eye. *Nope—still there.*

It was a face—no doubt about it. About four inches from his. Probably the most beautiful face he'd ever seen in his life, and one he'd seen before. But not like this. No, not at all like this—eyes closed…lips apart, but only slightly…skin wearing the soft pink flush of sleep. One hand, loosely curled, pillowed her cheek, in the way of very small children.

He must have moved…or maybe she felt, somehow, the intensity of his gaze. Whatever the reason, her eyes opened so suddenly he gave a small involuntary jerk, and for a long moment she stared in silence at the center of his face—at his nose, to be precise—before her gaze flicked up and connected with his.

He found he was holding his breath, his mind flashing back to a time in his past too distant to register as real memories… fragmented impressions of himself trudging through knee-deep cool-moist leaves while holding tightly to a large warm hand…a gruff voice softly warning…and then—a vision in dappled sunlight so miraculous it had remained intact and pristine in the attic of his mind for all these years—a doe and her twin fawns…newborn, damp and spindle-legged still. His heart pounded now as it had then, and he didn't breathe, lest even that stirring of air frighten her away.

The moment passed—they could hardly have stayed that way forever. Tiny muscles around her eyes and mouth…across her forehead and the bridge of her nose…quivered and stirred in a waking-up way. He began to breathe again…carefully…wondering whether she was about to smile at him or do what she'd done last time she'd awakened to find herself eyeball-to-eyeball with him.

Figuring he'd just as well get the suspense over with, he cleared his throat and gruffly murmured, "We're gonna have to quit meeting like this."

Chapter 6

He could have counted to four…maybe five…while she stared at him without moving, as if he hadn't spoken a word. Then her eyes widened, and he felt her breath swirl across his skin. The hand that had pillowed her cheek uncurled, her fingertips extended slowly and touched his lips, as if, he thought, she expected him to turn out to be a mirage after all. Evidently assured by her senses that he wasn't, she lifted her head, then her shoulders, propping herself on one elbow while she brought her other hand to his face.

He felt her warm hand cuddle his cheek, then lie long and gentle across his forehead. He was certain nothing in his life's experience thus far had ever felt so good—though it did occur to him there were possibilities that might grow from this moment that would feel even better yet. It felt so good he didn't want that feeling to end, and only the cocoon of clammy bedding he was imprisoned in kept him from putting his hand over hers to hold it where it was.

"Your fever's gone—I can't believe it," she said. The husky rasp of her voice sounded unbelievably sexy to him.

"That would explain why everything's soaking wet," he said with a smile to let her know he didn't hold her responsible.

"It is?" She scrambled up onto her knees and began tugging at the blankets. "Oh God—you *are*. Here—let me…get those—"

"Hey—not so fast," he protested in a desperate and feeble croak while trying to hold on to at least some of the blankets with his one good arm—that is to say, the one not folded like a broken wing against his bandaged side. "I'm *naked,* here."

It occurred to him that *she* was fully clothed—unlike the last time he'd awakened to find her sharing his bed—in sweats and a tank top.

She sat back on her heels and regarded him with amusement, the hands that had felt so good on his cheek and forehead now folded in her lap. "You really are feeling better. Who do you think found you yesterday when you passed out on the floor? Who got you back to bed? You didn't mind if I saw you naked then."

"Yeah, well, I was pretty out of it then," he muttered darkly, looking around him. "What the hell happened to my clothes?" Failing to spot anything that looked familiar, he pulled a clammy sheet around his shoulders. Dammit, he was shivering again. Like a little kid. He wondered if the cold was going to affect him like this from now on.

"What clothes? When I found you all you had on was a pair of shorts. Doc took them off of you. They were full of sand. He probably threw them away."

She scrambled backward off the bed and stood for a moment looking down at him and combing her hair back from her face with her fingers. In spite of the tumbled hair and sleep-flushed cheeks, it was clear to him the sexy sweetness of her waking up was already history. Fully alert now, she had that odd awareness about her again—that indefinable edginess that made his jaws tense and his insides quiver with wordless warnings.

He didn't know why, but in spite of the fact that she'd saved his life, he didn't in any way trust her. Not, as they used to say in the part of the world he'd been raised in, any farther than he could throw a bull by the tail.

Frowning and nibbling ingenuously at her lower lip, she said, "I'll see if I can find you something to put on, okay?" She moved to the door, where she turned and pointed at him like an empress issuing edicts. "*Don't* go anywhere. If you need to…whatever, just hold it until I get back, okay? I don't want you keeling over again. *Promise.*"

"Okay, okay, I promise." He raised himself on one elbow to call after her, "No flowered bathrobes, you hear? And I'm not wearing ruffles, either."

She looked at him over her shoulder, rolling her eyes in an *as if* kind of way. "That is *so* TV sitcom, don't you think?"

She went out, leaving Roy with silent laughter bumping against the sore places that still lurked through his insides.

Sweet, sexy or siren, he thought, the woman did know how to stir a man's juices and kindle fires where, by rights, there oughtn't to have been any fuel left to burn. While he still felt that lightness, that sense of well-being he'd woken up with, now he wondered how much of it was due to the fact that he'd fought a bare-knuckle brawl with death and won, and how much to the predictable effect a sexy and beautiful woman had on him.

One thing he did know. He'd lost—and was continuing to lose—precious time.

I have to call Max.

He was combing the room with his eyes for some evidence of a phone and trying to assess the odds he'd keel over if he got up to look for one when Celia came back.

"I found some sweats," she announced as she sailed into the room, trailing articles of clothing from both arms like a department store sales clerk. "They're going to be short on you, I'm sure. I don't care if you cut them off, so you don't go around looking like Alice in Wonderland after she nibbled the wrong cookie." She broke off, no doubt having noticed the fact that he was sitting upright and tense, with a frustrated light in his eyes. "What is it? Is something—"

Then, evidently sure she knew the answer: "Oh—duh. You need to use the bathroom—right. Do you need me to help you?"

Roy winced. "Lady, do you have any idea what it does to a grown man's pride to be asked that kind of question by a beautiful woman? Makes me feel about two years old."

"Sorry," she said, unrepentant, this time letting the compliment slip by as if it were no more than her due. She handed him the sweats. They were baby blue, with *UCLA* embroidered across the shirt in yellow script. "Here you are, then. If you need me for anything, holler." She turned on her heel and headed for the door.

Damn. "Wait—" So much for his masculine pride.

She pivoted back to him, eyebrows spiked up in a way he knew good and well was mocking him. "Yes?"

Reminding himself—again—that she had, after all, saved his life, he said grudgingly, "There is one thing you can do for me."

Something flared in her eyes, not long enough for him to figure out the subtle differences between gladness and triumph. "Sure. What do you need?"

He was thinking how it would be if he were himself, a healthy man, red-blooded and strong, sitting in bed watching a woman such as this come toward him with a smile lurking and eagerness in her eyes… His voice deepened and his smile came, naturally as breathing. "I sure could use a phone, ma'am."

"Oh—sure. I'll bring you the cordless."

Quickly, before she could turn away again, he added—only a little grudgingly, "Before you do that…if you wouldn't mind waiting until I get my pants on, I guess I could use a little help getting to that bathroom."

Again he caught that brief but unmistakable spark in her eyes, but she was either too good at shielding herself or too good an actress to let him know exactly what she was thinking.

"No problem," she murmured, hiding the light behind demurely lowered lashes. "Call me when you're ready."

Once again, he watched her walk away from him, feeling too frustrated to laugh, too weak to swear.

The truth was, beautiful though she may have been, she wasn't the kind of woman he'd normally have any interest in. Roy liked his women simple—not meaning lacking in intelligence, but in the sense of *uncomplicated*. He liked them warm and funny and accommodating and encumbered with a minimum amount of emotional baggage. He might be called shallow because of that, but he got plenty of intrigue and mental stimulation, and more than enough complications and challenges, in his line of work. When it came to women, what he wanted was recreation. He wanted to relax and enjoy himself—and them—which was not something he could ever see himself doing with a woman like Celia Cross. Getting involved with her, he had a feeling, would be like one big long sword fight—whether that meant the delicate thrust and parry of a fencing match or an all-out duel to the death, like in those old Hollywood swashbucklers.

No thanks—not for him. It made a shiver go down his spine just thinking about it.

Reasonably assured Celia wasn't going to pop back in on him to see how he was getting along, Roy shoved the damp bedding away and eased his legs over the side of the mattress. *Oof—still weak…still woozy.* He waited until the worst of the dizziness had passed before tackling the sweat pants. If anybody had ever tried to tell him how complicated a job it was to put on a pair of pants one leg at a time, he'd have thought they were nuts.

By the time he was on his feet and more or less upright, there was a howling wind blowing through his ears and a hollow drumming in his belly, and it was all he could do to summon the strength to croak, "Ready."

She must have been waiting outside the door for his call, because it seemed to him she was there in less than an instant. The muffled, "Thanks," he mumbled when he felt her arm come around his waist was both humble and sincere.

He was grateful, too, for the strong shoulder she tucked in under his arm and acutely aware of the feminine shape of her snugged up against his uninjured side. She was a good height for him, he noted; not an Amazon, by any means, but tall enough, sturdy enough to be a real help to him. And at the same time, soft where a woman ought to be. An observation…nothing more.

She turned her head toward him, her hair sliding across his arm like silk, and his skin shivered and his nipples hardened. "No problem," she said. "Just take it slow…"

"Is this how Nurse Suzanne does it?"

She gave that the answer it deserved—a short, mirthless laugh.

She guided him into the bathroom and left him holding on to the cold porcelain sink as if his life—or, at the very least, his dignity—depended on it. He waited until he heard the door close behind her before he lifted his head and confronted his image in the mirror. It was a good thing he'd waited, because what he saw hit him like a fist to the belly.

No wonder she's not impressed with your looks and charm.

He tried to make light of it, but the truth was, the gaunt, bearded and battered stranger looking back at him from the mirror shocked the hell out of him. His eyes stared at him from blackened sockets like wild creatures lurking in caves, and his nose was a different shape than it had been before. What it was, he realized, was his own mortality in the flesh, and he was feeling chastened and thoughtful as he attended to his most pressing need.

Back at the sink, he splashed his face with cold water, but while he was patting his dripping jaws dry with an embroidered hand towel, he studied the reflection of the tiled stall shower behind him with longing. Inevitably, as his various aches and pains diminished, he was becoming aware of secondary discomforts— the itch of sand, the sting of salt, the stickiness of blood. He knew he probably wasn't supposed to, given the bandages, the bullet wound, and all, but…

What the hell, he thought, and turned on the water.

He showered with his hands braced against the tile walls, letting the water sluice unimpeded over his bowed head…his upturned face…his aching body, bandages and all. Eyes closed… mouth open…teeth clenched in a grimace of overwhelming emotion…he let the water run and run, the pleasure of that simple thing so intense he wanted to cry.

Afterward, he crawled out of the shower and felt his way to the towels, bent over like an old, old man. He had to sit on the commode to dry and dress himself, but it had been worth it.

He pulled himself up and made his way slowly to the door; when he opened it, he found Celia there, gazing at him with luminous, unreadable eyes.

She looked at him for a long time without saying anything, and he looked back at her and didn't say anything, either. He wished he was better at reading her, because there were several times when it seemed to him she was on the verge of saying something…well, hell, he didn't know *what* he thought she was going to say, but something that was probably going to change his opinion of her for the better, put it that way.

Then she did speak, and instead of something sweet and nice, it was in her usual way—smart, cool, edgy. "You look like a member of the human race. Welcome back."

"Thanks," he said dryly as he moved past her.

"You're welcome." She came close to his side again but didn't touch him, and he made his way slowly back to the bedroom without leaning on her.

Then he felt humbled again when he saw the bed had been freshly made for him—lavender sheets with scalloped edges, no flowers this time. He crawled between them, almost chuckling aloud with the sensual pleasure of that smooth coolness against his skin, thinking he was never going to take such a thing for granted again.

Thinking how much he owed this woman, this beautiful stranger. So she was a little bit arrogant, a little bit nutty—so what? Considering what she'd done for him, he thought he could forgive her that.

After he'd gotten himself settled, she picked up a cordless phone from the nightstand and handed it to him without a word.

He took it and thanked her, then sat there and held it, wondering how he could ask her for some privacy without sounding too ungrateful. He looked up at her, hoping she'd get the message, but she was fussing around with things on the nightstand, tidying up…avoiding his eyes. He took a breath, then let it out with a little bit of a laugh as some help came from an unexpected quarter. His stomach growled. Loudly.

Her eyes flicked toward him and her lips parted in surprise. Then she, too, gave a laugh—a charmingly childlike giggle. He felt the easing of tensions he hadn't even been aware of, and it occurred to him she might have been looking for a way to ask awkward questions, too.

"Sounds like you might be ready for some real food," she said, avoiding his eyes again.

"Yes, ma'am, I believe I could eat," he said, falling back on his Southern ways.

She nodded, but before she could turn away, he surprised both of them by reaching out and catching hold of her wrist.

"I have to ask you somethin'."

It was a true statement; he didn't *want* to ask her, and all his training told him he shouldn't. But she'd mentioned Max. And that was something she shouldn't have known about. He had to find out how she'd come by that knowledge. He *had* to.

"A while back, you said something to me." *Yesterday? The day before? I've lost track of time.* "You asked me about Max." His voice grew rougher as he stared at her, willing her to look at him. "I want to know where you came up with that name."

She didn't answer, and her eyes stayed stubbornly on the place where his fingers were wrapped around her wrist. Following her gaze, Roy felt twinges of shame, enough to make him loosen his grip some, but not release it entirely, as he repeated with more urgency, "What do you know about Max?"

She hesitated, and he saw her throat move, her lips part. Then she lifted her lashes and her eyes met his head-on, and it felt a like getting slapped in the face by a cold ocean wave. He thought how easy it might be for a man to lose his bearings and his sense in those eyes…if there wasn't so much at stake.

"You talked about him," she said with an evasive little shrug. "When you were unconscious. Or delirious, I suppose."

Even though it was only his own fears confirmed, Roy felt himself go cold. Her wrist slipped unnoticed from his fingers. "I…*talked?*" He shook his head, not wanting to believe it. But there it was. He'd talked. "How much?" he finally asked, in a voice deep and hollow with dread. "What did I say?"

"Quite a lot, actually." Now there was accusation in her voice and in the lift of her chin. "You know, I have a question, too. I'd like to know how much of it was true."

He ignored that. "Did Doc—"

She gave her head an impatient shake. "He heard some—not very much. He just thinks you were out of it."

"And you?"

She looked at him for a long moment without speaking, then said quietly, "Well, there has to be some reason for the shape you were in when I found you. Doesn't there?"

And with that she left him there, staring after her and listening to the rumble of his career as an undercover agent of the United States government crumbling around him.

Eventually, he became aware of the weight of the phone in his hand. He glared at it, as if it were solely responsible for the mess he was in. Then, with his thumb, he savagely punched in a number he knew by heart. Swearing under his breath, he listened to the universal answering machine voice telling him to leave a message. When the beep came, he said in a voice as calm and expressionless as the recording, "Yeah, Max, this is Diver…just got back…guess I'll wait to hear from you."

Then, instead of hanging up, he pressed the handset against his cheek and closed his eyes, visualizing Max's computer running through its voice recognition software. After what seemed like a lot longer wait than usual, he heard a click, followed by a series of musical beeps, and a voice he knew well, sounding like nine miles of bad road.

"Diver? Jeez, where you been? I'd given you up for dead."

Roy laughed without humor, then wished he hadn't; he'd forgotten how sore his ribs and chest were. "Yeah, me, too," he said grimly. "Listen, Max—" it wasn't the man's real name, of course, anymore than Diver was Roy's "—I've got a helluva lot to tell you, but not over the phone. Okay? And, uh, I guess I'm gonna need you to come get me."

"Sure, absolutely. Just tell me where."

"Oh, *shoot*." He broke off, swearing, since he had no idea in the world where he was, other than somewhere on the Southern California coast. "Uh, wait—let me see if I can find—"

"You're in Malibu," Celia said from the doorway, in a firm, clear voice, projected to carry to the telephone receiver in his hand. "Off the Pacific Coast Highway." She continued talking as she prowled toward him, holding a tray before her like an offering to a pagan god, giving her address and some admirably concise driving directions, which she wrapped up just as she was bending over to place the tray on Roy's lap. Then, with her mouth roughly a foot from the phone's mouthpiece, she added, "Oh, and Max? You might want to bring him some clothes. Mine don't fit him all that well."

She straightened up, wearing a distinctly catlike smile of satisfaction, as Max screeched in Roy's ear, "Who was *that?*"

Roy closed his eyes. "You get all that?"

"Yeah, I got it." Max's voice was a good octave higher than it should have been, and Roy could hear him breathing. "Can I conclude from what I just heard that we might have ourselves a problem, here?"

"Yes, sir," Roy said dully, "you sure could do that."

He thumbed the disconnect button and carefully placed the phone on the nightstand. Celia went to sit on the foot of the bed and pulled her feet up under her.

"You're upset," she said. And she knew *upset* didn't come close to describing the man's state of mind just then.

It wasn't that she didn't understand, in her own heart, what he must be feeling—at least, she was pretty sure she did. An actress needed to be capable of recognizing and responding to a whole range of human emotions, and Celia considered herself more empathetic than most. But now it occurred to her that in terms of subtle shadings, the range of emotions she'd had to deal with in the past couple of days made all the rest of her emotional life so far seem like children's crayon drawings in primary colors.

She said mildly, "I don't know why you're so upset. Just because I heard you talking in your sleep."

"Delirious," he growled, tearing his gaze from the tray on his lap and throwing her a black look. "I wasn't asleep, I was out of my head. What you heard was garbage. It wasn't real." He picked up a fork and stabbed at a bite of pot roast.

"Max is real," she pointed out. And completely independent of the tense conversation she was engaged in, a warm little spring of happiness—primitive and uniquely feminine—bubbled up inside her as she watched him put the food *she'd* prepared for him—all right, she'd only microwaved it, but still—into his mouth, and chew and swallow it with obvious enjoyment. It was a whole new experience for her.

"Yeah, well," he said between quick, savage bites, barely tasting, "the rest of it isn't. So you can just forget about it, you hear? It's just…nightmares."

"Then why," she asked, "are you so upset that I know?"

He paused long enough to throw her another glare. "I'm not upset—just don't want you getting a bunch of wrong ideas."

His air of affronted masculinity amused her, and she couldn't resist saying, with exaggerated innocence, "Wrong ideas? Oh—you mean like, that you're a government agent working undercover trying to stop terrorists from bringing some sort of weapon of mass destruction into Los Angeles by boat? And that you were caught in the act of trying to sabotage some Arab prince's yacht—" She broke off when her patient erupted in a paroxysm of coughing and leaned over to pluck a napkin from the tray and hand it to him.

"Thank you," he muttered, voice muffled.

"You're welcome."

He dabbed at his eyes, tear-reddened and furious. "You…have one hell of an imagination."

"I do. I also have a helluva good memory," she said calmly. "Especially for dialogue—I have to memorize pages and pages of it every day, you know. I remember every word you said. It sounded like…" She paused to ponder it. "I think you must have thought I was this Max person, and you were giving him—me—a full report. With lots of details. In fact," she added, returning his stony stare, "there wasn't much left for me to *imagine.* Plus the cold hard fact that I found you washed up on the beach, half-dead from a gunshot wound." Celia hated being patronized and belittled. Anger embers flared as she nodded toward the damp bandages stuck to his chest with adhesive tape. "Tell me I'm imagining *that.*"

Then, as a new thought occurred to her, she caught her breath and leaned toward him to peer interestedly at the wounds. "You know…I just realized…Doc said the angle was strange. He couldn't figure out how the exit wound could be up *here,* and the entrance way down *there,* on your side. He said it was like you'd been shot from below. But you weren't! I can see it now—you were *diving!*" She was up off the bed and on her feet, now, acting out the scenario. "Someone on the boat shot you as you were diving into the water. *That's* the way it happened—right?" She spun toward him on the last word—then halted. "What are you doing?"

He'd set the dinner tray aside and was pulling his legs from under the covers. Aiming a smoky glare past her, he muttered, "Gettin' the hell out of this bed, that's what I'm doing. What does it look like?"

Her heart slammed against her ribs. "What does it look like?

It looks like you've lost your mind. You're not strong enough. You're going to—"

"I'm *fine*." Having succeeded in planting two bony bare feet squarely on the carpet, he transferred the glare to Celia. "Max'll be here in a minute. I'm not gonna have him find me lying here like some damn helpless invalid."

He'd never looked less like an invalid, in her opinion—or more like a buccaneer. Not a sick buccaneer, either, not any longer. The truth was, with his thickening beard and shower-rumpled hair, eyes throwing daggers, he looked more than capable of wreaking havoc on pretty much any venue he chose.

Her heart stumbled. She couldn't bear to look just then at the reasons for the irrational protests and denials that were screaming inside her head, so she told herself he was simply too weak, too sick to go. She told herself he needed her. Because she couldn't bring herself to admit the simple truth behind the protests, which was that it was she who needed *him*.

She stepped forward, reaching instinctively for him as he lurched to his feet, at that moment not sure in her heart whether she meant to help him…or stop him.

What happened next happened quickly. He swayed, uttering a muffled, "Whoa…" as his hands came up to clutch wildly at the only support within reach—which he did manage to grab hold of in the last instant before he toppled backward onto the bed.

As she felt his arms come around her, as she felt herself pitching forward, tightly wrapped in a surprisingly strong and wiry embrace, Celia had time for one electric flash of thought: *Oh, please don't let me hurt him.*

She heard a sharp exhalation—whose, she couldn't have said for certain—and the next thing she knew she was lying sprawled full-length on top of a hard masculine body. A thankfully no longer nude, but rather badly bruised, battered and recently gunshot body. A body, it further occurred to her, that had grown suddenly and alarmingly *still*.

Icy with fear, she carefully raised her head. Relief—and

warmth—flooded back into her when she saw her patient's eyes were open and focused. He appeared to be staring thoughtfully at the ceiling. Although she did think his breathing was somewhat shallow and constricted, and it seemed to her his heart was beating awfully fast. For that matter, so was hers.

"Are you okay?" she whispered. "I didn't hurt you, did I?"

She felt his abdominal muscles clench as he lifted his head in order to see her. He shook his head slightly, and his voice seemed to rumble inside her own chest. "Uh-uh…how 'bout you?"

"I'm okay." Which wasn't quite true. For starters, was that raspy croak *hers?* Then there was the way her heart was banging against the walls of her chest—for all the world, she thought in dawning horror, as if it were trying to get through it, to get closer to *him.*

In fact, her whole body, waking up from the numbness of shock, seemed overjoyed with the circumstances it now found itself in. All across the surface of her skin, happy little nerve endings were springing to delighted attention—particularly those lucky enough to be in direct contact with some part of *him.* Pulses pounded through her veins like excited signal drummers racing to spread glad tidings. And who could blame them? It had been a long time since they'd had anything much to get excited about.

"I *told* you you weren't ready," she said thickly, desperately trying to throw a net over her voracious senses. "Naturally, you wouldn't listen. What is it with men? Always think you have to—"

"Do you know," he interrupted in a conversational tone, "that you are a damned exasperatin' woman?"

Exasperating? For a moment she couldn't think of a response; she'd never heard that word applied to herself before. She decided she sort of liked it. Warmth crept through her and into her face, bringing a smile with it. "Thank you. That's very…John Wayne of you," she breathed, gazing down into his eyes. *Eyes…like dark vortices, pulling her in…*

Her perspective…her world…slowly narrowed until nothing

existed in it except for those eyes...then slowly it expanded outward again like a window spiraling open into a whole new world. A world that now included the hot, hard body beneath her, a furious pounding in her chest that seemed to leave no room for breathing, and the sweet, warm weight of his hands on her back. In this new world, she was deaf to reason and warnings of conscience. If, somewhere in the distant reaches of her mind, a voice was shrieking, *Are you out of your mind? He's injured, remember?* she didn't hear it.

And so, when his belly again tightened under hers, when his hand slid up to cradle the back of her head, when his head lifted and his mouth claimed hers, she was blissfully, eagerly waiting.

Chapter 7

The kiss tasted like pot roast and hot, hungry man, and all Celia could think about was how delicious it was, and how long it had been since she'd indulged herself with either of those, and how sorry she was about that now, and…what had she been thinking, anyway? Because this—the hungry-man part—was as good as anything in life ever gets, and she kissed him back with blissful abandon, unhurried, aching with the unbearable sweetness of it, like someone savoring a bite of chocolate cake after a long, wretched denial.

When he pulled away from her—though not far—she licked her lips and let go a careful breath, vibrant with regret.

"Wow." His voice was muffled, the word soft on her face.

"Yeah," she said, eyes still closed, still smiling—before she remembered she was *Celia Cross,* a TV star, for God's sake, and she ought to have some *pride,* dammit.

She opened her eyes and got them focused on the face so unnervingly near to hers, and was faintly surprised at the expression she saw there. *Puzzled,* she thought. Or maybe the word was…*bemused.*

"Tell me something…*Roy,*" she said, trying his name out loud for the first time—and again was surprised, this time by the queer little tremor that went through her when she said it. As when she'd seen his face in the light for the first time, it made him seem more real…brought her one step closer to knowing him…and did she really want that? She couldn't think—didn't want to. "Why on earth did you do that?"

His breath was warm on her face. "Tell you the truth, I'm not sure." He was frowning; his fingers moved in her hair as if testing the texture of some fine, rare fabric.

Shivers cascaded through her; goose bumps prickled her scalp and poured over her body. Her nipples hardened. Solemn as a doctor delivering bad news, she said, "You're badly injured, you know. You must've lost an awful lot of blood. You can't stand up without fainting." And then, sternly, "What were you thinking?"

"I dunno…something about…proving I'm still alive, I guess." His lips tilted in a smile of charming irony that affected her the way the smell of baking bread would a starving man. She swallowed as he went on, "*You* know—the drive to survive…something primitive like that."

She made a disparaging sound, but her heart wasn't in it. Maybe because his hand had found its way under her shirt, and his fingers were brushing her back in that exploring way…as if acquainting himself with the feel, the unique texture of her.

"But…doesn't it…hurt?" Her voice had grown breathless and hushed. His hand felt so good. "Your wound, I mean. I'd think—"

"Oh, *hell* yeah. But who—"

"Oh God—I'm sorry—you should've said—"

She was trying to shift her weight when his arms tightened around her with surprising strength. "Like I started to say, who cares?" His eyes seemed to smoulder as they looked at her. "Tell you what, though," he growled. "You really want to make me feel better, you can kiss me again. And this time, come here to me. I'm an injured man—don't make me come up there and get you."

He is *a pirate,* she thought, quaking with laughter and a strange and delicious fear. *At this moment, he could have just about anything he wanted from me, and I wouldn't know how to defend myself against him.*

And from somewhere far away, as she slowly dipped her smile to touch his, came the thought: *Why on earth would I want to?*

A pleased little chuckle bubbled up from her chest, and he answered it with one so fat with masculine smugness it should have enraged her—but didn't. Then the pressure of his hand cupping the back of her head closed the last of the distance between her mouth and his, and she gave up thinking entirely. She plunged into the kiss, the moment, the fantasy like a giddy child into a vat of ping-pong balls, fully aware that what she was doing bore about as much resemblance to real life as that.

But, oh, how good it felt! And what marvelous, wonderful fun it was…

And then, suddenly, it wasn't fun anymore. Oh, the desire still sizzled along her nerves and thumped in her body's secret places, but now, instead of joy, it was tears stinging behind her eyelids, and pain cramped her belly just beneath the places where the newly healed scars puckered her skin. Somewhere inside her, an anguished child was crying, *This is good—but it's not enough! I want* more!

She wanted him to make love to her, yes—so badly her whole body ached with it—and that in itself was astonishing. But at the same time she felt grief-stricken, because she knew if he did, it would never be enough.

I want more! I want…I want…

But she couldn't say it, not even in her mind. Because what she wanted was a fantasy not even she, who'd lived in a fantasy world all her life, could find a way to describe with words.

Roy knew the moment it went haywire. He felt a shudder go through her, which could have been good, but somehow wasn't. Instead of a vibrant, passionate woman, what this reminded him of was the way it felt to hold a captured rabbit in his hands.

"What is it? What's wrong?"

She'd torn her mouth from his and tilted her face downward, so his words emerged, rasping and guttural, against the watermark frown in the middle of her forehead. Her skin felt moist on his lips, as if she were coming out of a fever.

Her head rolled from side to side. In a muffled voice, she mumbled, "We can't do this. How *can* you, even? You've been shot…you almost died…."

"Why don't you let me worry about that?" Hell, how did he know? Some kind of biological imperative, maybe? Survival of the species? All he knew for certain was, he'd never felt a more powerful hunger for a woman than he did for her at that moment.

"Doc could walk in. Your friend Max—you said he'd be here 'in a minute.'"

"He's not my friend, he's my handler," he muttered. Then he swore softly and vehemently. After that, for a long time he didn't say anything, because he wanted in the worst way to deny the sense in what she'd said and was flashing back to a time in his youth when he'd tried hard to delude himself—and others—into believing it really was possible to die from unresolved arousal. But breathing in her scent, that light, sweet flower fragrance he couldn't place, he felt her body grow still in his arms. Inevitably, a similar acceptance came like cool rain to dampen his own raging fires.

After a while, he said in an aggrieved tone, "Did I mention you're a very exasperatin' woman?"

"You did." She said it without lifting her head, aiming the words at his chest, but he thought he could hear a smile come into her voice. "And if I recall, I took it as a compliment."

"Exasperating…and *weird*. When I said you were beautiful, which *I* thought was a compliment, you took it as an insult."

"Yeah, well…"

Regret sliced through him like physical pain as she eased

herself off of him, careful to avoid his wounded side, and scooted
to the edge of the bed. She sat there for several moments, hands
braced beside her, rocking herself slightly, face turned away
from him, letting the silence lengthen.

Consoling himself with the visual feast of her…the long, supple lines, the graceful curve of neck and shoulder, the rapturous
tumble of sun-shot hair, it struck Roy once more how beautiful
she really was—easily the most beautiful woman *he'd* ever met.
Holding her in his arms, kissing her, he'd managed to forget
that—and pretty much everything else, too, of course, including
how much every part of him really did still hurt, and the vital nature of the mission he'd failed to complete—but especially that.
Now, though, with the truth of it staring him in the face, the
thought smacked him upside the head: *Man, what were you
thinking?*

"What's up with that?" He pillowed his head on one folded
arm and aimed the question at her back, his voice an abrasive intrusion in a silence that had been allowed to linger too long. "I
thought women *liked* to be told they're pretty."

She threw him a fierce dark look over one shoulder, a look he
couldn't read. "It's nothing. Except, just *once,* I'd like—"

"*What?*" he demanded when she broke it off with a frustrated
exhalation. "Don't do that. *What* would you like? Tell me."

It was nervy of him to say that to her, he supposed, and for a
while he was sure she wouldn't answer him. She sat very still,
gazing along her shoulder at nothing, her profile revealing the
same sad look she'd worn before when he'd mentioned how
beautiful she was. He couldn't explain it, but he really wanted to
know why. He felt a strange certainty the answer was going
to provide an important key to what made this woman tick.

With an equally strange certainty, he knew he wanted that key.
What he wasn't sure about was what he might do with it once he
had it.

"Just once," Celia said softly, "I'd like to be admired for
something *I'm* responsible for. Do you understand?"

She shifted around to look at him then, a frown rippling the center of her forehead, and he forgot about the fact that she was an actress and thought about all the expressions he'd seen her wear on that lovely face of hers, and how none of them had tugged at his heart the way this one did.

"Listen. I look the way I do because I got good genes—big deal. My looks…and my acting ability…they were a *gift*. An inheritance." Her gaze shifted again, this time to the pictures on the wall. "I've been beautiful and famous since the day I was born. And don't get me wrong—" her smile was wry, now, but it didn't entirely erase the wistfulness "—I'm very grateful to my parents. But I'm thirty-two years old, and I'd like to think I've done *something* with my life that *I* could be proud of."

"Looks to me like you've done okay," Roy said gruffly, nodding toward the row of golden statuettes on the top shelf.

She followed his gaze and made a disparaging sound. "Those? Well, the Oscars are my parents', of course. As for the Emmys, let me tell you—"

But before she could, the doorbell rang. "That will be your friend, I'm sure," Celia said lightly, as she rose to answer it. And Roy, who not so long ago would have given just about anything to hear that sound, now found himself silently cursing Max for being so damn prompt.

Halfway across the room, she paused, turned, then nodded toward the row of Emmys. "You want to know how much those are worth?" she said in an amused, conversational tone. "I haven't appeared on the show I won them for in over a year. You want to know how much they miss me? To accommodate my 'indefinite' leave of absence, 'Nurse Suzanne' has been presumed to be dead after her plane went down somewhere in the Amazon jungle. Now—my contract comes up for renewal next spring, at which time one of three things will happen: *If* my contract is renewed and I decide to return to the show, Nurse Suzanne will be miraculously discovered tending the natives in some remote village. If it isn't, either someone new will be cast in the role, and

Nurse Suzanne will be miraculously resurrected following extensive plastic surgery to heal her terrible wounds, or no one will be cast in the role, and poor Nurse Suzanne will remain dead—'dead' being, of course, a tentative condition in daytime drama. Either way, with or without me the show goes on."

The doorbell pealed again, more insistently. Celia threw Roy a dazzling, movie-star smile and went out, leaving him dazed and wondering whether any of the emotions he'd just witnessed were for real, or if he'd just been treated to an Emmy-worthy performance by one of the best actresses he'd ever seen.

In the living room, Celia paused to rake her fingers through her hair and draw several deep, cleansing breaths. It's like being in a play, she told herself. All this adrenaline churning…butterflies rampaging… *Exit, stage left. New Scene—a few minutes later—Celia enters, stage right.*

Blowing out the last of the breaths in an explosive whoosh, she affixed a charming hostess's smile to her lips, marched to the front door and threw it open.

"Hel-lo," she said warmly to the man who stood there looking edgy, hand upraised to press the doorbell for the third time. "You must be Max. Won't you come in?"

The man appeared to be around fifty, about her height and wiry in build. Even though his nose was rather large and his grayish brown hair was thinning, he was attractive in a way, possibly because he had a very nice smile. He was wearing jeans and a Hawaiian print shirt and sunglasses, the last of which he peeled off to reveal an astonished stare.

He muttered a profane exclamation, for which he immediately apologized. "Sorry. You really *are* Celia Cross. I thought—hell, I don't know what I thought. My wife is never going to believe this…." He shook his head and his voice trailed off as he moved past her into the house, tucking the sunglasses into the pocket of his shirt and looking about him with undisguised interest.

In the living room, he halted, apparently transfixed by the

view. When Celia joined him, he turned to her with a gleam of amusement in his keen gray eyes and said dryly, "Nice place."

"Thank you." She smiled back and decided she definitely liked him.

"So." Deliberately turning away from the vast Pacific beyond the glass, Max took in a breath and lifted his eyebrows. "Where's my boy?"

My boy? Liking the man more by the minute, Celia hid her delight and murmured, "This way," as she made a graceful gesture for him to follow her. She was rather enjoying the role of gracious hostess as she led him to the room behind the stairs, knocked lightly as she pushed the door open, then stood aside like a well-trained housemaid for him to enter.

As he slipped past her, Max gave an explosive exclamation, the same one with which he'd greeted Celia at the front door. That was followed by, "Man, what the hell *happened?*"

"He was shot," Celia offered. "Among other things."

She thought Roy looked rather comical, actually, standing beside the bed with his head and one arm through the appropriate openings of the sweatshirt she'd given him to wear. The rest of the shirt was rolled up around his neck, leaving his chest and torso, complete with its Technicolor assortment of bandages, bruises and abrasions, mostly bare.

The look on Max's face as he walked slowly toward him was like someone coming upon a tethered leopard—equal parts dismay and awe, with a healthy amount of caution.

Celia's, as she gazed at the long, tapering lines of body disappearing into the sweats she'd once worn herself…sweats that now rode perilously low on narrow masculine flanks…must have reflected something very different. Remembering how that body had felt under hers, she had a sudden and terrible need to swallow—except she couldn't, because her mouth had gone dry.

"I can't lift my damn arm," Roy muttered, throwing her a furious glare, as though it was somehow her fault. Transferring the glare to Max, he immediately contradicted his first statement with a growled, "I'm okay—I'm *fine*."

"Yeah, I can see that." Like a patient father helping a child dress for kindergarten, Max calmly lifted Roy's arm and directed it into the proper sleeve opening.

Celia diverted herself to the easy chair where she perched on the arm and folded her arms across her waist. From there, she watched jealously as Max guided Roy to the edge of the bed and gently sat him down.

"Okay," he said, folding his arms across his chest and frowning down at Roy's glowering face, "let's hear it. What the hell happened?"

Instead of answering, Roy stared meaningfully at Max and jerked his head toward Celia. Then, switching to her and showing his teeth in what he no doubt thought was a winning smile, he said jovially, "Hey…Celia…could I maybe get a glass of water? Or better yet, how about a cuppa coffee? What about you, Max? You want something to drink?"

"Uh, sure," said Max, "that'd be great. Whatever you have." But he flicked her a look of apology that made her inclined to forgive *him*.

Roy, however… What did he think she was—*five?*

Max's eyes followed Celia as she rose with dignity, dipped her head in acquiescence and floated from the room.

"I can't believe you," he said in a low voice, after a long enough pause to make sure she'd really gone. "That's Celia Cross you just treated like the hired help. *Celia Cross.*"

Roy shifted around and scowled, trying to pretend he wasn't feeling uncomfortable about that himself. "So she's an actress," he muttered. "In a soap opera. Big deal. Anyway, she's been trying to get me to eat and drink stuff ever since she hauled me in here. She's probably thrilled I asked her for something."

"I can't believe you," Max said again. "Where've you been living, under a rock? Or are you just too young to remember?" he paused to shake his head dolefully. "God, I feel old…."

"You are old," said Roy, secure in the knowledge that Max had at least fifteen years on him. "Remember what?"

"Not what—*who*." He jerked his head toward the biggest of the pictures on the wall, a framed movie poster. "Frederick Cross and Alice Merryhill—just about the greatest husband-and-wife team ever to grace the silver screen. They were…Fred Astaire and Ginger Rogers without the music. Unforgettable." He sighed, shaking his head. "When they died—"

Sympathy kicked Roy under his ribs. Or maybe old memories of the daddy he'd lost too young. "What happened to them?"

"Plane crash—small plane, in Africa, I think it was the early Eighties. Celia would've been just a kid. Oh—yeah—" he paused to throw Roy an accusing look "—that woman you've been ordering around like the maid? She's their daughter—their only child. True Hollywood royalty, man."

"Well, hell," Roy said moodily, gazing at the poster, "I *thought* she looked sorta familiar."

Celia was pacing in the kitchen like a caged lioness. She was about as angry as she could ever remember being.

How dare he? I found him. Washed up on the beach like a chunk of driftwood. I saved his life. He talked to me—okay, he was out of his head, but still…I was there. He talked to me. How dare he shut me out now? Banish me like a child? I deserve a part in this, dammit! I earned it.

She stared down at the tray on the countertop in front of her, not seeing it, seeing instead images from the past thirty-six hours…a gaunt face, gray-frosted with sand…a bruised and battered body, dark against her flowered sheets…a naked body, lean and spare, coiled and tense, like a painting of some martyred saint. Remembering the way that same body had felt when she'd held it wrapped in her arms, sand—gritty and cold against her nakedness, and the strange, intense sense of *ownership*.

Okay…it was impossible to stay mad at him, remembering

what it had felt like to be lying on top of that body, hot and vital and strong…wrapped in *his* arms. Remembering his mouth…the heat… the taste of it…

You're pathetic, you know that? You've fallen for him. You have—admit it!

Impossible. I've known him what, two days? And most of that time, he's been unconscious. I'd have to be crazy.

Yeah, but we're not talking love, here. How long does it take to fall in lust? Face it, Celia. You're not mad because you're being excluded—you're scared you're going to lose him before you even have a chance to take him to bed. He's going to leave and go back to his life, as exciting and dangerous as that may be, and you're never going to see him again.

Celia found that she was shaking her head in silent denial. But even as she whispered, "No, uh-uh," she knew it was true.

You're like a little kid—"I found him, he's mine!" Finders keepers, right?

All right, she thought, maybe I have fallen for him. *Maybe I do want him. But it's not just* him *I want. It's the life he leads— a life that* means *something. Dammit, I want that, too.*

This…thing—whatever it is—he's involved in…there's a part for me in it, too. I know there is. I'm not going to be shut out. I won't let them shut…me…out.

She blinked the tray into focus and was surprised to find it laden with coffee cups and spoons and napkins. She had no recollection of having put them there. "Great," she muttered aloud, "all I've done the past couple of days is fetch trays from the kitchen—now I'm doing it in my sleep."

With that, she turned her back on the counter and the tray, opened the refrigerator, snatched up two bottles of gourmet iced tea—mango-flavored—and marched out of the kitchen.

Both men broke off talking when she entered the bedroom.

Ignoring their pointed silence and polite, waiting stares, Celia swept across the room and, like a grande duchess bestowing favors, handed each of them a sweating bottle of tea. Then she plunked herself down on the arm of the chair across from the two of them and folded her arms on her chest.

"You might as well let me stay," she said, with an airy toss of her head to disguise the way her heart was pounding. "I know everything anyway."

Max and Roy looked at each other. After a long and profound silence, Max said in an ominous tone, "Does she?"

Roy opened his mouth.

"Don't blame him," Celia said. "He was out of his head. He didn't even know I was there. Well—actually, I think he thought I was you. He made a very good report—very complete. At least, it seemed like it to me. Lots of detail."

Max tore his fascinated gaze from Celia and swiveled back to Roy. "Is that true?"

Roy cleared his throat. His eyes flicked toward Celia, and she felt an odd little thrill ripple through her. "I haven't heard it all," he said in a glum and resigned tone, "but from the part she's told me, I'd have to say…yeah, it probably is."

"Wow." Max ran a hand back across his thinning hair, then left it clutching the back of his neck, which he began to rub as if he'd just developed an ache there. "This…could be a problem."

"Tell me about it."

Celia slid from the arm of the chair into the seat and leaned eagerly forward. "Actually…I think I can help you with your problem." No stranger to the effectiveness of good timing, she paused, teeth clamped down on her lower lip, to let the suspense build.

Across from her, seated side by side on the bed, the two men exchanged "Is she for *real?*" looks.

It was Max who spoke, in a polite and wary tone. "And…what problem is it you think you can help us with?"

Celia delivered her money line, shivery with triumph. "You need to get someone onto Abby's yacht, right? Well…it just so happens…I can do that for you. I can get on board that boat."

Roy snorted and threw up his head like a startled horse. Max frowned and said, *"Abby?"*

"Yes—the Arab prince? Abdul Fayed Amir Abbas—or what-ever… anyway, it's Abby, to his friends."

"Friends…" Max said faintly.

"Good Lord," Roy exclaimed, staring at her, "you mean to tell me you *know* him?"

Celia flicked a gaze toward him, but it was like touching hot coals and she quickly brought it back to Max where she felt much safer. She wasn't used to having men look at her the way Roy did—unless, of course, such a fierce and smoky look happened to be called for in the script.

But this—this wasn't anything like having some actor stand-ing in front of her, reading lines, feeding her cues. And she had no lines to give back to him, lines cleverly written by someone else. She was on her own. This was real. She could almost feel the heat radiating from those eyes…hear the tension singing in that taut body. And she knew when she continued, whatever she came up with, her voice wasn't going to be as steady as she wanted it to be.

But I still…somehow…have to make them believe in me. I have to make them believe I can do this.

"I don't know him *well*," she said, locking eyes with Max and finding it was much easier if she pretended Roy wasn't in the room. "But I have met him. Several times. At parties, and things. Look—" she lifted a hand and gestured toward the pictures on the walls "—you have to understand—the house my parents left me is right up there in the part of Bel Air where Abby's is. It's like a small town. If I hadn't sold the house when I did—it was about the first thing I did when I turned twenty-five and came into my inheritance—too many memories…" She gave Max a shrug and a sad little smile. "Anyway…if I hadn't sold that house, Abby would be my neighbor now. But then," she added, turning up the wattage on the smile, "I wouldn't have had this place, and I wouldn't have been here to discover Roy washed up on the beach and saved his life. It's like…kismet…isn't it?"

"Did she do that?" Max asked Roy in an awed tone. "Find you on the beach?"

"'Fraid so," Roy said. It was the sound a dangerous animal makes, low in its throat…just before it springs. "I was about to tell you."

"Good God. How the hell did she get you in here?"

"Carried me."

"Not…by *herself*." Max's tone was flatly disbelieving.

"Well, of course not," Celia interjected, "I had help. But even with Doc, it wasn't easy."

Max's glare snapped back to her. "Doc? Who the hell is this we're talking about?"

"Yeah, that's *another* thing," Roy said ominously.

"Oh, never mind that now." She switched her focus to Roy, bracing herself, willing him to look at her. Then he did, and it was worse than she'd expected. Her heart stumbled and began to beat even harder and faster.

She said breathlessly, "I saved your life. Dammit, you—"

"Don't…say it—" His face squinched up in a grimace of extreme pain.

"—you owe me."

Roy clamped a hand over his eyes and let out a gust of breath. "She had to say it."

Max sat forward and clasped his hands together, elbows on his knees. "Miss Cross—"

"Oh—Celia, *please*." She flashed him her most radiant smile.

He coughed, looked at his hands, then back at her. She thought his eyes seemed intelligent…measuring. Unlike Roy's, which looked like something that could set off explosives. "Celia. What is it, exactly, that you want?"

She sat up straight and widened her eyes. "What do I want? Why…nothing, except what I said. I want to help, that's all. We're all fighting a war, right? I just want to do my part." She felt an odd little thrill go through her as she realized she meant it—absolutely—and she finished in a quieter voice, keeping her eyes locked on Max's, even though the words were meant for the person who was sitting next to him, simmering like an active volcano. "I can't do much, but I can do this. You suspect Abby's yacht is being used by terrorists, and you need to get someone on board to find out for sure. Well, I can get you there." She paused. "Are you telling me you're willing to pass up a chance like that?"

While Max studied her in thoughtful silence, Roy cleared his throat loudly. "You're forgetting something," he said, raspy anyway. "The prince's thugs got a *real* good look at me. By this time, they've probably got me ID'd, as well." Max looked at him. He lifted a shoulder. "I was about to tell you."

Celia laughed, a light ripple of sound. "You're forgetting where you are. I know people who can change your appearance so your own mother wouldn't recognize you."

"So do I," Max said, studying her thoughtfully.

Roy looked at him and made a disgusted sound. "I can't believe it. You're actually considering this ridiculous notion of hers. It's *crazy,* you know that. Lunacy. These people are dangerous. Trust me," he added darkly, "I know."

Max was gazing at Celia with narrowed eyes. "It's not like she's planning on joining special ops. Hell, during World War II, movie stars flew bombers. All she's wanting to do is what she does anyway." He gave her his very nice smile. "And very well, I might add. I don't see how there'd be any danger...."

"Yeah, well, you can't guarantee that. I'm not having any part of it."

"It's completely understandable *you* wouldn't want to go back there again," Celia said sweetly. "I'm sure Max can find someone else to go with me." Her gaze followed Roy as he pushed himself awkwardly to his feet—she just couldn't help it.

He stood glowering down at her, jaws black with beard, eyes black with fury, radiating heat and energy and danger...although...he did look a *little* silly, she thought fondly, with his hair all shower-rumpled, wearing baby blue sweats that were miles too short. But...with a shave and a good haircut, dressed in something...really classy...something elegant...say...Armani?

Oh, my. A wave of heat nearly knocked her over. She caught her breath audibly, and Roy instantly rounded on her with a suspicious, *"What?"*

She opened her mouth, then closed it again. "Nothing," she lied. She couldn't very well tell him she'd just gotten incredibly turned on from imagining him in *clothes,* could she?

Well, it's because I've already seen him naked, she told herself. *No imagination needed there at all.*

With a supreme effort of will, she tore her gaze away from images of Roy—both real and fantasy—and turned back to Max, who was also getting to his feet, though with considerably less devastating effect on her senses.

"Fact of the matter is, if she's right—" he nodded at Celia as he pulled his sunglasses out of the pocket of his Hawaiian shirt "—she can save us a whole lot of the one thing we don't have enough of, and that's time. We might not have a choice."

He jabbed a finger at the yellow *UCLA* scrawled across Roy's chest. "You—sit tight for the moment. Nobody knows you're here—it's a good safe house for you, until we know how badly your cover's blown. I'm gonna send a company doctor to look you over, make sure you're okay…get you some antibiotics. Meanwhile, I'll run this idea of hers—" he nodded at Celia "—by the director, see what he says. And, I'm gonna need to talk to this Doc character, too. Where'd you say—"

"Next door," said Celia, trying not to sound too eager. "Doc's okay—really. His name is Peter Cavendish. He's a real doctor, just…well—" she bit down on her lower lip and gave him a winsome smile "—not currently licensed to practice. But that's good," she added quickly when she saw Max and Roy exchange glances, "because it means the last thing he's going to do is tell anyone about this. Right?" She beamed at Max as she took his arm.

Roy thought he could actually hear his teeth grinding together. His knew his stomach was in knots, and the phrase *over my dead body* kept running through his brain. He really wanted to kick someone's butt—Max's, for instance—but was pretty sure if he tried it, he'd only fall flat on his own.

"I don't suppose you remembered to bring me some clothes," he called plaintively.

In the doorway, Max snapped his fingers and half turned to give him a shrug of apology. "You know…I didn't. Sorry—I was kind of in a hurry to get here." His grin went crooked and all the humor went out of it. "Hey, I thought for sure you were dead. When I didn't hear…" He cleared his throat, then tilted his head toward Celia. "She's right, you know." He smiled at her along his shoulder. "You do owe her. Big-time."

The two of them walked out of the room together, arm in arm, cozy as two kids heading off to the prom. Just as they disappeared from view, Roy heard Max say, "Could I get your autograph? It's for my wife—she's a big, huge soap opera fan…"

Chapter 8

Roy stood where he was and swore until he ran out of words. Then he figured the problem was he needed some air. He'd been laid up in bed, cooped up in a strange house with strange people, way too long.

How else could he explain the antsy way he felt, watching a woman he barely knew smile at his friend and handler that way. She was a *star,* for God's sake! Must have smiled like that at thousands of men. Probably didn't think twice about it.

He made it down the hallway and into the living room before he started to feel light headed and woozy and had to stop and hang on to the back of a cream suede sofa until his ears stopped ringing. Amazing, he thought, what being a few pints low on vital body fluids could do to a man.

Damn, but he hated the weakness. And he was going to have to get over it. Fast. Because Max was right about one thing—they were running out of time.

Just thinking about that gave Roy a queasy feeling in his

stomach, as if he were in some kind of vehicle moving way too fast and beyond his control. And *Max*. What the hell was he thinking? He had to be really feeling the pressure, too, if he was giving serious thought to Celia's hare-brained idea.

When Roy thought about *that*—when he thought about the man he'd come face-to-face with on the *Bibi Lilith*, the man who'd interrogated him, the man who'd shot him…touching Celia…smiling at her in that cruel way, looking at her with those dead eyes…

No. No way. He straightened himself up, gritted his teeth and fought off the dizziness with sheer willpower. He had to get his strength back. Had to get back in the game before that crazy woman convinced his boss to do something incredibly stupid.

Weaving like a 2 a.m. drunk, he made his way through the living room and out onto the deck, which was where Celia found him a few minutes later.

When he heard the sliding glass door open, he turned away from the view of sky and sea that was so different from the one he knew. Turned away, too, from the homesickness that had come upon him unexpectedly, along with thoughts of the beach house he'd left behind…gray-shingled siding with white porches, sitting tall on its stilts among gentle dunes tufted with sea grass…looking out upon endless sugar-sand beaches and sunny blue waters. Here, the beach houses of the rich and famous crowded close to the sand, yuppies jogged along the water's edge and teenagers threw Frisbees to one another, while surfers sat patiently on their boards beyond the breakers. But he knew those undulating, coppery swells hid dangerous rip tides, forests of kelp and jagged volcanic rocks, and the ever-hovering fog shrouded the horizon in a sinister curtain. The Pacific, he had reason to know, was anything but peaceful. It was cold, and vast, and lethal….

Suppressing a shiver, he braced his backside and his hands on the deck railing to steady himself and watched Celia come toward him, smiling, positively glowing with satisfaction, like a cat fresh from dining on a canary.

"You might as well wipe that smirk off your face," he said in a gravelly voice, "because you are *not* doing this. It's just a plumb crazy idea."

"Well, now," she said sweetly as she joined him, leaning her hands on the railing and lifting her face to the reddening sun and the chilling breeze, "it's really not up to you, is it? It's up to Max—and the director, whoever he is. And Max seems to think it's a *good* idea. Seems to think the director will, too."

"Seems to me," Roy said, scowling, "Max is way more susceptible to the influence and charm of a beautiful woman than a *married* man ought to be."

Her laughter seemed to sparkle like the sun out there on the water. She looked at him along her shoulder. "Seems to me," she countered in a husky voice, "you were pretty susceptible yourself not so long ago."

"That was before I knew what a devious woman you are," he muttered. "Before I knew you had an ulterior motive for kissing me."

She jerked as if he'd startled her, and an emotion he couldn't identify flashed like a seagull's shadow across her face. "I don't have any…*ulterior motives,* as you put it. It's like I told you—I just want to help. I want—" her breath caught and she turned back to the water, her blue eyes for a moment eerily reflecting its coppery glow "—I want to do something *I* can take credit for. Something…important. Something—okay, this is going to sound corny—something *meaningful.*"

"Fine," Roy said savagely. "Why don't you go volunteer at an old folks' home? Adopt an orphan from Bolivia? Why do you have to do something that could get you killed?"

The breeze blew her hair across her face when she turned it toward him. She lifted her chin as she fingered her hair back, revealing a sardonic smile. "You're being a bit melodramatic, don't you think?"

"Melodramatic?" His voice cracked on the word. "Lady, you tell me you listened to my nightmare ravings, heard every word.

You've seen *me*—living, breathing proof of how rough these people play. And you think I'm being *melodramatic?*"

"You were caught trespassing," Celia pointed out with airy confidence. "Obviously up to no good. I, on the other hand, will be Abby's invited guest. What danger can there be in that?"

Roy couldn't argue with her logic, and he couldn't find a way to explain his to her, either. Maybe he didn't have any. He just knew he didn't want Celia Cross—or *any* woman, he told himself—getting anywhere near the *Bibi Lilith,* Prince Abdul al-Fayad, or the thugs who'd tried their level best to put an end to Betty Starr's little boy Roy.

Finally, after working his jaw on it for a couple of minutes, he stuck his chin out in her direction and said, "Fine. Get me an invitation. That's *if* the director gives the okay. I'll take it from there."

Celia shook her head. "Oh, no. Not without me, you won't. I'm in on it, or no deal."

Roy felt his body go tense and still. He drew himself in around a humming core of anger and, with ominous calm, said, "What do you mean, 'No deal'?"

"I mean," she said, not the least bit impressed or intimidated, locking eyes with him, "you'll have to find another way to get on board Abby's yacht. You should also think about the fact," she added, leaning closer to him and dropping her voice to a seductive whisper, "that I know things you wish I didn't know. *And* I have mainline access to the media."

Roy's breath hissed between his teeth. "You wouldn't."

Again her smoky blue gaze didn't waver. "Don't bet on it."

He didn't know how long he stood there, staring down into those eyes, with his heart banging against the walls of his chest and his belly quivering with a hellish combination of physical weakness and cold fury. Dammit, she was so close...*too* close...and vibrant and sweet-smelling and beautiful and warm. Kissin'-close, if he'd been of such a mind.

Which he sure as hell wasn't. Right then, he'd have been more likely to strangle her.

Then, as abruptly as if someone had flipped a light switch, a smile burst over her face, dispelling the tension the way light eliminates darkness and causing a queer little kick in Roy's chest. "But why are we even talking about such things? It's not ever going to come to that. You'll see. Max is a smart man—he knows a good thing when he sees it."

She clapped her hands together, reminding him of nothing so much as somebody trying to distract a difficult child. "So—what would you like for dinner? That was it for the pot roast, but I've got…let's see…meat loaf, lasagna, and…oh yeah, chicken cordon bleu."

"I just ate," Roy reminded her, scowling. He was still smarting and the last thing he wanted to do was play her game, but, *damnation*, it was hard to resist that smile.

"Oh, I know," she said gaily, "but I'm planning ahead. It's all frozen, you see. I have to get something out to thaw." She paused for a moment to cock her head as if replaying that inside her head, then gave him an impish version of the smile. "I can't believe I thought of it, actually. Wow—I'm better at this domestic stuff than I thought."

He snorted—he'd be damned if he was going to let her make him laugh. If she wanted to declare a truce for the time being, fine, that was all right with him. But this war wasn't over. Not by a long shot. There was just no way he was going on an undercover mission with thousands—maybe millions—of lives at stake, with a soap opera star as his partner. *No way.*

"Yeah," he muttered, "you're a regular Julia Child." He didn't tell her he was surprised a TV actress would even *eat,* much less cook.

If possible, her smile grew even more dazzling. "Thank you." Then she added, in a chummy, conversational way, "I actually knew her, you know. She and my parents were good friends." She stuck out her lower lip in a regretful pout. "It's a pity, I suppose, they never asked Julia to teach me to cook. The truth is—" now the lower lip was captured by perfectly even white teeth "—I can't boil water. But—" and like the sun playing peekaboo with clouds, the smile reappeared "—I nuke fairly well."

Roy stared at her through the whole amazing display, and when she turned with a flirty little flounce to go back into the house, it was a beat or two before he could find his voice, to ask her the question that had come to him, whether he wanted it to or not.

"What was it like?" He knew his voice sounded harsh but didn't do anything to fix it. He waited while she paused to look back at him, then continued on the same gravelly way. "Growing up like that, I mean—in a Bel Air mansion, with famous movie stars for parents?"

She came back to him slowly, like a prowling cat, measuring him with her eyes. He watched her with a sardonic smile on his lips, fortified against her, now, expecting another performance. "Poor Little Rich Girl," maybe? But as she came closer, her smile seemed to grow wistful…then sad. And there was something in her eyes that made him think this time it—the smile and the sadness—might be real.

"It was…wonderful," she said softly. "More wonderful than you can possibly imagine. It was like…not even a fairy tale, because there was nothing evil or scary or bad. Ever. My life was always filled with laughter and love and music and…and the most *amazing* people. Everyone I knew was either beautiful or brilliantly talented or funny—sometimes all three—and it seemed as though everyone adored me. Everyone was always kind.…"

She was beside him again, hands resting on the deck railing, gazing out at the water, but closer than before. He jerked as her shoulder brushed against his arm; though it *seemed* accidental, it sent a shock wave through him and set off a thrumming beat low-down in his belly.

He looked over at her. The setting sun lent her skin and hair a summery warmth that contradicted a damp and chilly wind that was sharp enough now to redden her nose and spark tears in her eyes. At least, that was what he told himself was responsible for that display of apparent vulnerability. He didn't want to believe it was real. Didn't want to feel sympathy for the likes of Celia Cross. He didn't want to feel anything for her—to be truthful, not for any woman, right at the moment, but especially not a woman like this one. A woman as devious, as manipulative, as skilled an actress as this one.

"What about your parents?" he asked gruffly. "I'd think they'd have had to be gone quite a bit."

"They were." Since he wasn't looking at her, he felt rather than saw her nod. Heard the little catch of her breath. "When they could, they took me along. I loved that—I got to have a tutor, and when my parents weren't busy on the set, we had the most marvelous adventures." She flashed him a wind-whipped smile. "I've ridden on elephants and camels. And once, even in a rickshaw." She looked away again, across the water. "When they couldn't take me, they'd bring me back things…marvelous things from faraway places. You saw some of them—in the bookcase in my…in your room."

"It must have been hard," he prompted when she didn't go on. He didn't know why. Maybe he was thinking about his own daddy again. "To have all that end."

She flashed him a look. "Oh, it didn't end. I mean—there was a lot in my life that didn't change at all when my parents died. I'd always had an army of people looking after me—nannies, housekeepers, maids, cooks, gardeners, lawyers, business managers, music teachers, dance teachers…you name it. That went on the same as before, paid for by the trust my parents had set up for me. I went to the same school—private, but not boarding." Her smile was wry now. "I was driven to school every day in a limo and picked up afterward the same way. Which wasn't unusual for the school I went to, actually."

"So, you mean to tell me everything went on just the same? You didn't miss your parents at all?"

She flashed him another look, one that stung like a slap. "Of course I miss them. They were the only people in this world who loved me unconditionally. I miss them every day of my life."

Something tightened inside his chest, and he turned restlessly to face the water. "You don't have any other family?"

"Nobody." She shook her head, at the same time lifting her face to the wind and the dying light, as if, he thought, she were shaking off a cloak or a veil. Then she turned toward him and propped one elbow on the railing. "What about you? Are your parents alive?"

Distracted, he shook his head, then amended it with a shrug. "Well—my daddy died when I was just a kid. Momma's still goin' strong, though." He purposely said it in the accents of Oglethorp County, Georgia, where he'd been born and raised, and she smiled in appreciation.

"Any brothers and sisters?"

Grinning, he drawled, "A whole bunch. Three of each."

She seemed to absorb that for a moment, head canted as if she were listening to voices from far away. She straightened up and pushed away from the railing. "I hope you know how lucky you are," she said softly.

She left him standing there, alone, listening to the whisper and sigh of surf in the dusk. Muttering swearwords under his breath and wondering why it was he always seemed to feel off balance and uncertain about things after conversations with this woman. Particularly since the words *off balance and uncertain* weren't ones he'd ever felt obliged to apply to himself before now.

He didn't know how he felt about her, for one thing. Though he knew for sure how he didn't *want* to feel. Grateful to her, for one thing—although he was; he valued his life a great deal, and was more than glad she'd saved it for him. What he didn't like was being *beholden*—feeling as if he owed her something, and her being manipulative enough to hold that over him to get her way. Even if, in a way, he could understand *why* she wanted it…

Well, he for *damned* sure didn't want to feel sympathy for her. He didn't want to like her, either, not even a little bit, and he didn't want to fall for the charm and sex appeal she undoubtedly had—in spades. Especially the sex appeal. It was so damned blatant—and *still* he couldn't seem to help but respond to it. How stupid was that? Like seeing the damn pit trap right there in front of him and tumbling into it anyway.

The coastal evening chill was beginning to seep into his bones—something that seemed to happen to him a whole lot easier since his brush with near fatal hypothermia. He was about to abandon the uneasy solitude of the deck and head for the warmth of the house and more of Celia's company, aggravating as it was, when a light came on, illuminating the deck next door. That was followed by the sandy scrape of a sliding glass door.

"Well, I must say, you're looking a bit more chipper." The sardonic, English-accented voice drifted across from the neighboring deck as the man Roy had last seen bending over him with a stethoscope moved into the light. He was wearing what appeared to be a purple jogging suit that made him resemble a slightly wrinkled grape, which seemed appropriate, since he had a glass of wine in one hand and a cigarette in the other.

Some advertisement for a doctor, Roy thought.

"Yeah," he drawled with a half grin as he ambled over to the side of the deck that was closest to its neighbor, "I think maybe I'll live. I'd like to thank you, by the way."

Doc waved the cigarette in a dismissive way. "I didn't do much, I'm afraid. Not much I *could* do, under the circumstances—I'm sure Celia's told you. She's the one you should thank."

"Yeah," said Roy morosely, "so I've been told."

Doc chuckled and started to say something, then drank wine instead. Holding up the glass in a "Wait one moment" gesture, he made his way without haste down the wooden stairs to the sand. Roy waited for the other man to join him, then they both sat down in adjoining deck chairs.

"So," Doc said, leaning closer and lowering his voice, "I take it our Celia has been working her wiles on you."

"Wiles?" Smiling without humor, Roy shook his head. "I guess that's a pretty good word for it."

Doc drank wine, then settled back comfortably in the deck chair, seemingly impervious to the increasing chill. "I had a visitor a short while ago," he remarked, apparently changing the subject. "Fellow by the name of Max." He paused to take a puff from the cigarette, then added dryly as he exhaled, "I assured him I have no desire to become involved in anything, which might threaten the peace and solitude to which I've grown accustomed. He seemed to take me at my word—although by this time, I suspect he knows more about me than my mum and my ex-wife combined."

Roy carefully folded his arms across himself and leaned forward, trying to conserve what body heat he could. "Celia said you lost your license to practice medicine. How come?"

"Bad choices, my boy, bad choices." After looking in vain for an ashtray, Doc flicked the cigarette over the side of the deck onto the sand. "I lost a great deal by them, and have only myself to blame. But I have 'paid my debt to society,' as they say, and consider myself fortunate to have such a place in which to spend my exile." He waved the wineglass, taking in the deck and the dark ocean and sky beyond, then nodded his head toward the lighted square of window behind him. "Not to mention such charming company with which to share it. Although," he added enigmatically, draining the last of the wine and placing the glass carefully on the floor of the deck beside his chair, "it appears *that* may be about to come to an end. Ah, well—I always knew that, unlike mine, Celia's exile was only temporary."

"Exile? Celia?"

Doc's eyes widened. "She didn't tell you?"

"She said she had an accident. Somebody was killed?"

"Killed? Oh, yes." Doc sat up and shifted around in the chair to face him. "It was a terrible tragedy, really. And Celia very nearly died herself, you know. Broke both her legs…massive internal injuries—to put it in non-medical terms. She's not been back on her feet more than a few months, actually. But—well, the physical injuries weren't the worst of it. What really destroyed her was the way the media—and the public, goaded on by the media, no doubt—treated her. Attacked like a pack of wild dogs. There were rumors—and outright accusations, not just in the tabloids, but in the mainstream media—of drug use, alcohol abuse…all sorts of things. Absolutely none of which were true, of course." He made a disgusted noise. "It was a case of exhaustion, pure and simple. She'd been pushing herself to finish a guest shot on a prime-time show, at the same time her character on the soap opera was involved in a very demanding story line. She fell asleep at the wheel driving home from the set late one night. In itself a tragic mistake, obviously.

"But as for the other…Celia was totally unprepared for it. She'd always had it easy, you know, as things go in this business. She was charming, beautiful, talented *and* of royal blood—as you Americans consider royalty. Success and adoration came almost as her *due*. To lose it all, so suddenly…"

"She seems to have recovered pretty well," Roy said dryly.

Doc grunted as he pushed himself out of the chair. "Don't let her fool you. The lady is more fragile than she appears. Picture her stamped with the warning—" on his feet, now, and towering above Roy, he waved the wineglass to paint his next words in the air "—Handle With Care."

"Oh, I mean to do that," Roy said, mostly to himself as he watched Doc weave his way across the deck and start down the stairs, holding the empty wineglass aloft in a farewell salute.

Of course, he was pretty sure the way *he* meant it wasn't exactly what the doctor had had in mind…

"Oh—didn't I just see Doc out here?"

The melodic, slightly husky voice sent a shock through him, making him jump and setting off seismic waves of pain in his chest and side. Folding one arm across his waist to hold himself together, he pushed himself to his feet and carefully turned. "He was. Just left."

"Oh." Celia's lips formed a disappointed pout. "I was going to ask him to stay for dinner." The pout dissolved into an impish grin.

Watching her...the mouth, the pout, the grin...the smoky eyes, Roy was thinking, *Fragile?* Would that be the same Celia I know?

As far as Roy could see, the only likely application for the word *fragile* where Celia was concerned would be the way he felt when he was around her.

No—the doc had to be way off on that diagnosis. But even if—just supposing—what he'd said about her were true, it seemed to Roy it was just all the more reason why he wouldn't want the woman watching *his* back.

"Isn't it getting kind of chilly out here?" Celia said after an awkward little pause, studying him with a concerned frown. "Wouldn't you like to come inside, where it's warm?" A smile flickered across her face with convincing uncertainty. "I'm sorry—I don't mean to smother you. It's just that I keep remembering how *cold* you were."

"Yeah," said Roy, smiling crookedly, "me, too." In truth, what his mind was full of right then was a memory he hadn't even known he had until then. It was a memory of himself, cold...cold as ice...shivering. And her warm, warm body pressed against his...arms and legs wrapped around him...naked...warm.

Funny—right now he didn't feel the chill at all anymore.

He followed her into the house and made his way to one of the cream-colored suede sofas while she was drawing curtains across the expanse of dark glass.

"So," Celia said, turning from the windows with a bright, hostess smile on her lips, "would you like something to drink? Some...coffee, maybe? Or broth?"

Broth. That kicked in another memory, new and hazy like the last one. His head pillowed against something soft...firm... warm...and a heartbeat knocking against his ear. *Breasts. Celia's breasts.* Something hard pressed against his lips...salty liquid, warm on his tongue. A voice...*Celia's voice*...cracked and breaking. *It's all right...you're safe, now.*

"Coffee's fine," he said, his own voice dry and gritty as the sand he remembered chafing and burning his skin. "Black."

Then he put his head back against the sofa cushions and closed his eyes. *Max, where in the hell are you? What are you doing to me, Max? You've gotta get me out of here.*

"Are you okay?" She was back, standing beside him holding a steaming mug and looking concerned. "Shall I go get Doc?"

"Nah, I'm okay—just...tired, is all." He sat up and took the mug from her, sipped, grimaced, then said, "What's the story, there, anyway? You said the doc lost his license to practice medicine. So, what'd he do, exactly? I asked him, and he just said, 'Bad choices.'" He paused to put the mug down on a glass-topped coffee table in front of him. "I kinda think I have a right to know, don't you? I mean, if I'm putting my life in the hands of some quack who's committed malpractice—"

"Oh, no—it's nothing like that. Doc's a good doctor—really." She sat on the sofa that matched his, opposite him, the shaggy tumble of blond hair feathering around her face as she leaned forward. "It was..." she closed her eyes for a moment, then said it: "Drugs."

"*Drugs?*" Roy stared at her. "You mean the guy's a drug—"

"No, no—he didn't *take* drugs. Just...dispensed them. A bit too generously, it turned out." She let out a breath and sat back against the cushions, casually pulling one leg under her. "It was a few years ago. Doc had been prescribing painkillers for some very famous people who happened to be addicted to them. When those people went public with their addictions..." Her voice trailed off, and she shrugged. "What he did was wrong, but he's paid a very high price."

"Yeah," Roy said, "he told me."

"Anyway," Celia said, "he's a good doctor, and a good man. I don't know what I'd have done without him. Well—obviously, I'd have had to call somebody else for help—like the paramedics, for instance. And you'd be in a hospital right now, and the story would be in all the newspapers—Man Found Near Death On Malibu—"

"All right, all right, I get it." He held up a hand to stop the tumble of words. "I'm grateful, okay? I am. I swear."

She gazed at him, the fierce expression turning slowly to a smile. "His main concern was that he couldn't give you antibiotics," she said softly. "He was so afraid of infection. And when you turned feverish…"

"I did?" He felt feverish now.

She nodded, gazing into his eyes. "Yes. And Doc said if you weren't better by morning, we'd have to take you to a hospital. So I sat up all night and put cold towels on you."

"You did that?"

She nodded solemnly.

"Well…thanks." His tongue felt thick, his lips were tingling. He felt light-headed.

"You're welcome," she whispered.

And then there was stillness. Not *silence,* because he could hear his nerves humming and his heart beating and the waves thumping the beach outside. But everything seemed muffled and far away, as if he'd been closed up in a box…a box filled with soft golden light, cream-colored suede…and Celia. And it didn't matter that there were a couple of yards of space separating him from her, because a part of him—the essential part—seemed to have lifted out of his body and was floating across that space to where she was. He could feel her breath on his face…the soft caress of her skin…smell her light, sweet scent. He could see her eyes widen, her breath catch and her lips part. And in his mind— that essential part of him—he was kissing her, and she was kissing him back, her mouth opening under his, hot and hungry…

The doorbell rang.

Roy felt himself blow apart, then reassemble, all the essential pieces settling back into their customary places. Except he felt as if someone had set off a firecracker two feet from his head.

Celia said, "Maybe that's Max," and got up to answer the door.

Roy picked up the coffee mug, grimacing involuntarily as he took a sip of what had to be the worst coffee he'd ever tasted, and tried to figure out what in the hell had just happened to him.

He was a plain, down-home Southern boy. He wasn't a fantasy kind of guy. Or he never had been, before now.

Behind him, somewhere not far off, he heard an unfamiliar voice say, "I'm Doctor Chan. Max sent me."

And Celia's voice replying, inviting him in—ordinary words…everyday words that in her voice sounded like musical notes from some exotic instrument—a wooden flute, maybe.

It had to be *her,* dammit. *Celia.* Something about her wild imagination, and the make-believe world she lived in. If he wasn't careful, with all that beauty and charisma, the sheer power of her personality, she could very well suck him right into that world with her.

Chapter 9

Celia couldn't sleep.

Not that there was anything unusual about that—she almost always had trouble sleeping lately. Which, after all, was why she'd been out walking the beach at three in the morning the night she'd found Roy. Insomnia was insomnia. So, what was different about *this* night?

Well, for starters, she wasn't alone—which was not to say she wasn't *lonely*. There was a man—a stranger, and yet, somehow not a stranger—sleeping in the downstairs bedroom. The room that had been hers for almost a year. The room that held her past…her memories…her childhood. She'd been too busy to think about it, but now she realized because of the stranger's presence in that room, with all it meant to her, she felt *exiled*. As if she'd been shut out of her own place…her own past.

And it occurred to her that maybe that was part of what was different about *this* sleeplessness. Because normally it was the past that haunted her, and tonight it wasn't. It was the future.

Except, *haunted* wasn't the right word. *Preoccupied, perhaps. Excited. Galvanized. Yes—all of those!*

There was so much to do. Her mind was a jumble of plans…ideas. She couldn't wait for the new day to begin so she could get started—as soon as Max gave the go-ahead, which he would, she was sure of it.

Roy, of course, was another matter.

Her thoughts darkened, and some of the old, more familiar nighttime loneliness crept around her like a chilly draft when she recalled the way he'd looked when she'd made her proposal. *Angry, of course. And…betrayed?*

He'd called her devious.

He'd accused her of having an ulterior motive for kissing him. Implying he wouldn't care to kiss her if she did. The thought that Roy might not want to kiss her again made her feel unexpectedly bad. Hollow. Empty and lonely and cold.

But you're getting what you wanted. You're getting to be a part of something important. Something real.

Yes, she was. And Roy, after all, was only a guy. The world—her world—was full of guys, most of them much better looking than Roy. Well, okay, *some* of them. A few. Maybe. Anyway, guys were just…guys. She had to keep her focus on what was important.

And she really needed to sleep.

Not that she wasn't tired enough to sleep—she was, for a change, since she hadn't spent most of the day sleeping, as she'd become accustomed to doing in the past year.

This day had been a long and eventful one. Waking up with Roy…fixing food for Roy…fighting with Roy…*kissing Roy.* Meeting Max…convincing Max…fighting with Roy some more.

This evening, there'd been that unsettling conversation with him out on the deck—and what was *that* about, anyway? Telling him about things she never told *anybody.* About her childhood, and her parents, and how much she missed them. *Feelings. Real ones.* Celia never shared those particular feelings. Ever.

Then, later, in the living room…that strange tension between them. Had she only imagined it? She did have a…well, a rather active imagination, admit it. But it had seemed so strong, so *real*…the feeling that there was some kind of connection happening between them…as if he were reaching for her across the void…*touching* her, even when he wasn't.

But then Dr. Chan had come, and she would never know what might have happened if he hadn't.

After the doctor had gone, Celia had tried to recapture the earlier mood of intimacy. Since Roy seemed to be getting a little testy over being treated like an invalid, she'd set the dining room table for two—even lit candles. She'd microwaved the chicken cordon bleu for Roy, and made a salad for both of them—one thing she was fairly good at was salads. She'd even opened a bottle of very good chardonnay. But he hadn't wanted any, and after drinking one glass of it, she'd wound up pouring the rest down the sink drain. Conversation had been…awkward, to say the least.

Even after that glass of wine, she was simply too keyed up to sleep. And—which was weird, since it was her own—the bed she was in now felt strange to her. It had been a long time since she'd slept in it, true, but it was more than that. It was so…empty. Big…and empty.

My God, she thought, shocked to her very toes, I miss *him*.

It was true. She missed sleeping with Roy. For the past two nights, she'd slept cuddled up next to him—once practically naked, wrapped up with his chilled body cradled in her arms inside a cocoon of blankets. Then again fully clothed, on the outside of the blankets but close to him, with his body heat soaking through to keep *her* warm, and the reassuring thump of his heartbeat in her ear and her breathing timed to the slow, even tempo of his.

My God, two days and I'm hooked? Is that even possible?

She threw back the covers and got out of bed. Without turning on the lights, she found a pair of shorts and a tank top and put them on, then tiptoed downstairs. At the bottom of the stairs, she hesitated, and her heart quickened as she turned left, as she made her way silently past the kitchen and entryway, down the hallway to the den. Her room. Roy's room.

The door was only partially shut. She pushed it with one finger and it opened without a sound. With her heartbeat thundering so loudly she wondered he didn't hear it even in his sleep, she stood holding her breath and gazing at the dark mound of bedding, listening to the steady rhythmic breathing that was *almost* a snore.

Her mind filled with recent images and sensory memories, her body with a tight, hot arousal it hadn't known in a long, long time. She saw herself walking across to the bed, easing back the covers and slipping between the sheets, breathing in the warm, musky scent of sleeping man as she stroked his lean, hard body to wakefullness, delighting in the sudden awareness…the blossoming of heat…the slow, sweet murmuring welcome…

Her stomach lurched, a sensation like having the floor drop out from under her. Dizzy with that, and from holding her breath, she pulled the door to, leaving it exactly the way she'd found it. She let the breath out, then went silently down the hallway and back upstairs, where she put on a pair of fleece pants and a zippered jacket over her shorts and tank top. Downstairs again, she slipped through the sliding glass door and out onto the deck.

The fog was a chilly caress on her fevered skin as she skipped unevenly down the stairs to the sand, the muffled thump of the surf a familiar rhythm. The tide was out—just as it had been two nights ago, she remembered. Her muscles protested as she slogged across deep, dry sand, until her feet found the wet, firm strip near the retreating waves. Then she began to run.

Max rang the doorbell at eight o'clock that morning. Since there was still no sign of Celia, Roy let him in.

"Did I wake you?" Max asked, grinning with cheerful malice. He took off the sunglasses he'd been wearing, even though the sun had a long way to go before it would break through the thick layer of coastal morning fog, and stuffed them into the pocket of his brown leather jacket.

"Nah," said Roy easily, waving him inside, "I've been up a while. No sign of Sleeping Beauty, though. Want some coffee?"

Max raised his eyebrows. "Making yourself at home?"

"Self-defense, trust me. The woman makes the worst coffee I ever tasted."

"Can't have everything, I suppose." Max followed Roy into the kitchen where he accepted a steaming mug, declining milk and sugar with a shake of his head as he hitched himself onto a stool next to the counter. He nodded at Roy's chest. "You're looking a whole helluva lot better. How's the wound?"

Roy rotated his arm experimentally, touched his side, then shrugged. "Better. Ribs are the worst. I'll live."

The two men sipped coffee in comfortable silence for a few minutes before Max said, "So, aren't you gonna ask me about the director's decision?"

Roy shrugged again. "Do I have to? He went for it, right?"

Max lifted his cup, drank coffee and put it down again. "How'd you know he would?"

"Because," Roy said, pulling out a stool for himself, "it's what I'd do. Hell, it's the only thing to do. The stakes are high, we're out of time, we have to use what's available in order to get the job done. End of story."

Max gave his head a wry half shake. "Gotta say I'm surprised. Relieved, but surprised."

"Look—" Roy got comfortable on the stool "—if Celia says she can get us an invite into the prince's social circle, if she thinks she can actually get us on board that yacht, then we'd be crazy not to let her try."

"I'm sensing a 'but' in there somewhere."

Roy swiveled to face him, frowning. "Okay, look—when the time comes for serious business, I don't want her anywhere near that boat. That's where I'm drawing the line."

Max stared at him, eyebrows lifted. "You're 'drawing the line'? What's this? If I didn't know you so well, I'd think you actually care about her."

Roy snorted. "Sure, I care about her, but not the way *you're* thinkin'. The woman saved my life—now I'm gonna repay her by gettin' her *killed?* Besides—she's a civilian—an actress, for God's sake. She's got…I don't know, romantic notions, like this is some kind of spy game, and she's Mata Hari." He picked up his mug and scowled into it. "Be like having a five-year-old tottering around in a war zone dressed up in her momma's—"

He broke it off, warned by Max's none-too subtle throat-clearing. That was followed immediately by, "Speak of the devil…" spoken in a ventriloquist's undertone behind the toothy, "Good mornin', sunshine" smile Max aimed past Roy's head.

Roy swiveled around on his stool and even though he'd been warned, he couldn't help but react—like he would if somebody had thrown a play punch at him and held up at the last second— with a catch in his breathing and a little squirt of adrenaline in his blood that made him tingle all over.

Celia was coming down the stairs…slowly…one step at a time, looking sleepy-eyed and tousled. All she needed, he thought, was a pair of footy pajamas, and she might have actually resembled that five-year-old he'd just been comparing her to. However, wrapped as she was in a slinky, slithery ice-blue robe, with some sort of satiny high-heeled slippers with silvery fur puffs on the tops that peeked through the front slit of the robe with each step she took, it was obvious the look she was going for was more along the lines of old-time Hollywood glamour queen. Names like Mae West or Carole Lombard came to mind. Maybe Rita Hayworth? One of those. Anyway, sexy as hell.

And Roy, watching her in appreciative silence, nevertheless couldn't help but think of what he'd just been saying to Max, about a five-year-old playing dress-up in her momma's clothes.

Meanwhile, as he sat in spellbound silence, Celia produced a warm smile and a husky, "Hi, Max," and joined them. And was it Roy's imagination or did the wattage of the smile dim a notch or two when she shifted it his way?

Then he thought he must have imagined the coolness, because

when she said, "Oh, lovely—you made coffee. Is there any left for me?", her voice had a warm and furry quality that made him think of something he'd like to nuzzle his cheek next to.

Without saying a word, Roy got a mug out of the cupboard and filled it for her. While he was doing that, she floated around the end of the counter and into the kitchen, trailing blue silk and a faint hint of fragrance and raising the temperature in the room by measurable degrees. She began opening doors, taking out little packets of artificial sweetener and flavored creamers, and a spoon to stir them with. Naturally, all this required Roy to keep dodging and sidestepping her, which he managed to do without once touching her or either of them saying a word.

All of which Max observed wearing a look of utter fascination. Roy decided then and there if Max said one word about it, he was probably going to have to deck him, whether the man was technically his boss or not.

"Sorry to wake you so early," Max said, looking not sorry at all. "Thought you'd want to know as soon as I got the word."

"Oh…yes…tell me," Celia breathed, lighting gracefully on a stool and leaning toward him in a seductive way that elevated Roy's temperature to simmer. "Did the director—"

"He did—and it's a go." Grinning, Max lifted his coffee cup toward her. "Looks like you're 'on,' dear."

She gave an excited wiggle accompanied by a delighted peal of laughter—then naturally couldn't resist throwing Roy a little "I told you so" look across the rim of her cup.

"However," said Max, pasting on a stern expression, "there are going to be some conditions."

"Of course," Celia said solemnly, picking up her cue from him like an eager-to-please child.

"First, there will have to be a security check—"

She gave a short, ironic laugh. "That shouldn't be hard. My life is an open book—literally. Just check out the tabloids."

"Then, you'll need to learn some basic undercover skills. Call it a crash course in spying."

Celia made a snuggling movement and murmured, "Cool…" as she caught her lower lip between her teeth to hold back a smile.

Roy couldn't help it—watching her flirt like that made his mouth water. To cover it up, he gave an out-of-sorts *"Humph."*

"And," Max said, looking stern again, "there're going to be some ground rules. Understand?" Celia nodded gravely. "Okay. Rule number one: You don't do anything—and I mean *anything*—without running it by me first. You got that?" He waited for her nod before adding in a conciliatory tone, "That's so we can get security measures in place—surveillance, backup, and so on." He paused to put his tough-boss scowl back in place again, which Roy happened to know meant absolutely nothing anyway. "Rule number two: You make no contact whatsoever with these people—I mean al-Fayad, or anybody connected with him—unless Roy, here, is with you."

Smoky blue eyes, veiled and unreadable, shifted toward Roy, and when they touched him, he felt a shiver go down his spine.

"Yes, boss," she murmured.

Max stabbed a thumb toward Roy. "Uh-uh—in the field, *he's* the boss. He's the guy with the training and experience. You do what he says, no questions asked, you got that? Lives could depend on it—one of 'em could be yours. Other than that—the both of you answer to me. I answer to the director. Any questions?"

Roy saw Celia's throat move and he thought sardonically, *What's that she's swallowing, her pride? How hard must it be?* After a moment, she shook her head. Roy tore his eyes away from her and looked over at Max and pointedly cleared his throat.

Max shot him back a look. "Oh, yeah—one more thing. This goes one step at a time. Which basically means, if at any stage along the way, we decide the situation looks bad, if we don't like the risks, we call it off. We pull you out. Understand? We will not take any chances that might put you in harm's way."

He placed both hands palms down on the counter. "So—those are the rules." He ducked his head in order to snare Celia's eyes, which were studying her mug as if there were something in it far more fascinating than coffee. "Still want to play?"

"Yes," she whispered, then cleared her throat and lifted her eyes to his as she repeated it in a normal voice, nodding, "Yes—of course."

There was a bright smear of color on each cheek, but Roy didn't know what that meant. *Anger? Excitement?* He didn't know her well enough to read her. Considering how good an actress she was, he thought gloomily, most likely, he never would.

Max took a swig of coffee and waved his mug at her. "Okay, so…what's the plan?"

In contrast to how subdued she'd been during Max's "briefing," Celia sat up alertly. "Plan?"

"Yeah—what now? You told us you can get yourself invited on board al-Fayad's yacht. How do you propose to do that? What's the plan?"

"The plan—" she drew it out as she threw a frowning look over her shoulder at the digital clock on the microwave oven "—is to call my manager. He'll know what's going on in town right now—where the best parties are, what everyone's doing. But he'd kill me if I call him this early. So, I guess…" She swiveled toward Roy, wearing the well-fed kitty-cat smile along with a gleam in her eye that made the skin on his arms and the back of his neck tingle. He wasn't exactly sure what hackles were, but he figured if he had some, they'd have been rising. "The first thing we should do," she continued, "is figure out who you're going to be."

Roy wished he knew for certain whether the way her robe slipped open as she was moving around on that stool was as accidental as it seemed to be. As much as he didn't want it to, his gaze dropped as if it'd had lead weights attached to it, down, down into the deep, narrow slash in the top half of the robe—a slash that had fallen more to one side than the other, so that it revealed one almost-hemisphere of soft round breast. Then a movement of her legs commanded a further shift in his line of vision. Down it went again…and down…

He felt a jolt, as if somebody had punched him under his ribs.

Because, in the long, inverted *V* below the robe's belt, where he'd expected to see the graceful line of feminine calf and knee and thigh clothed in creamy skin, lightly tanned, perhaps…instead, there was the ugly red weal of a scar.

He thought he'd done a pretty good job of disguising the involuntary check in his breathing, and he knew his face wouldn't betray the shock he felt—or the shame. Nevertheless, with a seemingly casual movement of hand and body, she twitched the robe shut, hiding her legs and the scar from his view.

"You can't be *you,*" she said—and was it his imagination, or had her voice suddenly gone breathless? "You said yourself, Abby's people got a good look at you and might even have identified you—I don't pretend to know how they'd do that, but if you say so, I'm sure it's true. So we have to give you a new identity, right?"

Though she hadn't addressed the question to Max, he shrugged and made a gesture that said, basically, "This is your ball game—go for it."

She slipped off the stool and walked slowly around Roy, studying him in a way that made his heart pound and his breath go shallow. He couldn't have described the way he felt, but he sure as hell knew he didn't like it. It was like…being in a car going way too fast, with somebody else driving—somebody whose driving he didn't entirely trust. Come to think of it, he'd been having that feeling a lot lately.

Then she stopped directly in front of him, and—he couldn't help it—his breath hissed between his teeth as she reached up to finger his hair back from his forehead. "The easiest way to change your appearance, would be to make you…older," she said softly, and her eyes brushed past his to follow her exploring fingers. "We can give you gray hair—a nice silvery gray, right here at the temples, which will be very striking with your skin…and so distinguished. We can add a few wrinkles here…make your eyebrows a little heavier…"

Her fingers moved over his skin, light and cool as flower petals, touching each feature as she cataloged it, while he glared at her in helpless fury. His temperature rose and his pulse thumped low in his belly.

"Maybe a few more crow's feet—contact lenses, naturally, to change your eye color." Her own eyes seemed to shimmer…or was it *his* vision beginning to go, flickering like a faulty lightbulb? Her voice was a hypnotic murmur, like a cat's purring. "Blue, I think—it will look stunning with the silver hair. You already have a little bit of a bump to your nose…no time for plastic surgery, but a mustache, maybe, to hide the shape of your mouth…" Her fingertips traced the still swollen and tender bridge of his nose…outline of his lips, and he felt a growl forming in the back of his throat as he held himself rigid and fought the almost overwhelming urge to capture those tormenting fingers in his mouth.

But almost as quickly as the impulse formed, the fingers moved on…the backs of them, now, lightly brushing the quarter inch of stubble on his jaws. Shock waves of shivers rippled down his back. His face felt on fire. His fingers curled, wanting to reach up and grasp her wrist so badly, it was all he could do to hold himself still. He curled the fingers into fists and fought to keep his eyes from closing, glaring into hers instead and seething helplessly.

"Or…maybe a goatee? No—wait! I know…" Something flared in her eyes, then smoldered. "A scar—right here." Her fingers traced a line down the side of his face, from his cheekbone to his chin, her eyes never wavering from his as she said softly, "The thing about a scar, you see, is that it draws the eye, and people tend not to look past it. They see the scar, not the person. That's what makes it the perfect disguise."

She whirled abruptly back to Max, leaving Roy shell-shocked. A little humiliated. Definitely weak in the knees. "What do you think?"

"Sounds doable to me," Max said, not even trying to hide his grin of delight.

After a moment, maybe in response to the murderous look Roy threw him, he coughed and got serious again. "Okay—what about a background story? We'll need to get our people going on the paperwork as soon as possible."

"I don't see why I have to be *old,*" Roy muttered, picking up his coffee cup and scowling into it. He didn't know quite what had just happened to him, but he felt like an invalid who'd been out of bed too long. Not to mention itchy and out of sorts, and vaguely abused. "What am I supposed to be, your father?"

"Of course not," Celia said, giving him her kitty-cat smile. "You're going to be my sugar daddy."

Max guffawed. Roy choked on a swallow of coffee. "Like hell! Who'd believe that, anyway? You're the one who's rich, maybe you should be my...my—what the hell would you call it—my sugar momma?"

"Obviously," said Celia dryly, ignoring Max, who was laughing so hard he had tears rolling down his cheeks, "you don't read the tabloids. If you did, you'd know I'm supposedly broke." Both men stared at her. "Oh, yes—after having squandered the fortune my parents left me on drugs and fast living. Trust me— showing up on the arm of a mysterious older man who also happens to be a millionaire will fit the public's expectations of me to a *T.*"

"So," Roy said gruffly after a moment, folding his arms on his chest and glaring down his ruined nose at her, "I'm a millionaire?"

She prowled closer. "Billionaire, probably. Nowadays, millions aren't all that impressive. Canadian, I think—"

"Canadian!" Gun-shy, this time he reared back from her like a nervous horse. "Woman, you're forgetting. I'm from Georgia— and I've got the accent to prove it."

She paused, her smile flickering...and were the shadows of uncertainty in her eyes for real, or the products of her art...or merely his imagination? "Only a slight one, actually—most of the time. Anyway, we're supposed to be disguising you, right? You want your new background to be as different from your real

one as possible." She tilted her head and studied him thoughtfully. "The real problem is going to be your actual *voice*. Voices
are harder to disguise than faces."

"She's right," said Max.

"I know—how's this?" Though she was obviously speaking
to Max, her voice was low and intimate, and her eyes never left
Roy's. "He can't talk. He can only whisper. He was injured—in
an accident. A hunting accident—in the Northwest Territories.
That's how I met him, you see—in rehab. We helped each other
through…difficult times…and of course, it was inevitable that
we should fall in love." She whirled away from him, leaving him
with the sensation of a man teetering on the edge of a cliff.

"And it explains the nose and the scar, too," she said breathlessly to Max. "Oh, this is perfect. Americans don't know anything about Canada, so any accent he might have, any odd habits,
they'll just think it's because he's Canadian."

"You're something else, you know that?" Roy said with half
a laugh, desperately trying to ground himself. "Forget acting—
you should be writing fiction."

"I've thought about it, actually," she said, throwing him a
look that *seemed* to be serious—as if she really did want him to
understand. "They're not that different, writing and acting. Both
are about making up characters and then crawling inside their
skin. Getting to know them. Figuring out what makes them tick.
Then, you figure out ways to let the audience in on the secret."
She gave a half shrug, along with a faint smile. "That's all acting is. And maybe fiction writing, too."

"Got it all figured out," Roy said in a grating voice.

He wasn't sure when his heart had begun to beat so fast, when
he'd begun to feel like a hunted man, dodging through the woods,
looking for a place to hide. He knew he didn't much like the idea
of *anybody* getting inside his skin…figuring out what made him
tick…knowing him that well. And as for a woman like Celia…it
scared him to death. Just as well the character she was trying to
crawl inside of was only some fictitious Canadian billionaire and

not the real *him*. So, fine, he thought, let her do that—so long as she lets Roy Starr and *his* secrets the hell alone.

The momentary fog of panic cleared from his vision slowly. He found that he was staring down into Celia's eyes—dangerous waters if ever there were any—and a new question seemed to be lurking in those mysterious depths. He could hear echoes of it vibrating in the waiting silence.

"What?" he muttered thickly.

"A name," Max said patiently. "You need to pick one."

"Oh." He frowned, thinking about it, but the only name in his mind seemed to be the one he'd been answering to for thirty-five years.

"I rather like…Cassidy," Celia murmured, again not taking her eyes from Roy's, but smiling this time. "It has a nice outdoorsy ring. Rugged."

"Cassidy? Not bad…first or last?" It was Max's voice, coming from far away.

Roy shook himself. "Last," he said crossly. "Why can't I use my own first name?" It was what he usually did when he was under deep cover—less chance of slipping up that way.

Both Celia and Max were shaking their heads decisively. "What's your middle name?" Max asked him.

"Jackson," Roy said, eyeing him warily. "As in, General Stonewall."

"Initials," Celia said, with a smile like a burst of sunshine. "R.J.—how's that? R. J. Cassidy, Canadian millionaire." She stood back to look at him, like an artist surveying her creation—which, in a way, she was.

She clapped her hands over her mouth, stifling giggles.

"What?" Roy glared at her, unreasonably affronted. Then he looked down at himself.

Well, hell—he supposed it did look a little ridiculous for a billionaire—Canadian or otherwise—to be wearing a pair of baby blue UCLA sweats several sizes too small for him.

"Max," he said plaintively, "tell me you brought me my clothes."

Chapter 10

"She took me shopping," Roy said morosely. "On Rodeo Drive." He paused to take a swallow of beer from the longneck bottle he'd been cradling against his chest before continuing. "Do you know the last time a woman took me clothes shopping? It was my momma—I think I was 'bout eight."

"She's got good taste, you gotta admit," said Max, nodding at the slacks, pullover and leather jacket Roy was wearing.

They were sitting on Celia's deck and although the sun still had a ways to go before taking its nightly dive into the Pacific, there was a stiff wind blowing and a December chill in the air. The weather reports had said there was a storm moving down from the Gulf of Alaska that probably wouldn't arrive until tomorrow, but in the meantime it had blown away the fog.

Roy looked down at himself and snorted. "I get a shock every time I walk past a mirror. Shoot—I look like my own daddy." He didn't, though. From what he recalled of his daddy, Joe Starr had been a man with considerably less hair and all the outward signs of a lifetime of good down-home Southern cooking.

Max studied him for a moment from behind his sunglasses. "What's with all the complaints? You've been undercover before. You've put up with disguises a lot worse than this."

"Yeah? I've never had to be somebody's 'boy toy' before."

Having been completely unsuccessful at stifling a snort of laughter, Max turned his head away, still snickering.

"Okay, laugh, but I'm tellin' you, it's not funny from where I'm sitting. Hell, I was supposed to be the millionaire—"

"Billionaire."

"Whatever. She's supposed to be my mistress—so how come I feel like I'm the one being *kept?*"

"Poor baby," Max said with absolutely no sympathy. "By the way, is that your new set of wheels I saw out in the driveway?"

Perking up a bit, Roy said, "You mean, the Land Rover?" Then, since it was obviously a rhetorical question, he shrugged. "Celia's idea—she seems to think it goes with my 'rugged, outdoorsy image.' Canadian…north woods…all that…stuff." He snorted and took a swallow of beer, wondering what Celia would think of his damned image if she knew his idea of "rugged and outdoorsy" was hooking a marlin on a warm, sunshiny day on the Gulf of Mexico.

"I sure never expected I'd be driving a Land Rover," he said, shaking his head in a wondering way. Then he looked over at Max and had to grin. "Never expected I'd be living with a soap opera queen, either. But what the hell—it's just make-believe, right?" He lifted his beer bottle in a sardonic toast to the sparkling view.

"You sure about that?"

Roy snapped Max a look. Max nodded toward the small figure jogging toward them from far down the beach. "That's one gorgeous and sexy woman you're sharing a house with. Sleeping in her room—hell, in her *bed.* I won't say I'd approve, given the fact that you're working together, and the seriousness of the situation, but I couldn't entirely blame you, either."

"Come on." Roy waggled his shoulders impatiently. "She sleeps upstairs, I sleep downstairs. Anyway, are you nuts?" He watched the jogging figure for a moment, and he could feel a heaviness building inside his chest. When he spoke again, his voice had grown gravelly. "Even if we weren't in the middle of an operation—forget it. She's from a different world. Hell, practically a different species. I'm a small-town Southern boy. She's—*you* said it—she's Hollywood royalty."

"Can I ask you something?" Since that was such an unusual thing for Max to say, Roy nodded out of pure curiosity. "You're... thirty-five, right? How many girls—women—would you say you dated in the past twenty or so years, while you were growing up...living in that small Southern town?"

His curiosity growing, Roy said warily, "I don't know, quite a few, I guess—why?"

"And yet...you're not married. Why is that?"

Feeling vaguely annoyed, Roy shrugged and wriggled around in his deck chair. He didn't like the way the conversation was going. He'd been called to account on the subject of marriage by various members of his beloved family enough times that it was a sore subject with him. He gave Max the same answer he generally gave, which was the shortest and simplest, not necessarily the most truthful. "I don't know—why does anybody not get married? Never met the right woman, I guess."

"Ever think maybe that's because those small-town Southern girls weren't what you wanted? Maybe what you want is someone different. From a whole different world, even."

Roy stared at him for a moment, then grunted and shook his head. He looked down at his beer bottle, but it had lost its appeal. For a moment, he toyed with the idea of telling Max how he felt about the choices he'd made in his life so far. How for him, choosing a career as an undercover agent pretty much meant there was never going to be a Mrs. Roy Starr and a bunch of little Roy Starr Juniors waiting for him back home, all cozy in a little house with a picket fence. From what he could see, undercover agents made lousy husbands and even worse daddies. He said, "That's pure fantasy, man."

"Maybe." To Roy's great relief, Max seemed to have finished

with the subject. But a moment later, just when Roy was starting to relax, he said, with the air of somebody starting a whole new subject, "Ever think about the fact that actors, even Hollywood royalty, even soap opera queens, are just people, too?"

Roy couldn't help it—he burst out laughing. "That is truly lame, you know it? You're as bad as she is."

Max gave him a long look he couldn't read at all, thanks to the damn sunglasses. One thing he was sure of, though—it wasn't even close to being a smile. "I'm serious. She's just a woman, Roy. Okay—prettier and richer than most, but a woman all the same. Smart, too. And funny. Not to mention, nice…"

"Jeez," Roy said, with a grimace of severe pain, "you sound just like my momma." He made his voice high and singsong. "Roy, you know, Lena Grace Osmond's youngest, you remember her—Jolene? She is just the *nicest* girl—pretty, too, and *bright*—"

"Okay, okay." Laughing, finally, Max held up his hands in surrender. "Just as well you're not interested. Should make it easier to keep your mind on the job. Speaking of which," he said, casually shifting gears, "any progress on that front?"

He didn't add the obvious—that the holidays were fast approaching, which meant they were running out of time.

The intelligence "chatter" had been growing more ominous by the day. *Something* big was being planned for around the holidays—just no specific word, yet, on what…or where.

The terror alert hadn't been elevated, but it would be soon—most likely the week before Christmas. The thinking was if the alert was raised too soon or too often, it would lose its effectiveness—like the boy who cried wolf.

Roy shifted and straightened up as Celia approached the bottom of the stairs, flashed them a smile and a wave, then paused to do some cooling-down stretches. Without taking his eyes off of her, he said to Max in a low voice, "She's got some party we're supposed to go to tomorrow night. It's at some producer's house up in Bel Air. Seems to think there's a good chance al-Fayad'll be there…"

The truth was only part of his mind was engaged with renegade Arab princes, luxury megayachts and international terrorists right then. The rest was thinking about the long, slender body doing toe touches and waist swivels down at the foot of the stairs, covered from neck to ankles in sweats, tank top and zippered warm-up jacket. Thinking, too, about the scar he'd glimpsed in the slit of her robe, and wondering if she was hiding it from herself, the world or just him.

He didn't know why, but more than her beauty or fame or personal history or anything else he'd learned about Celia Cross in the short time since he'd met her, more than how much he wanted her body—and any red-blooded male in his right mind would— that scar intrigued him. Which should have been a warning to him, right there.

"It's around the next bend," Celia said. She could hear the strain and tension in her own voice—small wonder, since her whole body felt as if she'd been encased in concrete, and her jaws as if they'd been wired together. She concentrated on taking slow, deep breaths and mentally reciting a yoga mantra she remembered. "The gate should be open—you'll see it on the right. Just drive on in—there'll be a parking valet…"

Roy nodded, his expression grim in the Land Rover's dashboard lights. He didn't say anything or glance her way, for which she supposed she should be grateful. She would hate for him to guess how nervous she was. *No—not nervous. Terrified.*

It's only a party, she told herself, for the umpteenth time. *These people are your friends.*

Friends? Even as she formed the word in her mind, she wondered if it was true. In her world friendships, like love affairs, tended to be transitory. Like treasures from the sea, she thought. They usually vanished with the changing tide.

They were pulling up in front of the huge Spanish-style, wrought-iron gated entry, and a valet was opening her door. She gave him her hand and a dazzling smile.

Roy came around the front of the Land Rover, and she thought, *No, not Roy. I must remember to call him R.J.!* As she watched him, she felt an alarming upside-down sensation in her chest. Switching to her painted-on smile, she inquired brightly under her breath, "Ready for your debut, R.J.?"

He gave a noncommittal grunt and touched her elbow, guiding her up the walkway in a proprietary way. It felt astonishingly good, him doing that, and her heart began to thump and her skin felt hot, as if she'd stayed too long in the sun.

"I feel like a damn performing gorilla," he muttered, leaning his head close to hers.

She laughed and whispered back, "Welcome to my world."

The thought came to her: *This is opening night. You've always wanted to do live theatre, right? Well, it's curtain time. So, you've got a few butterflies? It's not as though you've never had them before.*

"It's a private party—I'm still supposed to tip the guy, right?" Roy whispered, bending closer.

Celia gave a little hiccup of laughter and wondered whether the delight she felt was because his naiveté amused her, charmed her or, in some indefinable way, touched her soul. "To tell you the truth, I have no idea."

"Well, I did, anyway," he growled, now that they were inside the mansion's courtyard entry and for the moment, at least, alone. "Figured I couldn't go wrong—might even have made his day." He paused in straightening his shoulders and resettling his jacket to give her a suspicious frown. "What?"

"What? Nothing." She gulped the denial, embarrassed by the fact that she'd been caught flat-out staring at him, practically mesmerized by his unconscious grace. *Girl, you've got it bad. If just looking at the guy makes you go weak in the knees...*

"Just checking," she said archly, looking away.

"You sure I'm dressed right for this? I mean, the jacket's okay, but I still think—I mean, come on. *Jeans?*"

She looked back at him warily, knowing how dangerous it

was. Sure enough, the endearing uncertainty in his frown made her heart flutter in a maddeningly adolescent way. "I told you," she said crisply, "this is Hollywood. In this town, jeans will take you anywhere—except maybe the Academy Awards." She turned to face him and, after a moment's inner struggle against the urge to hurl herself at his chest and weave her fingers through the gleaming silver hair at his temples, stepped closer and reached up to brush at his lapels. "Trust me—you look…perfect."

His blue contact lenses glittered oddly in the torchlight as he stared down at her. "I must've gone undercover in a dozen different situations," he said in a low, rumbling voice. "Never felt like I didn't know what the hell I'm doing before. Hell, I don't know if I'm gonna blend in, or—"

"You don't have to blend in, darling," Celia said softly, touching the fake scar on the side of his jaw, surprised at the ache of secret pleasure that simple action awakened. "You're Canadian, remember? Just don't forget to whisper."

She heard a faint intake of breath—or was it only wishful thinking? Imagination? And did she also imagine the moment stretching…and a kind of building suspense, with breaths held, humming under the skin and a far-off thumping of pulse beats? She did see his lips move—no imagination there. And she was mesmerized by his mouth. The memory of how wonderful it had felt…tasted…made her throat ache and her eyes smart with unexpected tears of longing.

Somewhere nearby, a door opened, leaking sounds of voices and music and laughter into the courtyard.

Close to her fingertips, Roy's lips formed a smile. He dutifully whispered, "Yeah, Canadian. Right."

She snatched her hand away from his face and they turned together to walk on through the courtyard, Celia feeling lightheaded and fluttery in her stomach, wishing he'd take her arm again. Wondering if she should take his…

Just as they reached the door, he looked down at her and said gruffly, "You look nice, too."

Such an innocuous thing to say. But he said it with a kind of innocence and sincerity that was rare in her world. She caught a shaken breath, once again unprepared for the ache that clutched at her throat, the sting in back of her eyes.

But there was no time to reply. For Celia, time had begun to stand still. She took a deep breath, drew herself up. I'll get through this, she thought. *I will.*

Then, she was standing with Roy in a great tiled entryway, looking down into a huge sunken living room filled with people. Faces turned toward them. There was a break in the hum of sound, then a ripple, as if a breeze stirred through the crowd. She could hear individual voices. It took all the strength she possessed just to lift her head high.

"Look—isn't that…"

"My God, it's Celia Cross."

"Didn't she—"

"I thought she was in rehab!"

"She looks—"

"…amazing—you'd never know she almost—"

"Who's that she's with? You don't suppose…"

"Who knows? Never seen him before…"

"…think maybe he's her therapist?"

Roy felt those hackles he wasn't sure he was supposed to have rising again. He couldn't believe the things he was hearing. Who the hell did these people think they were? Far as he could see, there wasn't one of 'em who could hold a candle to Celia Cross when it came to looks, style, elegance, class.

As if to confirm what he already knew to be true, he glanced over at her, and it shocked him to see, instead of her usual cool, calm, breathtaking beauty, that her blue eyes were shimmering deep in smudgy sockets, that her face had gone deathly pale.

He didn't know how or why, but in that moment his own nerves and uncertainty vanished, swept away in a wave of protective fervor.

Without knowing he was going to, he put his hand on her back and gave her waist a reassuring squeeze. And he got his second shock of the evening when he felt her tremble.

But before he could begin to process that phenomenon, a short bald guy with a reddish-gray goatee came sweeping toward them, crowing, "Celia, my darling—you look incredible! I can't tell you how delighted I am to see you."

With a trill of laughter and a light and musical, "Hello, Arthur, I'm glad to see you, too," she floated away from Roy's supporting hand and moved forward to meet the bald guy. They exchanged air kisses, and then Celia turned to Roy. "Darling, I want you to meet Art Milos. This is his house. And his party. Art, this is my friend, R. J. Cassidy. He's Canadian."

She said it all with a smile so playful and eyes so serene, Roy felt confused and a little bit foolish—sure, now, that he must have been mistaken about the trembling.

He shook his host's hand and—remembering to whisper—produced some apparently adequate answers in response to the man's standard questions: *Canadian, huh? What part? What business are you in? Where did you two meet?* At least he hoped he did. If anybody'd asked him, he'd have been hard-pressed to remember one word of what he said. His eyes and most of his mind had wandered off with Celia as she moved into the crush of people, pausing to speak to someone, then moving farther afield to take two wineglasses from a tray borne by a passing waiter.

"What is it?" he asked in a growly undertone when she returned to hold out one of the glasses to him.

She was already gulping from the other like a thirsty child. She considered, licking her lips. "Chardonnay, I think."

"You don't suppose they'd have any beer?" Though he said it in a whisper, Milos, who was already moving on to the next arrival, evidently heard him anyway, and turned back long enough to point toward a wall of arches that opened onto a stunning view of the L.A. lights.

"Foreign, domestic and weasel piss—otherwise known as lite

beer. Bar's outside on the patio." And he was gone—swallowed up in the crowd.

"That's for me," Roy muttered. Celia, having drained the first glass of wine, smiled at him gaily, shrugged and took a sip from the other. "Back in a minute," he said under his breath, and as he began to make his way toward the arches, he was thinking, I'm here five minutes and I already feel like I'm making a prison break.

Outside, he found the bar with no trouble and selected a bottle of Mexican beer. While he waited for Celia to join him, he strolled across the tiled patio, carrying his bottle of beer in his usual way, close to his chest. One of those aluminum and canvas affairs had been set up to keep out the rain, and there were several tall aluminum outdoor heaters holding off the December chill. Between them, people stood around in small groups, laughing and talking in the mellow light of torches…drinking…a few eating—nobody smoking, though, he noticed. In Hollywood, evidently, healthy living was In.

Some of the people gave him curious looks as he passed; a few nodded and smiled, just in case he was somebody important. Most ignored him.

He saw some people he recognized, and some others he thought he probably ought to have recognized, if he'd been more up on the latest goings-on in the world of entertainment. But it wasn't his world. Truth was, he felt more out of place in it, more conspicuous and exposed, than he ever had mingling with street thugs, underworld bosses and international arms dealers.

Wondering what was keeping Celia but reluctant to go back inside where the bulk of the noise and the crowd were to find out, he wandered to the edge of the patio, to the point where it dropped away in an impressive series of Spanish-tiled terraces, hot tubs, pools and fountains toward a carpet of city lights. Tonight, the distant spangles seemed to blur and shimmer in the lightly falling rain, and Roy found himself thinking about another night not so long ago, a warm, clear night, when he'd stood on a hill above Los Angeles Harbor with Max, talking of boats, and unthinkable acts of terror.

Was it only coincidence that a cold, damp breeze should skirl in out of the darkness and rain just then to find its way under the collar of his new leather jacket and make him shiver?

"Darling—*there* you are!"

Something leapt inside him at the sound of her voice. As he turned, he wondered if it would show in his eyes. Prayed it wouldn't.

An instant later, that momentary spark was snuffed out, and a professional chill settled over him; his body stilled and his features froze into what he prayed would be an unreadable mask of calm. Impassive as a granite statue, he watched the small group of men come toward him. They were swarthy skinned and darkly dressed, and at their center, Celia, laughing and lovely, looked like a shimmering golden topaz set in onyx.

The man beside her caught and held Roy's attention first, possibly because he had one arm draped around Celia's shoulders. He was tall and, Roy supposed, would probably be considered handsome, in an exotic sort of way, with a hawk nose, gleaming black eyes and a perfectly trimmed goatee. (And what was it with these Hollywood people and goatees? He was glad he'd won the argument with Celia on that score, at least, and was, for the moment, clean-shaven.) He didn't know whether it was the damned goatee or the arm around Celia that irked him, but he felt a sudden primitive urge to slug the guy.

Still…*he* wasn't the reason Roy had gone still as stone, with every nerve and sinew vibrating with a primitive cognizance of danger. After the first second, his eyes had moved on to the four men arrayed in a rough semicircle behind Celia and her escort. They were much alike, of a type Roy happened to know well. Though formally dressed in seemingly identical dark suits, gleaming white shirts and black neckties, there was about them a certain alertness…and something more. Ruthlessness and even cruelty…a suggestion in their taut muscles and impassive faces of violence kept under tight rein.

And one of them, at least, he'd seen before. It had been dark that night, but he'd known he'd never forget the face of the man who'd shot him on the deck of the yacht *Bibi Lilith.*

"Darling…" It was Celia's voice again, breathless and tipsy, reaching toward him across the black, echoing void that had opened up in his mind. He focused on her and saw her hand extended gracefully toward him. "This is…" she sang the name, punctuating each syllable with a wave of her nearly empty wineglass "…Prince Abdul Abbas al-Fayad—but everybody calls him Abby—don't they, darling?" Her laughter was a silvery sound that twanged against Roy's razor-edged nerves like aluminum foil on a sensitive tooth. "Abby, this is my friend, R.J., from Canada."

"Your highness…" Roy returned in a grating whisper, smiling a clenched-teeth smile, extending his right hand. At the same time, he caught Celia's outstretched hand with his left. He heard her breath gust sharply as he pulled her to his side.

Seemingly oblivious to that not-too-subtle demonstration of possession the prince raised his eyebrows and waggled a finger at his own throat. "Your voice—it is…?"

"An injury. It's getting better…slowly." His voice would have been sandy, he thought, even if he hadn't been playing a part. He considered it a wonder his vocal cords worked at all.

Danger. Suddenly it was all around him; he could feel it. Inside his new designer clothes he was cold…sweating. Images… sensations still fresh in his memory played again in his mind. The searing pain of the bullet ripping through his flesh…the blackness of the water, the deathly, mind-numbing cold…

Had the bodyguard recognized him? There was no outward sign in those impassive black eyes. *Don't look too closely. Can't risk looking him in the eyes. Mustn't give him the chance to look too closely at me…*

"R.J. and I met in the hospital—in rehab," Celia said, and reached up to kiss his cheek.

He didn't know where the impulse came from. Some primal directive of male biology predating civilized competition by millennia, maybe? He felt her lips brush his cheek, her breath warm and smelling of wine. In the next instant, he'd hooked his arm around her waist and brought her hard against him, turned his head and caught her mouth in a deep, claiming kiss.

He felt her lips…their warmth, flavor and texture…burst under his like ripe fruit in the heat of summer. Sensation flooded his senses and, for a moment, drowned all thought, infused his system like a potent drug, leaving him shocked, reeling, disoriented.

It lasted no more than seconds. Not nearly long enough…much too long. *What the hell was that? What did I just do?*

She swayed a little when he released her, as if something she'd been leaning against had been removed suddenly.

"Darling—" Incredibly, her voice, her lowered lashes, her smile, still seemed sultry, sexy, intimate. Then she lifted her lashes, and he saw that behind their camouflage her eyes were fierce and bright. With confusion? Anger? And yet…when she continued, her voice and smile gave no sign. "Abby's been telling me all about his boat. He has the most amazing yacht…"

"Really?" Mentally reeling himself in, Roy showed the prince his teeth.

With Celia tucked close against him, he could feel the tension humming in her body. Or maybe the humming was only in his. Every nerve, every instinct was telling him to run like hell, to get away from there before he was found out. Any moment now, the prince or one of his bodyguards would see through his charade. *If they haven't already. How could they not?*

He'd never felt so exposed.

Meanwhile, maddeningly, Celia was chattering away, oblivious to the danger, asking questions about the yacht in her sexy, sultry voice. And Prince Abdul, dividing his attention between both members of his audience, was regaling them with the boat's dimensions and specifications. Roy tried to listen with the right amount of interest, just a touch of awe, but he was restless and on edge. It was hard to concentrate when all he could think about was the danger he'd put Celia in, if, in fact, he'd been made. And when and how he could end the interminable small talk and get the hell out of this place.

At the same time, inexplicably and unforgivably, but in a very visceral way, he was thinking about the kiss. Thinking…not with his mind, but with the elemental pulse-pumping, heat-making part of him…about the thump in his belly…the fire in his loins. And how much those parts of him wanted to feel like that again.

Be careful, the thinking part of him warned. *Don't let them know you're edgy. Don't let them see you sweat. They'll know something's up. And for God's sake, don't let them get a good look at your face.*

Celia's shoulders were rigid against his arm as he turned her slightly and, with a casually possessive, almost languid motion, lowered his head to one side of hers. With her face between his and the bodyguards' watchful eyes, as the conversation continued, he lazily stroked her hair with his chin…blew his breath along the intricate whorls of her ear…

He felt her shiver. Swaying, as if in a dance, she contrived to turn her head toward him, her smile quivering at the corners, her eyes questioning. But when he tried to explain silently—*I have a reason…play along…please…trust me!*—he could see the desperate appeal in his eyes bounce off the confusion and anger in hers, like pebbles thrown against a wall.

Or had it? A moment later, she managed to deftly and charmingly bring the conversation to a close, by waving gaily to some distant someone and explaining to the prince, with a wry smile and rolled eyes, that she'd promised her agent she'd say hello to this certain producer… The prince, being familiar with the ways of those in The Business, laughed and kissed her cheek, shook Roy's hand…and he and his retinue moved on.

So did Celia and Roy, making their way with excruciating slowness through the crowd on the patio, then the living room, pausing often to exchange gracious greetings, introductions, small talk and good wishes with a whole lot of beautiful and famous people, much of which, to Roy's mind, even seemed sincere.

Meanwhile, his neck, shoulders and jaws screamed with tension and a feral desire to bolt for the exit like a spooked deer. He could feel a similar tension in Celia whenever he touched her, a kind of minute vibration running like an electrical current through her body, and he marveled at how relaxed she appeared, how naturally she moved through what to Roy seemed an impossibly complex and utterly alien world.

Then he thought, *She's an actress. She's in her element. These are her people.*

Besides, he told himself, *she* doesn't have to worry about a killer recognizing her face.

It was while they were making their way through the entryway, saying their goodbyes, waiting for Celia's coat, that Roy caught a glimpse of her in an ornate, Spanish-style mirror that took up most of one wall, some distance away. For a moment he thought, *Who's the old guy with her?* And he was actually glancing around when the realization hit: *Holy... Jeez—it's me!*

Okay, so he was an idiot. As the tension drained out of him, he felt shaken and foolish. What had he been so worried about? It was just as Celia had said: the way he looked right now, his own mother wouldn't recognize him.

Chapter 11

Celia sat hunched in the passenger seat, listening to the steady thump of windshield wipers and fidgeting to hide the shudders that rippled through her from time to time. She could feel Roy's glance dart her way, but kept her eyes steadfastly focused on the raindrops that spangled the Land Rover's windshield and hood like diamonds.

Stopped for a light on Sunset Boulevard, hands relaxed on the wheel, he looked over at her and said quietly, "You're not sayin' much."

She looked at him and lifted a shoulder. The last thing she felt like doing was talking. Her mind felt drained…empty…exhausted. And yet her body was humming with tension, with an excess of energy, as if, she thought, forces beyond her control, alien forces, had taken it over.

"You did good," he went on, and she could hear the wryness in his voice. "Damn good. Surprised the hell out of me, in fact." The light changed, and so did the direction of his voice as the Land Rover moved forward. "You might just be a natural."

"Thanks," she said dryly, and she was thinking that a week, even a day ago, she'd have been quivering like a puppy over a compliment like that.

Instead, anger rushed over her unexpectedly, making her feel off balance, the way a wave did when it swirled and sucked around her feet, then slid dizzily away.

"Apparently, I have a few things to learn." She'd meant to say it lightly; the tight, hard edge she heard in her voice, and its tendency to tremble, shocked her. She closed her eyes and concentrated on controlling both the anger and the trembling.

Roy's chuckle was oblivious. "Maybe one or two."

"About working with you, I mean." Her voice was hers again, light and only mildly curious. "For instance, what was with that kiss? Some kind of ploy, I suppose, but you might have given me some warning."

She heard a soft snort and then, for a long, unbearable time, silence. Ashamed of the need, she managed to steal a quick look at him before setting her gaze on the windshield again. When she swallowed, she was surprised at how much it hurt.

Finally, he exhaled and said in a low, half-muffled voice, "Yeah...well. Didn't have much time to discuss a game plan with you. It was the best I could come up with at the moment."

"Really? Game plan...for what, exactly? I mean, I know I'm supposed to be your mistress, but the rest of the evening you barely touched me. Was that kiss just a declaration of ownership for Abby's benefit? 'Hands off, this woman is mine.'? Not that I mind—it's definitely not the first time I've been kissed according to script. I just like to know my motivation."

"For God's sake," Roy said harshly, his body leaning toward her as he took the hard right turn onto the Pacific Coast Highway. "Not Abby—*the bodyguard*. I was trying to keep him from getting a good look at me. And...like I said, it was the only thing I could come up with at the time."

"The bodyguard?" She stared at his profile, grim in the highway lights.

"I was afraid he might…I was afraid he'd recognize me." His voice sounded tight, as if his teeth were clenched. "He'd seen me before—on the boat. He was the one who shot me."

She paused to let that sink in, and to consider whether it made any difference. Deciding it didn't, she said, "And…the thing with my hair…and my ear?" Breath, in mysteriously short supply, sifted from her air-starved lungs.

He glanced over at her and lifted a shoulder. In the erratic light, his face seemed like a mask. "Like I said."

She sat for another time in silence. The rain was coming down harder, now, the way it can in California, sluicing over the windshield and side windows and curtaining them inside in their own little bubble of quiet, alone with the tension of misunderstanding and a thousand unspoken thoughts.

She drew a breath. "He wouldn't have recognized you."

"Yeah," he said, somewhere between a drawl and a growl, "I think I know that…*now.* Can't say I did then, though."

She listened to the echoes of irony. Though far from being an apology, it made the silence seem less electric, somehow.

After a while she asked carefully, "Is it always this—" she coughed "—forgive me, but are you always this nervous when you go undercover?"

He gave an unexpected bark of laughter. "You wanna know the truth? This is the hardest thing I've ever done—bar none."

She stared at him. "Seriously? Why? These are just…people. Showbiz people. Actors, directors, producers. It's not like they're…dangerous." She listened, head tilted wryly, to a replay of that, while Roy echoed her thought.

"I can think of at least one who is."

He drove for a while without speaking, then threw her a frowning glance. "I don't know if I can explain or not, but…see, normally, if I'm going to be 'made,' it's because of some screwup on my part—not doing my job right. Those things I can pretty much control. My face…well—not much I can do about that. I've never had to worry about being recognized before. I guess I felt…I don't know…naked. You know—exposed."

Naked… Celia stared straight ahead through the rain and didn't say anything. Her throat felt achy and tight.

She could feel him look at her. "Guess you know what that's like, don't you?" His voice was deep with unexpected sympathy.

Her impulse was to laugh—why, she didn't know. Some sort of defensive mechanism, she supposed. "Why would you say that? I've never been undercover before."

"No, I mean, the face thing. Being recognized even when you don't want to be. I guess, unless you want to go around in a disguise all the time, wherever you go, you're always going to be Celia Cross."

She didn't know what to say. Who would have thought he'd understand? She said dryly, "More likely Nurse Suzanne." Then, after a short silence, looking away from him again, "Actually, this past year I've gotten fairly good at disguises."

Again she felt his glances, asking questions he didn't quite know how to put into words. She let the silence settle around her—like fog, cloaking, insulating, protecting and, at the same time, making her feel chilled and lonely, so that when she broke it to say, "That's my turn up ahead," even her voice sounded muffled to her own ears, the way it does in fog.

Roy made the turn without comment. He drove slowly down the steep, narrow, winding street and pulled into Celia's driveway. He turned off the motor, and the roar of rain and the whump of distant breakers rushed to fill the space where the engine and wiper noise had been, keeping time with her heartbeat.

He took the keys from the ignition, but instead of opening the door, said in a gruff voice, "Something I can't figure out."

She waited for him to continue, her heart quickening. He turned toward her, a dark silhouette against the silvery sluice of rain on the windows. "Why were you so nervous tonight? I mean, it's not like you were in disguise, worrying about being recognized. You were…you—Celia Cross. Everybody there knew who you were. But you were shaking. When we first went in. I felt it. How come?"

Her heart gave a lurch, her breath caught, and to hide it she gave another light laugh. "Obviously, you don't know much about showbiz. Of course I was shaking—it's excitement, it's adrenaline. I was about to go 'on'—as in, on stage, you know? It's normal, it's…energy."

"I heard what they were saying—those people—when we walked in," he said roughly. "You did, too. Don't tell me you didn't."

She shrugged and looked away, and the movements felt awkward to her, as if her body were a marionette controlled by an inept puppeteer. Through stiff lips, she said, "Oh well, I expected that. I told you about the rumors…the newspaper stories…the tabloids. The first time I appear in public…after… there were bound to be comments."

"The first time…bound to be comments…you 'expected'—" He broke off, muttering. Glancing at him, she saw that his elbow was propped on the steering wheel, his hand clamped over the lower part of his face. He shook his head and snapped her a look, blue contact lenses glittering in the meager light. "Why in the hell didn't you tell me?"

She tried the laugh again, this time with a lift of her chin, hoping it would be enough. "Why would I? What could you have done?" *Why do you care?* Her heart thumped and her skin shivered with something that felt like fear.

"Hell, I don't know—" he made an angry gesture, frustrated and typically male "—but you're my partner in this, dammit, if you've got something goin' on, I need to know about it."

Smiling, patient and gentle, she said, "I haven't 'got something going on,' as you put it. It's no big deal. It's just the way things are in this town. You develop a thick skin or you don't survive. Look—I got through it—it's over. Finis. Done."

He looked at her, saying nothing. She looked at him, and her whole body seemed to hum…background noise, an undercurrent to the restless stormy nighttime sounds.

In a sandy whisper, barely audible above the shush of the rain, he said, "You're really something, you know that? One hell of an actress…"

Clinging desperately to her smile, Celia said nothing. *I must be,* she thought, *or you would know how vulnerable I am right now. You'd know how much I want you to hold me…warm me with your body, the way I warmed you. Kiss me…make love to me…make me feel strong and good…make this aching go away.*

And she thought, *Oh, God, I'm glad you don't know that! Because if you were to touch me right now I'd come apart in your arms and cry on your shoulder. I sure wouldn't want to do that!*

Oh, God…how I want to do that.

Please…touch me.

"Well, you definitely had everybody there fooled tonight," Roy said, reaching for the door handle. "Sure as hell fooled me."

Celia let out a breath and opened her door, gasping, "Thanks," as the cold rain hit her face.

Yes, she thought, *I surely did fool you, didn't I?*

In the days that followed, Roy grew to appreciate the one good thing about having a deadline coming at you way before you were ready for it—it made time go by a whole lot faster.

Although, he'd probably have to admit, at least part of that could have been due to the fact that much of what filled his days—not just events, but images, sensations, emotions—was new to him.

Every day, he and Celia put in an appearance at some trendy restaurant or other on Melrose Avenue or in Beverly Hills. Lunch at Morton's, maybe, where the prices made it hard for him to swallow his steak and fries, even with the ketchup the place thoughtfully provided. At other times, it was dinner at some romantic garden hideaway where he felt underdressed even in the silk Armani suits Celia insisted on buying for him on their shopping forays to Rodeo Drive.

At those times, it was Roy's job to look rugged and outdoorsy and enigmatic—Canadian, he surmised—and Celia's to appear the love-struck celebrity—starry-eyed, effervescent, radiantly beautiful. No great stretch for her—not the last one, anyway. As for the first two, well…it just made him admire her acting ability all the more when he saw how the stars faded from her eyes and the effervescence went flat as three-day-old beer as soon as they were alone together.

Admiring…awed…hell, yes. Where Celia was concerned, he had no trouble justifying all those feelings. It was the let-down-disappointed blues that came with them he couldn't understand.

As far as Roy was concerned, it was all getting too damn complicated. In his past life, B.C.—Before Celia—whenever a relationship showed signs of developing complications he'd put an end to it in a hurry. Which he figured was probably why he'd managed to remain friends with so many of his old girlfriends, most of whom were currently happily married to other people. But this thing with Celia—in the first place, of course, it wasn't even a real relationship. It was all playacting. Make-believe.

Or was it?

That was where it began to get complicated. *Could* things ever become real between Celia and him? On her side…truth was, he didn't know. Normally he considered his instincts to be pretty good, but in this case…for starters, there was the acting thing. He'd seen firsthand what the lady was capable of. How was he supposed to tell whether the feelings she was letting him see were real or not?

Lately, every waking minute it seemed his mind was full of images and sound bites: some grainy and flickering like old black-and-white film clips—Celia blowing on a spoonful of broth before touching it to his lips…sitting cross-legged on the foot of his bed, laughing…tumbling with him onto the sheets…kissing him; others warm and glowing with color—Celia painting a scar and goatee on his face with her fingertips…mugging in a purple fedora in a Rodeo Drive menswear shop…sniffing a gardenia and smiling at him across it with her

eyes in a candlelit garden café. Still others made him feel restless and uncomfortable, like watching a sad movie when other
people were around who might see him cry: Celia saying, "Of
course I miss them!" And her eyes shining with unshed tears…a
scarred leg peeking through the gap in a silky robe…Celia walking along the water's edge, pausing to throw a stick for a passing jogger's dog, laughing…then looking up to see Roy watching
her and the laughter fading to a bleak and lovely mask, impossible to read.

If only he could make some sense of it all! But the memories
flashed by too quickly, always changing, so he never got a close,
clear look, a chance to figure out what they meant. If only, he
thought, memories could be more like photographs, so he could
shuffle them around, lay them all out like snapshots in an
album…maybe that way get a sense of the overall picture.

And supposing he *did* figure it out and, from Celia's view-
point, the answer was yes…what then? Would *he* want a real relationship, considering all that was sure to come with it?

From a purely physical standpoint, the quick and easy answer
was: what red-blooded male in his right mind wouldn't?

But again, this was where it got complicated. And Roy didn't
like complications, particularly where his own emotions were
concerned. Having a "real" relationship with the likes of Celia
Cross—meaning not make-believe—was one thing; having a
real relationship, as in one that might put *his* heart in danger—
that was something else.

The way Roy saw it, as long as he and Prince Abby al-Fayad's bodyguards were walking around loose in the same city, he
was in enough danger as it was.

Prince Abby al-Fayad…danger…loose in the city…

Sometimes he could almost manage to forget the nightmare
cloud that might even then be approaching L.A.'s oblivious millions, hidden in the hold of one of the thousands of apparently
innocent sailboats, fishing boats, pleasure craft and yachts that
floated regularly in and out of Southern California's marinas

and boat harbors. He could almost believe his own nightmare on board the yacht *Bibi Lilith* and in the chilly waters of the Pacific had been only that—a bad dream. The fantasy role Celia and Max had created for him became less alien to him once he got used to the idea that nobody short of a mind reader was ever going to connect the battered, shivering wretch in the frogman suit, shot and thrown into the deep, dark ocean, with the silver-haired Canadian billionaire with a scarred larynx and a movie star mistress.

The truth was it should have been an easy part to play, putting him in no imminent physical danger, demanding nothing of him except that he appear at Celia's side, present in her scene but not a part of it, indulgent and a little aloof, like a patient and loving parent watching children in a playground.

He did have a bad moment the first time photos of the two of them appeared in *People* Magazine.

"Shoot, my momma reads *People*," he told Celia in an outraged growl. "What am I gonna do if she recognizes me?"

For an answer, she turned the magazine around and showed him the picture, snapped by some paparazzi on Rodeo Drive, then waited in silence while he studied it. After a long time, he nodded and muttered, "Well, okay, then…"

It was like seeing himself in the mirror at Art Milos's party all over again. After that, he pretty much accepted the fact that Betty Starr's little boy Roy was no more—at least until the current operation was over.

But, while the operation put little or no pressure on him personally, he was well aware that the same could not be said of Celia. After all, she'd claimed—bragged, really—she could get the two of them invited on board al-Fayad's yacht. No doubt she would, eventually, but the problem was, it had to be sooner rather than later. According to Max, intelligence chatter was growing ever more insistent about a major west coast "event" planned for sometime during the "holidays." And Celia and Roy had had no contact whatsoever with the prince and his retinue since the night of Art Milos's party.

No one nagged—it wasn't Max's way, or Roy's, either—but it was obvious to Roy that Celia was feeling the pressure. He was certain that was the reason for her growing moodiness, and her habit of sneaking out of the house at night to go for long walks alone on the beach, maybe even the way her smile faded whenever she looked at him…the way her eyes darkened and slid away from his. She's afraid, he thought, that she might fail.

What surprised Roy most was, for reasons having nothing to do with terrorist threats against a sleeping city, he didn't want her to fail.

In any event, as the Christmas holiday approached, Roy's and Celia's social calendar got busier and busier. The parties were bigger and glitzier, and nerves more and more on edge.

"Why can't you just impound the damn boat?" Roy exploded one day to Max as they sat drinking beer on Celia's deck. "I don't know…make up a reason."

"Wish we could," said Max with a gloomy shrug. "But the man hasn't broken any laws. Technically, he's a member of the ruling family of a country friendly to ours. We can't just confiscate a hundred million dollars worth of yacht on a hunch."

"What about the guys that roughed me up—the bodyguards?"

"Nothing on them, either. Sorry."

"Sorry?" Roy jumped up to pace in the confines of the deck, arms folded and shoulders hunched in spite of the fact that three straight days of Santa Ana winds had pushed the temperature into the low eighties. "What's 'sorry' gonna do? Christmas is…what, four, five days away? And what am I doing? I'm going to *parties.*" He made a disgusted noise, then rounded suddenly on Max. "Send me back in. Let me check out the damn boat. Look at me—my wound's pretty well healed, I'm strong…I'm *fine.* Getting caught last time was a fluke—I'll be more careful this time. Come on, man…"

Max was shaking his head. "Even if I was willing to let you, you'd never make it. Security's too tight—you found that out. The only way to put that yacht out of commission—other than *her* way—" he tilted his head toward Celia, who they could see on the other side of the sliding glass door, talking on the telephone "—would be with several well-placed packs of C4. And don't even think about it," he added, with a wry smile at the look on Roy's face, "because we can't just *blow up* a hundred million dollars worth of yacht on a hunch, either."

"Why on earth would you want to blow up Abby's yacht?" Celia asked innocently as she joined them, placing the cordless phone on the table among the beer bottles, as if it were a gift she'd brought them. She waited, returning their frowns with a maddeningly angelic smile.

Finally, when neither one of them asked who was on the phone, she relented, first helping herself to a sip from one of the beer bottles—Roy's, as it happened. She wiped her lips, then said, "That was my—" she coughed delicately "—a reliable source, who tells me on good authority—" her smile came out like an irrepressible child playing peekaboo "—that Abby is planning to attend the premiere party tomorrow night."

Max looked at Roy. "I take it this is one on your agenda?"

Roy nodded. "Yeah. I get to wear a tux. Can't wait." But a strange little quiver was running through him. Excitement? Foreboding? Anticipation? He lifted his bottle to Celia in a silent toast and saw warmth bloom in her cheeks.

At the time, he was sure he understood why.

"You look nice," Celia said.

Under the circumstances she thought she might be forgiven the enormity of the understatement; Lord help her—help both of them—if Roy ever found out how her body warmed at the sight of him…how her heart stumbled and her skin prickled with the dangerous impulse to step close and feel his arms around her….

Instead, she gave his lapel a pat and moved one pace back, tilting her head judiciously to one side as she gazed at him. Amazing, she thought. Nude, his naturally thin, hard-muscled body had made her think of Greek statues and portraits of mar-

tyred saints. Clad in a classic tux, that same wiry grace assumed
a natural elegance that brought to mind images of fairy-tale
princes.

"You sure this thing's okay?" he asked, tugging at his neck-
wear in a potentially destructive way. The white silk cravat was
a compromise; he'd absolutely refused to wear a bow tie.

She slapped at his hand. "Leave it alone. You'll probably set
a trend."

"Yes, ma'am," he said with a mock-serious frown, staring over
her head like a soldier at inspection. Then his gaze flicked downward and his features relaxed. "You look nice, too," he said
softly.

"Thank you." She smiled as she looked into his eyes, remembering he'd said those same words the night of Art Milos's party,
the first they'd attended together. And when he smiled back, she
knew he was thinking of that night, too. His teeth gleamed in the
lights that cast a daytime brilliance over the theater's entrance
and the crowd of celebrity watchers gathered there, and though
the silvered hair and blue contact lenses softened his pirate looks
somewhat, her heart gave a queer little bump just the same.

His smile slipped, became crooked. "So," he growled under
his breath, "we gonna do this, or what?"

She drew a meager breath. "Ready when you are, R.J."

He offered his arm. Celia tucked her hand into the bend of his
elbow and when his hand came to cover hers, felt a shiver ripple
through her. Behind them, the limousine purred quietly away, and
they stepped together onto the red carpet. She felt the cool tickle
of her mother's favorite diamond-and-topaz earrings on her neck
as she lifted her head to smile at the waving, cheering crowd.

It was something she'd done—oh, many times before, the first
when she was all of five years old, decked out like a princess and
clinging proudly to her father's hand. But how, she wondered,
must Roy be taking all of this? Surely, the glitz, glamour and celebrity must be a little overwhelming to someone from…where
was it? Oglethorpe County, Georgia?

She glanced nervously at him. He said something out of the side of his mouth, something she couldn't hear, and she whispered, "What?" and leaned closer.

"I said, this reminds me of my senior prom," he growled, showing his teeth like a ventriloquist.

She gave a laugh, half surprise and half…something else. Envy, perhaps? "I've never been to a prom," she whispered, gazing at him as new layers of awe, of emotions unnamed, wrapped themselves around her heart.

"I've never been to a premiere. Guess we're even."

She felt heavy inside…half-suffocated. She thought, *This is terrible. What am I going to do? I adore this man…*

Then they were inside the theater, making their way through a vast, crowded lobby decorated in the plush-carpeted, gold-painted opulence of recreated "Old" Hollywood and, of course, some larger-than-life statues of the movie's major characters. Ushers came to show them to their seats. The theater darkened, the audience grew quiet and the movie began.

Roy hoped nobody asked him what he thought of the movie, because the truth was, he didn't remember one thing about it.

Maybe it had something to do with what he'd said to Celia about the whole thing reminding him of his senior prom. For some reason, sitting there beside her in that dark theater, it was as if he were back there again, in high school, sweating through a Friday night movie date, and his mind more on what he might manage to convince the girl to let him do with her later on than anything up on the screen. There'd been a lot of girls….

His prom date—what was her name? *Jennifer…something. Jen…Jennie Dooley—that was it.* He recalled they'd done some fooling around that night—not as much as he'd have liked, probably more than she'd intended—and he'd taken her out a few times after graduation. But evidently she'd been saving herself for somebody with more to offer her than some sultry summer nights, because she'd gone off to college in the fall unsullied—

at least by him. Last he'd heard, she was married to a state sen-
ator in Atlanta and had three or four kids.

He thought about the girls he'd known, where they were
now…what they were doing. Sitting there in the dark theater, remembering them the way they'd been, it didn't seem all that long
ago. When had he got to be thirty-five?

It hit him then—if it hadn't been for the woman sitting next
to him, his life would have ended right there, at thirty-five years
old. And what had he got to show for it?

A tiny *frisson* of…something…rippled through him—loneliness, maybe? Regret?

*Not regret—I made my decisions, chose my path with my eyes
wide-open. I've done good things…made some difference,
maybe. And maybe I'm gonna make some more. So, no—no re-
grets. But loneliness? Okay, maybe. But hey—that's life. Right?
Sometimes you have to make sacrifices.*

He shifted restlessly and glanced over at Celia. He wondered
what she'd think if he were to put his arm across the back of her
seat…then let it sort of slide…forward…onto her shoulders…take her hand and pull it over onto his thigh, the way he
used to do back in high school.

Yeah, right. Smiling to himself in the darkness, he faced the
giant movie screen again.

Chapter 12

After the movie, an endless line of limos moved in to whisk everybody off to the party, which was being held in some swank hotel in Beverly Hills, in a huge ballroom fixed up like a set from the movie, with pillars and palm trees, ferns and fountains, and a whole lot of fancy food and champagne. It was loud with music and congratulatory chatter, bright with dazzlingly beautiful people and bathed in a rich golden light.

In the midst of the splendor, Roy stood like one beleaguered, with his back to a pillar that looked like marble but he was pretty sure was actually made of something lightweight, like Fiberglas or maybe plastic foam. He was sipping champagne—which he'd never liked, much—and supposedly keeping an eagle eye out for the prince and his retinue.

Instead, at the moment, he was watching Celia. Small wonder. Even in the company of beautiful people, she caught the eye…ensnared it…commanded it.

Taken piece by piece, he supposed, she wasn't that much

more striking than any of the dozens of gorgeous women there. Her dress was slinky and all but backless, but elegant rather than sexy, her hair upswept…elegant…leaving her long neck bare. Her hair and her dress were both the exact color of the champagne in his glass, come to think of it, and shimmered like it, too, and the jewelry she wore…diamonds and some kind of deep golden stones—topazes, maybe?—caught the light and threw it back like sparks. Her body, of course, was perfection in his opinion, all long slender lines and dizzying curves.

All those things taken together…*bright…beautiful…rich… elegant…* She was, he thought, like a shaft of golden sunlight slashing across a landscape of muted purples and grays.

He pushed the fantastic thought away. To help it stay there, he drained his champagne glass in one angry gulp and went back to scanning the ballroom for Prince Abdul Abbas al-Fayad. That was what he needed—to keep his mind on his job. Just let me find him, he thought…let Celia work her magic—*or, as Doc puts it, her wiles*—get us invited on board the damned yacht, then we can go home.

At least he no longer felt so much like a fish out of water, paralyzed with worry about somebody recognizing him from his former life. Actually, except for the fact that, at the moment, his feet were killing him, he'd grown fairly comfortable in his new role. It happened like that in undercover work. If he stayed in a situation long enough, sometimes the lines between his undercover life and his real one got blurred, his old identity slipped further and further away. Sometimes it even got misplaced temporarily, shoved into the back cupboards of his memory. Until he happened to stumble across it again, the way he had tonight. Those were the danger times, when the memories, voices, people he loved from his past life nagged at him, distracted him, made him feel restless and off balance. Maybe guilty, too, for letting himself get sucked too far into the new life. For forgetting who he was…what was real and what was not.

"R.J., darling…*there* you are…" Celia swayed into him,

gracefully holding a champagne flute aloft, cheeks dusted with golden mist and eyes sparkling. A prickling blanket of sexual awareness enveloped him, as impossible to deny or ignore as the compulsion to sneeze. "Come with me," she murmured, warm and husky with muted excitement.

What could he do? In his experience, a beautiful woman with too much champagne in her was pretty much a force of nature; he knew arguing with her, even if he'd had a reason to, would be an exercise in futility.

With a wry smile and an indulgent shake of his head, he allowed her to sweep him from his quiet eddy and into the mainstream of the party. Caught up in her magnetism, bemused by the power of his attraction to her, he was barely aware of the path they followed, or whom they spoke to. Faces he'd seen on TV and movie screens floated close, smiling and making self-conscious conversation, then drifted away again. People he'd met casually during the past two weeks gave him air kisses, cheek hugs or handshakes. Through it all, Celia clung devotedly to his arm or dipped and swayed at his side like a rowboat on a choppy sea as she laughed musically and charmed with effortless grace.

Then suddenly, ungracefully, she tripped, lurched, uttered a decidedly unmusical squeak and threw out a hand to clutch for support—not from Roy, standing right next to her, but instead the purple-jacketed arm of a man with his back to her, engaged in conversation with someone else.

The man jerked around, reflexively reaching to steady her, and adrenaline squirted through Roy's body and turned his nerves to electrical charges and his blood to ice water. Man, he thought, she's good. Damn good...

"Oh—I'm so sorry," Celia gasped—then, switching to a squeal of delight: "*Abby*...how lovely to *see* you!"

Prince Abdul al-Fayad's liquid brown eyes widened and warmed in recognition. Keeping her hand possessively sandwiched between his, he drew her close and kissed her cheek. "*Celia*—my beautiful little Celia—how *are* you? We meet again!"

"You remember R.J.—you met him at Arthur's party…"

"Yes, yes—I remember." The prince reached past Celia to shake Roy's hand, then, showing very white teeth, made the same finger-waggling motion toward his own throat he'd made before. "The throat—the voice—it is better, yes?"

Roy managed a lopsided smile as he replied in R. J. Cassidy's sandy whisper, "Ah, well, they tell me this is 'bout as good as it's gonna get."

By this time, he'd located the quartet of bodyguards, standing in a cluster near a grove of potted palms, looking out of sorts and uncomfortable, wearing their uniform dark suits and holding plates filled with hors d'oeuvres.

At least, thank God, the adrenaline had blown away the sexual fog that had been clouding up his brain. He was back on track, nerves on edge, senses humming…but prickling still with a peculiar residual irritation, which, if it wasn't so alien to his nature, he'd have said was jealousy. Watching Celia "work her wiles" on al-Fayad, he felt torn between admiration and the need to keep reminding himself to unclench his teeth.

"Abby, I'm so disappointed…" She was cooing to him now, swaying her body sinuously…almost but not *quite* brushing against al-Fayad's. At the prince's look of stark dismay, she put out her lower lip in a charming pout—subtle as a truck, Roy thought, but the prince seemed to be buying it all the way. "You know, you promised to show me your beautiful yacht. I've been waiting, but I haven't heard a word from you. Please, don't tell me you've forgotten…"

The prince's mouth popped open, but before he could get a word out, Celia rushed enthusiastically on. "Actually, R.J. was saying he'd like to see it, too. He's thinking of buying one—aren't you, R.J.?"

Roy gave a *harumph* and a shrug of masculine modesty. "Ah…well, from what I hear, nothing near so big as what you've got." And Lord, even playacting, it was amazing how hard it was to say those words. "Wouldn't mind having a look, though. Maybe you can give me some ideas…advice…"

Abby, his face lit with smiles, burst in with, "Oh, but Celia…R.J., of course, you must come on my cruise!"

"Cruise?" said Celia breathlessly. Roy felt his heart begin to tap against the satin front of his waistcoat.

"Yes, yes—for the New Year holiday. We will cruise down the coast to Mexico and back again, and finish it off at Avalon—you know, on Catalina Island? We will have the greatest New Year's Eve party ever—the party to end all parties. All my friends are coming—many you know…so many famous people. Of course you must come! Both of you—I will reserve a stateroom for you—the best one! Please say you will come…" His eyes implored, with a childlike enthusiasm that seemed completely innocent.

And yet… *New Year's Eve…a yacht filled with famous people…Avalon Harbor…the party to end all parties…* A cold chill settled between Roy's shoulder blades…a knot in his belly…a sickness at the back of his throat.

Dear God. This is it. It has to be. This time the "chatter" is real.

From a great distance he heard Celia exclaiming her delighted acceptance of the prince's invitation. He heard his voice—R. J. Cassidy's voice—seconding that and adding thanks. Words floated back and forth. More handshaking and cheek hugging, and then he and Celia were moving again, moving through the glittering crowd like water in a stream flowing past clusters of people standing motionless on the shore.

"I did it," Celia said as they walked together side by side, when they had left the prince safely behind. She was looking straight ahead, her voice husky and low in her throat.

Roy swallowed, then answered the same way. "That you did."

"Told you I would." With a defiant little toss of her head, she snagged two glasses of champagne from a passing waiter and handed one to him.

He took it, clinked it gently against hers. "Done good."

"Yes, I did." She held his eyes while she said it, then tipped back her head and drank, nearly draining the glass in a few thirsty gulps. Afterward, her gaze slid away from his, as if she felt awkward with him, suddenly. He thought her face seemed pale, too. As if she was feeling ill…or scared.

If she was, he pretty much knew how she felt. He had a sudden impulse—a need—to draw her close and hold on to her—to gather close to everyone he cared about, the way primitive people once huddled together against the terrors of the night.

The limousine rolled through holiday traffic like a migrating whale, unhurried and unfazed. Inside, isolated and insulated behind tinted windows and an aura of privilege and mystery, Celia sat and watched Christmas lights and crowds of last-minute shoppers flash by in a kaleidoscope of gaudy color and frantic motion. And music. In her mind a song was playing over and over, one line in particular, from "Silver Bells"—the one about city sidewalks decked out in holiday style…

But where, she wondered, was the "feeling of Christmas" that was supposed to be in the air?

Her mind felt as disconnected from the emotions and sentiments of the season as her body was separated from the busyness and bustle of it by the limousine's steel-and-glass shell. She had no room in her head for Christmas! Her thoughts, her whole being felt crowded, stuffed full, overfilled, like a balloon in danger of bursting, and all the more in chaos because so many of the thoughts and emotions filling it seemed to be in conflict with each other.

And her fertile and imaginative mind, being perhaps overly fond of allegories, reminded her that it was conflicting forces in nature that created tornadoes and hurricanes.

Her life forces were pounding inside her head and chest, loud, distracting, unsettling, like storm winds or heavy surf. Nerves pricked her skin like wind-driven rain. Her scalp tightened, as if warning of some unseen danger. Her breathing was shallow and her muscles tense, as if preparing her for imminent flight.

She felt exhilarated…and at the same time, in despair.

She wanted to run as fast as she could on a wide-open beach, put back her head and scream at the empty sky.

She'd never felt so alone, or wanted less to be.

Beside her, inches away, Roy sat in infuriating, and typically masculine, oblivion. How, she wondered, could he not be aware of the turmoil that was in *her?* How could he not understand what she must be feeling? *How can he not know how much I want him?*

Done good.

That much at *least* he must know—how much she'd wanted to do this thing…how much it meant to her to have succeeded. And then… "Done good," he'd told her—like a grudging pat on the head.

That's not enough, damn you! I want more! Though how *much* more, she couldn't bear to say, even in the privacy of her mind.

Then, assailed by that actor's familiar malady, insecurity, she decided if Roy somehow "didn't get it," it must be her fault. She was an actress, after all; it was her job to communicate thoughts, feelings and emotions to her audience. If her audience—Roy— didn't understand, it was because she'd failed. She was a lousy actress.

No! Stomach flip-flopping, she quickly rejected that. She'd won Emmys, after all. She only had to try harder.

Sunk deep in ivory plush and the darkness of his own thoughts, Roy gave a start when Celia suddenly unbuckled her seat belt. "Hey, where y'goin'?" he asked, reaching for her.

She threw him an enigmatic smile over her shoulder. She murmured, "I *know* this limo must have some champagne…." as she opened the bar.

"I'd have thought you'd had enough of that stuff already," he muttered, but she ignored that. Naturally.

She slid back into the seat beside him, triumphantly holding up two glasses and a champagne bottle. "I feel a need to cele- brate," she announced, smiling the way she sometimes did, with her teeth pressed down on her lower lip, like a little girl doing mischief.

Well, damn. He hated when she did that. Because no matter how much was on his mind, that look, so at odds with the ele-

gant clothes and hairstyle she wore, her sultry beauty and probably a queen's ransom in jewelry, made something twinge in the
back of his jaws, as if he wanted to smile, too, and maybe do the
same mischief right along with her.

Not trusting himself to come up with anything intelligent to
say, he snorted and accepted the glasses she gave him to hold
while she expertly opened the bottle. Naturally, she had to give
a little squawk when the cork popped and laugh as she licked the
spillage from the back of her hand.

Resigned, he offered the glasses, and she put her hand on his
to steady them while she poured. She tucked the bottle into the
corner of the seat behind her, then turned back and took one of
the glasses from him. She held it up and faced him across it, the
champagne's liquid effervescence washing sparkling golden light
over her smile.

"A toast," she said.

Roy said, "Humph," and added an unwilling, "Okay—what to?"

She opened her mouth, then paused, looking uncertain, and
instead gave a one-shouldered shrug. "I don't know—to us. To
the mission. To success!" She clinked her glass half-defiantly
against his and drank.

He felt a spurt of anger and tasted bitterness at the back of his
throat at the thought of what might still lie ahead of him. He lowered the glass without drinking. "The job's not done," he said
harshly.

She waved her glass, lips glistening with champagne. "My
part is—" her eyes flew wide "—No—wait—I didn't mean—"

"Well, I'm sure as hell glad to hear you say that," he said, smiling darkly at her.

She leaned toward him, earnest and dismayed. "I didn't mean
that. It's not done—just this part of it is. You still need me—you
know you do. He invited both of us."

Furious with her, he said, "Why do you insist on being in on
this? You're like a little kid trying to get into the big boys' game.
Dammit, Celia, this isn't a game."

"I know it's not." She burped softly and looked away. After a moment she brought her eyes back to him, and he saw in them something he'd seen before—he couldn't remember, now, exactly when it had been. Pain and wariness, and maybe even fear.

She licked her lips, then said in a hard, quiet voice, "Have you ever killed anyone?"

He jerked and spilled champagne on his hand. "What the hell kind of question is that?"

"It's a question. Have you?"

He took a drink of champagne, shifted his shoulders. "No. Of course not. I'm in the information-gathering business. We don't kill people."

Her gaze was dark and steady. "I have."

Again he jerked, irritably, as if she'd poked him with a stick. "Come on."

"No, it's true—I told you."

"For God's sake, Celia, that was an accident!" Clumsily, he polished off the rest of the champagne and set the glass on the floor. "That's pretty melodramatic," he muttered angrily, "even for you."

"Maybe…" She exhaled softly and once again her gaze slid away. This time, when she brought it back to him, there was something in her eyes that tugged at his heart in new and uncomfortable ways. His anger with her drained away like waves in the sand.

"Do you believe in fate? *Destiny*, I mean."

"Jeez, Celia…" He ran a hand over his hair as he sat back against the seat, then let out a hissing breath. "I don't know…I guess so…maybe. Tell you the truth, I never thought about it."

"Think about it." She sat forward, hunched and intense, the champagne forgotten, one hand resting on his knee. "Two women…driving alone along a highway…one crosses over the line—never mind whose fault it is—and the two cars collide head-on. One woman lives, one dies."

She looked down at the glass in her hand but found it empty. She said softly, "She had a husband and three grown children,

do you know that? The woman who died. She was about to become a grandmother for the first time." Her voice broke, and she
cleared her throat.

She lifted the gaze once again, and Roy's heart stumbled. Her
eyes…dammit…they reminded him of a lost dog confronting a
possible rescuer…full of confusion and fear, and maybe a glim-
mer of hope. He tried to think of something to say to her that
might help, but he was no healer. Her pain was beyond him. He
felt helpless, frustrated, useless—ways no man wants to feel.

After a moment, she cleared her throat again and, in a low,
husky voice, went on. "I used to wonder about it…why I lived
and she didn't. I felt so awful…"

"Survivors' guilt," said Roy, nodding, pleased with himself
now, like a kid in school who finally gets a question he knows
the answer to. "I guess that's normal."

She nodded. "That's what I was told. I don't know that it
helped much." She drew a deep breath. A smile flickered, then
grew brave. "Then…I found you. And I thought, *That's why!* I
thought, it's all a matter of destiny. I lived because I was needed
to be there, on that particular beach, on that particular night, so
I could save your life. You see? *But then—*" she held up a hand
as if to keep him from interrupting her, though he couldn't have
spoken if his life had depended on it "—later on, when I heard
you talking, and I knew what was at stake, and I figured out it
was Abby's boat you were investigating… *Then* I thought, *This
is why I lived!* Because anybody walking on that beach that night
could have saved your life, right? But only *I* could get you onto
Abby's yacht."

When she finished, her voice was hoarse with emotion, her
eyes fierce—a heroic effect that was spoiled an instant later
when a tear tumbled swiftly, like an escapee, down her cheek.
She sniffed and wiped at it, then continued thickly, "So, you see
why this was so important to me. Why I—" she hiccuped loudly
"—had to do it. *Have—*" she hiccuped again, then muttered a
small, "Oh dear—have to do it. Don't you?"

She gazed at him, waiting, and he stared back, unable to think of a single thing to say. And at that moment, with timing worthy of the best of Hollywood directors, the limo, with a polite jerk and a discreet squeal of brakes, came to a halt in Celia's driveway.

His eyes flicked to the windows and he blinked, momentarily disoriented by the half-lit shapes of houses and cypress trees he saw beyond them. His lips moved and sounds came from them, but rusty and viscous, as if they'd been kept in the heat too long.

"We're home," he said.

She flinched and threw a look randomly into the night, like a startled animal uncertain which way to run. She caught a breath and said with desperate lightness, "Yes, I suppose we are." Even without touching her, he knew she was trembling, her body's vibrations stirring the air in some strange way that he felt in his soul rather than his senses.

The door opened and the limo driver stood there. Celia leaned forward to take his hand, and stepped from the car with the easy grace of someone who must have done such a thing a hundred times before. Roy followed somewhat less nimbly, his attention distracted, as he dealt with the driver, by Celia, who had gone ahead of him down the curving path. He could see her floating there in the near darkness, arms extended to each side as if she danced to music only she could hear, the distant surf a muted drumbeat. He paid, tipped and thanked the driver, then hurried after her, swearing under his breath. Behind him, he heard the limo growl quietly away.

Just as he caught up with her, she pivoted tipsily toward him—and stumbled. She gasped and lurched sideways as one of her high-heeled shoes twisted and collapsed under her, and even though he remembered all too well the way she'd worked that particular trick on the prince earlier tonight, Roy did the only thing he could do, under the circumstances. He caught her and swept her up into his arms.

And miraculously, didn't drop her a second later; he'd forgotten about his half-healed ribs. Fortunately, his hiss of pain was lost completely in Celia's gasp as she hooked her arms around his neck and stared up at him with wide, shocked eyes.

"Thank you," she whispered in a slow, wondering way.

"No problem." His voice was tight and air-starved, but she didn't seem to notice.

She licked her lips and said thoughtfully, as he tottered with her the few remaining steps to the front door, "I think…maybe I've had a wee bit too much champagne."

"Ya *think?*" On the steps he halted and croaked, "Keys."

Her lips curved, catlike. "You have them, remember?"

"Oh, yeah…" Because Celia didn't like pocketbooks, he'd taken to carrying her essential feminine odds and ends in his pockets. He thought about it now, frowning over the logistics of it because he was going to have to put her down in order to get to the keys. He was frowning, too, because the pain in his side suddenly didn't seem so bad—either that, or sexual arousal trumped pain—and as a result, putting her *down* had become the last thing he wanted to do.

"I've had too much champagne," she said, gazing into his eyes with a curious intensity, "but I am not drunk."

"Okay…" He barely heard her. His head was swimming…all at once he felt as if he were drowning in her scent, her heat, her *energy*. The shape and weight and warmth of her in his arms crowded every other thought from his mind. Desire for her pounded like thunder in his temples. Wanting zapped across his skin like heat lightning.

It seemed almost an inevitability when she kissed him…a consequence of natural laws. She seemed to flow upward in his arms, like warm air rising, and her lips came to his as if gravity itself compelled them. He closed his eyes, and night spun into day. Heat engulfed him. He opened his mouth to hers…and flew headlong into the sun.

A long time later, he felt her body slide along the front of his, but molded to him still as if the heat from the kiss had melted them into one.

"Do you know how long I've wanted to do that?" she whispered brokenly, her breath flowing over his lips and making them tingle, like warm champagne.

"How long?" His hands, helpless and awed, stroked her back.

How long? All my life. All my lives before this one. Maybe even forever.

She was numb with wanting. Dazed with wanting. Nothing else mattered, not even pride. "Since the first time. I've wanted so much…for you to kiss me again. But you didn't. I thought…you didn't want to."

He stared fiercely over her head. His voice was guttural. "I wanted to."

Her fingers curled against his shirt front. She wanted to pound on it and scream at him, and her jaws ached with fighting that impulse as she whispered, "Then why didn't you?"

He laughed the way people do when something hurts. "Do you really want to get into that now?"

She was silent, listening to opposing wants colliding inside her head like bumper cars. Oh, she did very much want to get into this with him. She needed desperately to understand him. But right now…*oh, right now,* she simply *wanted* him.

Needed him.

She drew a shuddering breath. "No. I want you to kiss me…again. Please." Her voice caught. Her smile flickered—pure reflex. "I don't normally have to ask."

Frowning, he held her face between his hands, stroked her cheeks with his thumbs and looked deep into her eyes. "Not now," he said harshly. "Not here."

Fear and anguish coiled around her throat. *I want you so much. Why don't you want me? Don't make me wait again…please.* In that constricted voice she managed to ask, "Why?"

His warm lips touched her forehead. "Because," he said with a rasping sigh, "I'm not gonna make love to you on your front doorstep. What would the neighbors think?"

A single joyous note, one bright bubble of laughter burst from her, beginning the unraveling of the tangle of doubt and frustration and confusion and despair that had been inside her for so long. Laughing, she stood on tiptoes and held his face between her hands. She heard, "*Wait—*" but it was muffled and far away, and lost completely when she kissed him.

He leaned into the kiss, gasped and pulled away, then groaned and plunged back into it, all the way this time. His hands roamed frantically over her body, then abandoned the struggle and folded around her.

And suddenly warmth and strength surrounded her. She felt euphoric and giddy and frightened, like a baby on a swing…and at the same time, grounded in that lovely warmth and strength, she felt entirely safe. Because, though she knew it was *only* for that moment, for that moment, at least, she felt…*loved*.

"Celia…"

"I know…"

"We can't…"

"I know…the key…"

Somehow…gasping and trembling, overcoming obstacles like clumsy fingers and randomly placed kisses, they managed to remove the key from his pocket and open the door, tumbling into the shadowy quiet like puppies, oblivious and uncaring what parts of them touched where. That they *did* touch each other was all that mattered. For Celia, separating from him, even for a moment, even for such necessities as walking and undressing, seemed intolerable.

Articles of discarded clothing marked their progress through the house: her shoes and his jacket just inside the door; his cuff links and cravat on the kitchen counter; his shirt on the back of the couch. Even the silky tickle of his hair on her skin and the hot promise of his mouth couldn't hold off the cold jangle of alarm she felt when he found the abbreviated zipper in the back of her dress and pulled it down, when she felt the fabric relax around her waist and the thin straps slither over her shoulders.

She gave a laughing gasp and caught the dress with her arm

as it slipped below her breasts, before it could fall all the way to the floor. Roy, preoccupied with what had been uncovered, seemed not to notice. By that time, they were in the hallway where the light was dimmer, then in the bedroom where there was almost no light at all, and Celia relaxed and let herself become wanton again....

Chapter 13

Thought spiraled away into joyous light and heat and giddy, shivering excitement. His shirt hung open and her hands found the tight, hard muscle of his torso and she laughed with delight at the answering heat she could feel rising inside him...feel it burning through his skin and scalding her fingers. Daring in the darkness, she let the dress fall to the floor and leaned into him, pressing her palms against his ribs and her soft breasts against his hardness.

And felt him *flinch*. Heard him utter a sharp hissing sound, quickly silenced.

She jerked back, heart knocking sickeningly with frustrated wanting. "Oh God—your ribs—I'm so sorry—"

"Ssh...it's okay..." His fingers rubbed their gentle and uniquely masculine abrasion over her back, from the base of her spine to her shoulder blades, sanding her from scalp to toes with goose bumps.

"But...your wound—I forgot—" She was shivering...bereft.

"Celia." His hands lay heavy and comforting on her shoulders. He exhaled as he rested his forehead gently against hers. "Say g'night, Nurse Suzanne…"

Her suspended breath erupted in a single bubble of laughter, like uncorked champagne. "G'night," she whispered, but still trembled as she eased back against him and tilted her face to find his mouth.

Relief and happiness and gratitude filled her; it had been harder than she'd expected, this throwing aside of pride and a lifetime of habit and expectation to ask for—no, *demand*—that which had always come almost as her due. To place so much trust in a man she knew so little had seemed to her a tremendous and terrifying gamble, and her awe at finding that trust vindicated now all but overwhelmed her.

I love you, she thought, knowing as she said it in her mind that in the long run it probably wasn't true. *Don't make too big a thing of it,* she warned herself. *It's probably only gratitude.* But for that moment she allowed herself to believe it.

She believed it…because the sweet-hot demand of his mouth made her melt inside, and her legs go soft and trembly. She believed it…because the cool, silky feel of his hair on her skin made her want to cry. She believed it…because of all the times and all the ways she'd been touched, nothing before had ever made her feel so cherished.

His kisses were hot…slow…searing…almost more than she could bear. Laying her back on the bed with exquisite gentleness, he kissed her throat, her earlobes, the nape of her neck…not rushing, as if they had all the time in the world. And when she lifted her hands to the clasp of her necklace to give him clearer access, he smiled against her skin and murmured, "Leave 'em on. I'm gonna love you wearing nothin' but diamonds…"

"They're mostly topazes," she whispered as he drew the last remaining scraps of her clothing away, her throat half-choked with wanting him.

"Okay…them, too."

He touched her then, intimately…deeply and unhurried,

watching her all the while with eyes so somber…mouth so tender…and a sweet dusky passion haze like velvet on his skin. She lifted her hands and filled them with the thick, silky textures of his hair…and tried to keep her eyes open because she wanted to watch him, too, while he touched her that way, the intensity of her desire building on the intensity in his gaze.

But that became too much…too quickly. No longer hers to control, her passion-weighted eyelids drifted shut. She arched into him, breathing in panting gasps. Her hands flowed like liquid over his skin…

His skin felt sleek and feverish to her, like the hide of some magnificent animal, his body hot and hard and vibrant beneath. *I love your body,* she thought, but couldn't bring herself to say it. Because it was so much less than what she meant. And, she told herself, he'd probably heard it so many times before…

My God, you're beautiful, he thought, but remembered not to say it as he gazed down at her face in the almost-darkness. Somehow he knew, though he couldn't really *see* her, that her eyes had closed, that her mouth would be blurred and soft from his kisses…her skin rosy and misted with desire. But he realized as he looked at her that what was so beautiful to him wasn't anything he could have seen with his eyes anyway, but rather, a picture of her he'd been carrying around in his mind for a while now. A picture that had no particular age or expression, that wore no special makeup or hairstyle—or perhaps it was a composite of all the ages, expressions and styles, not just of the Celia who was *now,* but all the Celias who had been or would be. In short, it was simply…Celia.

And he wondered when he'd stopped thinking of the woman in his arms as Celia Cross, TV star, extraordinarily beautiful woman, every man's fantasy and way out of the reach of a simple Georgia boy—and when she'd become that…simply *Celia.*

Dazed and overwhelmed, he lowered his head and kissed her, and was just in time to capture her whimpered moan in his mouth. The sound punctured his heart like a lance, and he tore his mouth from hers and drew a quick, gasping breath. "Want me inside you now?" he asked her in his torn, devastated voice. "Celia...sweetheart...shall I love you now?"

Her reply caught in a high little laugh. "Oh—yes...please. I thought I was going to have to take desperate measures..."

Laughing, relieved, he nipped her lower lip, while his mind whirled with a strange effervescent happiness like a pinwheel shooting off sparks. "Such as?"

"Such as—" between words she lifted her head and took his mouth in hungry bites "—jumping on you and ravishing your body..."

"Aha..." He kissed her throat, then lifted his head to drawl tenderly, "And you think you could do that?"

"I thought—" her gasp, as he closed his mouth over one tight, hard nipple, delighted him "—in your weakened condition..."

"Weakened, am I?" He'd never felt stronger or more sure of himself. He lay back on the mattress like a Roman emperor being pleasured by handmaidens. "Then give it your best shot..." The words felt good mixed with laughter, vibrating deep inside, and he wondered if this was what cats felt like when they purred.

Then her hair and her laughter were flowing over his skin... along with her hands and her mouth, and the sharp, cool kiss of diamonds. *And topazes...yes, them too.* And he wondered if he was losing his sanity, and if there could possibly be such a thing as too much pleasure.

"Celia..." he murmured, cradling her head between his hands.

"Mmm...wait..." She lifted her head, leaving the moisture from her mouth to cool his heated skin. "I'm not done ravishing you yet..." She sounded like a sleepy lioness.

"Yeah...well, feel free to pick up where you left off another time. For right now...that's about all the ravishing I can stand— if you know what I mean..."

She gave an ecstatic little gulp as he took hold of her under the arms, just below the soft pillows of her breasts, and ignoring sharp protests from his mending ribs, brought her up along his body, then in one swift motion rolled her over and under him. Rocking them both onto their sides, he swept his hand down her back, over her bottom and along the back of her thigh, and she hooked her legs around him and arched, panting, to make a place for him. She raised herself, reaching for him, whimpering. Her fingernails raked his back and her teeth nipped at his shoulders, her urgency only mirroring his.

But hot and hard and eager to be inside her as he was, somewhere in the back of his mind a voice was warning him to go slow…to be careful with her…that most likely it had been a while for her, too.

And somewhere else inside him was another voice whispering that maybe, just maybe…this moment might be one he'd like to hold on to, and remember.

So, he held himself back, entered her body slowly, drawing out the moment as long as he could, though it took all the self-control he had when every instinct wanted to plunge into her with jubilant abandon. The pleasure…the sensations…shivered through him like the prickling fire of Fourth of July sparklers. After the first shock of penetration, she gave a long sigh and began to move as he did, slowly, sinuously, opening to him by degrees, as if she understood how he was feeling, and maybe felt the same.

At some point—he didn't know when—he'd laced his fingers through hers, and by the time he felt himself settled warm and deep inside her, his arms had begun to tremble with the strain of holding himself away from her. Now, dazed, he stared down at her face in the darkness and wanted to tell her how good she felt…how good *he* felt, joined with her that way.

Once again, he couldn't say it. He couldn't, because it hit him that he'd never before thought of sex that way—as a *joining*. And how that could be, when wasn't that what the whole thing was about? Hadn't he known that? Surely, he must have. Maybe he just hadn't understood. Hadn't *felt* it before. In his heart. *Joining…two people coming together to make one.*

The wonder of that filled his chest. He opened his mouth, but nothing but air came out.

"What?" Celia whispered, sounding breathless in the darkness and touchingly young.

"Nothing…" He lowered his head and kissed her mouth, then her forehead, moist with desire. "Just…you feel so good…"

She reached with her mouth to find his again. "So do you…"

Again, her body moved in perfect harmony with his, and he gave up trying to understand it…to make any sense of it at all.

Though, to say he gave himself up to what was happening inside him…well, that would have been like saying he'd given himself up to an avalanche. Because he didn't have a whole lot of choice in the matter. The feelings just took him. Overwhelmed him. Buried him. And at the precise moment when he felt that tremendous power engulf him, he knew a moment of utter terror…then acceptance…and finally, peace.

Waking in the humid warmth of a shared bed, Celia knew first a purely hedonistic contentment…like a cat stretching languidly in a pool of sunshine.

That was followed by a lovely sensation of *lightness,* then a thought that struck her so sharply, so sweetly it was almost like pain: *This is happiness. I…am happy.*

Then, with a thoughtless, childlike anger: *I want this always. I want this forever!*

Raising herself on one elbow, she gazed down at the unguarded face of the man who still slept beside her. Her fingers tingled with a desire to touch him. Such strong bones he had, sparsely covered with flesh…he'd be magnificent, she thought, even when he was old. Rich dark hair, artificially frosted with silver…the newly straightened brows and the temporary scar she'd given him. His brutally altered nose. Jaws and chin rough with a night's growth of beard…and oh, she was glad he'd talked her out of the goatee. It would have hidden his mouth…his wonderful mouth, that smiled so seldom and so wickedly. *Like a pirate…*

Her vision blurred, like watercolors in the rain. Thoughts and comparisons flew out of her head; there was only awe, and a love so intense it almost overwhelmed her.

I want this, she thought. *I want him. Always and forever.*

Maybe she'd trembled or given a start; maybe he felt the weight of her gaze…or her thoughts. In any case, the thick, dark lashes flew open. She caught her breath, and was momentarily disconcerted by the blue-eyed glare until she remembered he was still wearing his contacts. Until he surged upward, like a sea mammal surfacing for his first breath, to claim her mouth.

"Mmm…'morning," she murmured huskily into the kiss, smiling at the unbearable sweetness, the impulsiveness of it.

"'Mornin'…" And his hand was already hooking around her neck, pushing under her hair as he pulled her down to him, and his mouth was opening under hers…hot and hungry…famished…

Desire twisted violently in her stomach, skated along her skin and began to throb in the part of her already swollen and sensitized to his touch. Dizzy with it, she thought fleetingly of things that would once have seemed important to her: *What do I look like? Is my makeup smudged? Do I have morning breath?* In the next moment, on a wave of stunning heat and joy and ardor, those thoughts simply vanished, along with others she probably should have remembered. Laughing and giddy, she followed him down into the tumble of pillows and flower-sprigged sheets, raining kisses on his cheeks and beard-roughened jaws, and down onto his neck and chin.

But when she would have carried her hungry forays even farther, to his chest and torso and belly and beyond, as she had the night before, he stopped her with a growl, and a guttural, "No, you don't, darlin'—my turn now…" as he rolled her deftly onto her back.

Delightedly vanquished, she lay with her eyes closed while he trailed kisses across her throat and then her breasts, biting her lip to keep from whimpering, shivering and trying not to, her body wanting to arch with every touch, like a cat being petted. He kissed her nipples, first one then the other, and the sensation…unbearable pleasure…knifed through her. She drew up one knee and curled herself toward him, seeking him…her hands gathering in the silky thicket of his hair…urging him… begging him.

Answering her need, his head, and his mouth, moved lower, while his hand swept down across her belly to cup the hot, aching place between her thighs.

And something in her woke to a faint and distant cry…of warning…of dismay. *Too late.* She already felt his questing mouth, roving unrestrained, touch the numbed ridges of the scar on her abdomen.

Her hands clutched in his hair, her body spasmed inward, and panic burst from her in a single anguished cry. He lifted his head, brow furrowed. "What is it—did I hurt you?"

"No!" She could feel his hand on her belly, a heavy, aching weight. Squirming helplessly under it, she gasped, "Yes…I don't want you to—please…don't…"

Something in his eyes kindled…and burned. "You mean… this?" She could feel his fingers opening wide across her stomach, spreading warmth like healing balm. "Did you think I didn't know about it?" As penetrating as his gaze was, his voice remained gentle…even wondering. "You told me, remember?"

"About the accident. But…you haven't *seen*—"

"And you thought…*what*—I was gonna run screaming at the sight? Get turned off by it? That it?"

Too miserable even to nod, she lifted one arm to cover her eyes. Her face burned, though her body, except for the place where his hand was, burned with a cold sharper than ice.

"Celia—open your eyes. Look at me." Now his voice was harsh…commanding; she wouldn't have thought of disobeying it, though she wished she could have. Even through the ice-blue contact lenses, the hurt in his eyes stabbed at her, so fiercely she flinched. "Lady, I know you've got some strange ideas, but I'd have thought you'd have more trust in me than that."

She held her breath, unable to reply because of the sob that waited shuddering just beneath the words. *I'm sorry...*

"Celia..." His voice softened as he lowered his head to lightly brush his lips across her stomach, then grew ragged as he lifted it to say it again: "Celia..." And then, "I'm going to touch you now, love. Don't stop me. Don't think about anything..."

He lowered his head once more. She felt his mouth on her belly. His tongue stroked her with liquid warmth. And as he did that, his hand was gliding up and down her legs with a touch both sure and gentle, relaxing her, easing her until her inner shaking ceased and she opened for him without thought.

His fingers moved over her delicate, heated flesh in the most intimate exploration...slowly and with exquisite care, sometimes a feathering touch that half maddened her...sometimes deeply, rhythmically, pushing...throbbing with the beat of her own pulse.

Her breathing unraveled in a series of gasps and mindless whimpers. And just before all thought left her and her body spiraled completely and deliriously out of her control, she heard him say, in a voice as smug and thick and sweet as syrup, "From now on when you think of your scars, I want you to remember this...."

Later that day, after Max had come and gone, Roy went with Celia for a walk on the beach. It wasn't something he normally did—that particular beach had some less than pleasant associations for him—but on this occasion, for some reason, when he saw her heading out into the evening in her bare feet and jogging clothes, he felt a strange sort of yearning...a disquieting reluctance to be separated from her. A need—dangerous though it was, to be alone with her for the first time since breakfast that morning.

Roy had put in a call to Max before he'd even showered, knowing how much there was to do and only a week to do it in. It had been hard, coming straight from Celia's bed, with the scent of her still in the pores of his skin and the taste of her in his mouth, to know what to say to the man who'd been his handler, mentor and friend, just about from the first day he'd joined the DHS. Guilt made him edgy; he was sure Max was gonna take one look at him and know.

And if not him, then Celia for *sure*.

Once again, though, he'd underestimated her. Or he'd forgotten how good an actress she was. By the time Max showed up, she was fresh out of the shower and looking about nineteen, with her cheeks scrubbed and her hair tied up in a ponytail, and that incredible body—of which his intimate knowledge gave him continuous guilty and haunting images—hidden away in its customary T-shirt and jogging pants camouflage. And if she seemed a little bit more than usually excited and keyed up, Max would most likely put that down to the obvious fact that the operation was heating up—looked, in fact, to be heading for its conclusion, whatever that might be.

Which was a thought that gave Roy cold chills. For a whole lot of reasons.

In any case, after the briefing in Celia's living room, the only comment Max had made as he'd taken his leave was a stern and cryptic, "Stay focused, you two."

Which, Roy told himself, could mean just about anything.

Stay focused. Which went without saying. And was easier said than done.

It wasn't that late by the time Max left, though at that time of year it seemed the day was already almost gone. Only a few days past winter solstice, the twilight would come early. Still, the air was unusually balmy, thanks to the mild Santa Ana that had been blowing all day. The sunset promised to be spectacular. A nice evening for a walk on the beach.

Especially since, walking on the beach at sunset, it was easier to pretend things hadn't just drastically changed between them. Easier to avoid saying things that had to be said.

Though even the most difficult things couldn't be avoided forever.

"It's going to be a beautiful sunset," Celia said, as they paused to watch waves break against a jagged ridge of volcanic rock. Her voice had a kind of tightness to it that told him she'd most likely been wanting to break the silence, but hadn't known how, and had finally given up hoping he'd do it for her.

"Yeah," Roy said dryly, "it's because of all that air pollution the Santa Ana wind just blew out there."

She laughed and threw him a crooked smile. "You're in a romantic mood."

"Got a lot on my mind." He said it gently, because he'd heard vulnerability in her voice, too.

"Yeah, me too."

There was silence, then, while he struggled with the temptation to simply let it go, knowing she must be doing the same. Then a stray puff of wind carried her scent to him, and he was hit with a wave of memory so powerful he had to catch his breath. The taste, touch, and feel of her…images, the way she'd looked this morning, so vulnerable, so frightened…and flushed with desire for him, too…

He couldn't let it go. Couldn't pretend it hadn't happened when it was in his mind every waking moment. Couldn't let it happen again no matter how much he wanted to. How much they both wanted to.

"About last night—" They both began at the same time, then broke off with uneasy laughter.

To give them both time to rebuild defenses, Roy bent down, picked up a piece of driftwood and hurled it into the surf. Aiming a wry grin at the brilliant horizon, he said, "Yeah, that's definitely one of the things on my mind."

He glanced over at her, but she, too, seemed to find the western horizon intensely fascinating. Her expression seemed thoughtful. *Or guarded,* he thought.

It occurred to him then that no matter how good an actress she was, there were times he was starting to be able to read her. Times when he could tell what was real and what wasn't. He never doubted last night had been as…he tried to think of a word for it, but the only thing he could come up with was *real*. As real for her as for him. And as certain as he was of that, he was just as sure right now that she was going to use all her acting skills to try to keep him from knowing that.

She's in love with me, he thought. *Or thinks she is.*

Which made it that much harder for him. If she believed it, it would be too easy to let himself believe it, too.

And if he did believe it? Where did that leave him? Given his lifestyle, the choices he'd made? Loving someone—*really* loving—knowing they loved you back, belonging to someone, making a life together…*joining.* Being responsible for—and to—someone…

He gave his head one hard shake. No way. Not for him. It just didn't compute.

But there was last night. This morning. How in the hell was he supposed to make himself forget about that?

He took a breath, stared at a retreating wave near his feet and said gruffly, "What Max said…"

Her own quick intake of breath interrupted him, as she rushed to be the first to say it and he paused to let her. "Yeah. I know. He's right. What were we thinking?"

He looked at her and she looked back at him, the question she'd asked lying unanswered between them. But though her face…her eyes…seemed outwardly composed…even serene, with his newfound ability to read her he found the signs easily enough: the bruised, transparent look of the skin beneath her eyes…the blurred softness of her mouth. *She's in pain,* he thought. *I know. I can feel it.*

Then, he thought, who the hell am I kidding? *That's not her pain I'm feeling. It's mine. I'm hurtin', too, dammit. I guess we both are.*

He swallowed, and even *that* hurt. "Bad idea," he mumbled.

"Yeah," she said, "bad idea."

Then they simply looked at each other in helpless silence, and in the faraway calling of the gulls he heard aching denial, and the question they couldn't bring themselves to ask: *Why? Why is it so bad when it feels so good?*

"Not so much a bad idea, as bad *timing*," Roy answered it gruffly. Regret, because he couldn't give the answer they both wanted so much, made his voice harsh. "We've got no business getting…you know, emotionally involved. Not in the middle of an operation. Not with God knows how many lives at stake. Like Max said—gotta stay focused."

"I know…" She said it on an exhalation and turned her face to the setting sun, not before he caught the tiny spasm of pain that shivered through those delicate tissues around her eyes.

She reached up, and with a swift, almost violent motion, pulled away the elastic band that held her hair in its ponytail, then gave her head a shake that tumbled her hair into the wind.

Watching her do that—face lifted to the sun, and her fingers scrubbing that Santa Ana wind into her hair—made Roy think of a song from his childhood; his momma had been a big fan of Broadway musicals, so he'd been a captive audience for probably every Rodgers and Hammerstein movie ever made. Right then he was thinking of "I'm Gonna Wash That Man Right Outta My Hair."

Which was maybe why, when she turned to walk on again, he didn't take her hand, although the impulse to do so was a powerful ache inside him.

After a few minutes of watching her bare feet make prints in the wet sand, she caught a quick, lifting breath and said, "Do you think maybe…" He glanced at her, waiting for the rest, but she looked away and shook her head, smiling a little.

He was pretty sure he knew what she'd almost asked. *Do you think maybe…after this is over?*

He knew, too, why she hadn't finished it. Neither of them dared to think that far ahead.

Drawing a breath to quell the queasiness in his stomach, Roy said with false brightness, "So—what's on our agenda for Christmas?"

Celia squinted at him, shading her eyes with her hand against the setting sun. "We were going to party-hop. We've got several different invitations. But now I'm thinking—" she shrugged "—you know, what's the point?"

"Yeah…" They'd accomplished their purpose; that part of the job was done. He watched his feet for a few steps, then glanced over at her. "So…you don't much feel like partyin', is that what you're sayin'?"

"Not really," she said warily. "Do you?"

He gave a dismal huff of laughter. "Hell, no."

Fact was, he'd never felt less like partyin' in his whole life. He'd never felt less like Christmas, either. What he did feel was heavy and dull and sad. He'd never been much of one for moods—sure as hell couldn't recall ever having been depressed before. He wondered if this was what depressed felt like. Because if it was, he could kind of understand why people made such a big deal about it.

"Then let's stay home." There was a gay lilt in her voice that, though masterfully done, didn't fool him. After a little pause just for effect, she added slyly, "I'll cook dinner."

Because he knew she wanted him to, because she was trying so hard, Roy laughed, rolled his eyes, groaned and said, "Oh, my Lord, save us…" in his very best Southern drawl.

Chapter 14

"**I**'m serious," Celia said, and her eyes gleamed bravely. "I, Celia Cross, am going to cook us a traditional Christmas dinner. With all the trimmings—whatever that means."

"Tell me the truth, you poor little Hollywood princess, you," he said, grinning skeptically at her. "Do you even know what a traditional Christmas dinner is?"

She gave him an insulted look. "Of course, I do—I've read *A Christmas Carol*. I know all the songs. Aren't you supposed to cook a goose? And roast chestnuts, right? Then there's something called figgy pudding—I have no idea what that is, but I bet I could find a recipe for it online. Did you know, there's this wonderful thing called Google…"

"Turkey," he said with a sigh.

"I beg your pardon?"

"That's what we always had—turkey, roasted in the oven. Sometimes a ham, too, with pineapple rings and those little cherries stuck all over it. And candied yams with little marshmallows melted over 'em, and corn bread stuffing and mashed potatoes with giblet gravy. Collard greens…little baby peas. Cranberry sauce, and Grannie Calhoun's homemade rolls…pumpkin and apple and mince and pecan pies with real whipped cream…"

Celia stared at him in pretended horror, but the truth was, the look of hunger and yearning on his face made her skin shiver and chest warm as if she'd swallowed brandy. "Oh, my God," she breathed, coughing a little, then laughing a little…all to cover the fact that she wanted very much to cry.

She wrapped her arms around herself and drew a shuddering breath. "What's it like—for you?" she asked with desperate brightness. "Christmas, I mean. Normally."

For a moment or two he was silent, watching the shoreline and the little spindle-legged birds running in and out, chasing the re-treating waves. Then he smiled crookedly and lifted his head, and the wind feathered his hair back from his forehead so that, in spite of the silver in it, he looked impossibly young.

"Well, let's see… Most times, everybody gathers at Momma's. The ones that live some distance away, like I do, generally stay at her place, or with one of the brothers that live close by. Momma's place is a mess—wrapping paper and decorations all over the place, and the kitchen…let's just say it's a place you want to steer clear of, unless you're into choppin' up stuff and crackin' pecans and the like, because Momma'll put you to work, right quick. The ones that get there early usually have to help her with the tree-trimmin', too, and puttin' the leaves in the table, because she never gets it done on time." Celia laughed softly when he did.

"Christmas Eve, Momma goes to church. Usually some of us go with her, because it makes her happy. Christmas Day, that's when it gets crazy. Momma's got to have everybody on the prem-ises put out a stocking, which she gets up at the crack of dawn to fill, so first there's that. Then people start showin' up, every-body bringing some kind of food, plus armloads of presents, not to mention kids. There's a whole *lot* of kids. When the weath-er's nice, they can run around outdoors, but if it's not, then they're just pretty much underfoot. The menfolk wind up out on the porch no matter what the weather, just to escape the noise. The women, naturally, they gather in the kitchen and catch up on the gossip—everybody talkin' at once, it always sounds like.

"'Round about noontime, the house gets to smellin' so good, you just about want to die. Sometime in the midafternoon, things finally get sorted out and the food on the table—tables, I should say, because there's always too many to fit in the dining room, so there's card tables set up in the living room, and then the little kids, of course, they eat in the kitchen, because of the mess.

"Then in the evening, after the food's packed up and the dishes done, and the kids and the menfolk have had their naps, everybody gathers in the living room, which is jam-packed with the tree and presents and everybody, kids sitting on the floor, people overflowing out into the dining room, wherever they can find room. Momma likes everybody to sing Christmas carols, so we do that for a while, because it makes her happy. After that…well, somebody starts passing out the presents—it's mostly ours to Momma and hers to us, because the families have their own Christmas at home, too—and it's noisy, and messy and crazy, and…after a while everybody packs up their stuff and their half-asleep kids and heads for home." He shrugged, eyes on the crimson-washed horizon, the last slanting rays of the sun casting sad purple shadows across his face. "That's about it."

That's about it? As if, she thought, it was nothing much at all. And to her it seemed like a Christmas fantasy…a holiday special on TV, a painting by Currier & Ives. She tried to imagine herself part of it—*really* part of it, not playing a scene, and any minute the director was going to holler "Cut!" and she'd return to her real life. *Living it.*

An impossible fantasy, she thought. Never happen.

Celia forced a breath through the heaviness inside her. "You must miss it."

"Yeah," he said quietly, still not looking at her, "I do. It's kinda hard, you know, this year… I haven't been able to contact anybody. Let 'em know I'm okay. They're used to me being gone from time to time, but…" He looked over at her with a jerky motion, as if shaking himself loose from the thoughts in his head, and gave her a dogged smile. "What about you?"

The smile was too painful; if she went on looking at him, she was going to lose it for sure. She looked away and said lightly, "I don't really have any Christmas traditions. Can't miss what you've never had."

"Even when you were little? When your parents were alive?"

She shook her head. "Every Christmas was different. Sometimes we'd be where it was cold—lots of snow…skiing—I don't know, Switzerland, maybe? Other times we'd be someplace warm—like Hawaii, or Palm Beach. Or exciting, like Paris. Once, I remember, we were in New York City for Christmas. I remember we went to see the tree in Rockefeller Center. My dad carried me on his shoulders." She caught a quick, hurting breath and gave him a smile she knew must be as bad as his. "*That* was cool."

"What about now?"

"Now?" She shrugged. "Usually I spend the day with friends… Whoever I'm…" she smiled wryly "…*with* at the time. We either go to some restaurant, or maybe somebody's house. Exchange a few gifts. You know—the usual stuff."

The usual stuff. Yeah, right, Roy thought. Skiing in Switzerland…surfing in Hawaii…Christmas in New York…Paris…who knows where. Christmas, Hollywood-style. Fantasy stuff. Try as he would, and in spite of the role he'd been playing the past few weeks, he couldn't see himself ever being a part of all that. It wasn't him. R. J. Cassidy, maybe, but not Roy Starr. Never would be.

Even if he did decide to settle down…someday…it wasn't going to be with someone like Celia. Couldn't possibly be. So it was just as well they had a good reason to call a halt to…whatever this game was they were playing. Because that's what it was—all it could ever be—a game. A fantasy. And both he and Celia were too damn old for games.

* * *

The next day was Christmas Eve, and Celia was up at the crack of dawn. When Roy wandered into the kitchen to make the morning coffee he found her already sitting at the counter making out her list, all got up in her grocery shopping outfit—meaning sweats and T-shirt, baseball cap and sunglasses, which she thought made her unrecognizable, but which in Roy's opinion just made her look like somebody beautiful and rich trying to look like a beach bum.

After breakfast, she drove off in her SUV with the list and a credit card in her pocket, a determined set to her chin and a fanatical gleam in her eye.

After she'd gone, Roy hauled the wind chime he'd bought for her at an artisans' fair in Topanga Canyon during one of their "outings" as R. J. Cassidy and mistress out from under the bed. Actually, he supposed it was both a wind chime and a prism, consisting of a bunch of little crystal teardrops hanging from a big crystal heart, and everytime the wind blew they made tinkling sounds and scattered little tiny rainbows all over everything. He'd told Celia at the time he was buying it for his momma, but he'd intended it for her all the time. He didn't know why, but it just seemed right for her, somehow.

Since he had an idea wrapping paper was probably one of the items on Celia's shopping list, he wandered over to Doc's to see if he had any he could borrow. To his surprise, considering it wasn't noon yet, Doc was up and about, sort of, dressed in his purple silk bathrobe and looking, as folks would say where Roy came from, as if he'd been rode hard and put up wet.

After rustling up some tissue paper and a gold foil gift bag that was shaped suspiciously like a wine bottle, Doc asked if Roy wanted to join him in a breakfast glass. Roy declined the wine, but maybe because he knew it was apt to be before Celia got back from her shopping trip, he felt inclined to hang around and shoot the breeze with Doc a while.

For some reason Celia's house this morning seemed unbelievably empty without her in it. He told himself it was because it was Christmas, and he was used to a whole houseful of people and noise. He'd talked about it yesterday, which had made him think about it, and now he missed it. Simple.

So, after Doc had lit up a cigarette and poured himself his breakfast glass of wine, and the two men had settled themselves on the deck in the warm December sunshine, Roy asked Doc what he was doing for Christmas.

Doc looked at him with bleary-eyed amusement. "Having dinner with you two, actually."

"Ah." Aware he'd missed something and trying to cover for it, Roy frowned and said, "That's great. Uh...she called you?"

Doc chuckled dryly and nodded. "Last night. Quite late. But don't let it trouble you. We're fellow insomniacs, Celia and I."

Roy gave him a sideways look and decided to let the inference go by. "She tell you she's cooking dinner?"

"She did." Looking even more amused, Doc lifted his wineglass in a sort of salute. "Should be an interesting holiday."

"Yeah…" Interesting was one way of describing it, Roy thought. He stared at the gold foil bag lying on the chaise lounge beside him, then gave it a nudge. "Hope this is okay. Didn't know what to get her. I mean, she's pretty much got everything." What did you get someone who spent her Christmases in places like Paris, New York or Hawaii?

Doc blew a stream of smoke sideways as he stubbed out the cigarette. "Don't worry, she'll love it." He shot Roy a look, still half-amused, but half...something else. "She will, you know— whatever it is. Celia's not about *things*. Thought you'd have figured that out by now. Doesn't care a fig about things—tends to give them away, in fact. Be prepared—she'll give you something marvelous for Christmas, but odds are it won't be something she paid a pot of money for." He waved a hand toward the house. "I, for example, have a small fortune in Frederick Cross memorabilia in there, things she's given me over the years. Things that would make any entertainment museum green with envy."

Roy picked up the gold foil bag and stared at it as he turned it over in his hands, seeing instead all the expressions on Celia's face that had mystified him during the past few weeks…thinking about all the times he'd caught…*something* in the depths of her eyes, just before she'd turned them away from him. "What is she about?" he asked gruffly. "You tell me."

"In a word, my boy." Doc paused for a swallow of wine and another soft, ironic chuckle. "What Celia's about is feelings."

Roy waited, expecting more. When it didn't come, he scowled and said, "That's it?"

Doc shrugged. "That's it. Keep that in mind, and you'll have a fairly good idea what makes our girl tick."

Celia returned in the early afternoon with the back seat of the SUV piled full of shopping bags. Tied onto the luggage rack was a large scraggly-looking Christmas tree. When Roy untied it and stood it up and gave it a kind of thump, the way you do with a tree, it dumped roughly a third of its needles on the doorstep.

"It was the only one they had left," Celia said defensively before he could say a word. "It's a Charlie Brown tree—you know, from the *Peanuts* TV special movie? It's going to look great once we get the decorations on it. I got *lots* of decorations—everything was on sale," she added happily. "Half price—can you imagine? Come on—leave it a minute and help me unload all this stuff."

What could he do? Something about the way she was grinning, and the flush on her cheeks and the wisps of blond hair falling out from underneath the baseball cap made him want to grab her and kiss her breathless, then roll her onto the nearest friendly surface and make love to her, laughing and carefree as a couple of kids, and afterward, feeling warm and happy, hold her in his arms and talk about whatever came to mind….

"Be careful of this one," Celia said, handing over a large plastic bag. "It's—" he took the bag from her, not expecting the weight of it, and it sank to the pavement with an ominous *clunk,* as she finished, "—the turkey."

It was, too. About twenty pounds worth, by Roy's estimate, and frozen solid as a chunk of concrete.

He stared down at it, then looked at Celia. "It's frozen."

Her mind on the packages she was gathering from inside the SUV, she gave a distracted sigh. "I know, but it was the only one they had left." She paused, laden, to smile at him. "Don't worry—I'll defrost it in the microwave. I've gotten really good at defrosting."

Roy hastily grabbed up the turkey along with several other bags and followed her into the house. "I don't want to rain on your parade, darlin'," he said when he caught up with her in the kitchen, "but unless you're thinkin' about goin' after this thing with a hacksaw, it's never gonna fit in that microwave." To illustrate his point, he hoisted the bag containing the turkey onto the countertop beside the microwave oven, where it rocked back and forth with a quiet, rhythmic thumping sound.

She looked at the turkey, then at the oven. Her mouth popped open, but no sound came out. After a moment she turned to him, the watermark frown wrinkling the center of her forehead. "So…what do we do? How long does it take to thaw a turkey?"

"One this big? I'm no expert, but I seem to recall…days."

"But we haven't got 'days.'"

Dammit, he couldn't stand it. The tension in her body…the pinched look of disappointment around her eyes… Well, *hell.* He could feel his stomach knotting up and his breath coming short and shallow. He didn't know why it was so all-fired important to her, but at that moment he'd have taken a blowtorch to the damn bird if she needed him to.

He ran a hand over his face, "Uh, look, don't panic, okay? I sort of seem to remember my momma, one time, puttin' a bird in the bathtub to thaw—in water, you know? Don't know how long it takes that way, how much faster it'd be, but we can try it." The way she looked at him then made him feel as if he were eight feet tall and wearing shiny white armor. His heart did a little happy dance against his breastplate as he gave her an "aw, shucks" shrug. "What've we got to lose, right?"

She handed over the turkey without a word, those incredible dark-fringed blue eyes of hers full of trust, never leaving his face. He carried it upstairs to her bathroom—unknown territory for him, and filled with her own unique scent and all her mysterious feminine lotions and potions and secrets.

"Cold water, not hot," he cautioned her as she knelt beside the Jacuzzi tub and flipped the switch to plug up the drain.

She gave him a look but didn't question his judgment, just turned on the cold tap full blast. He knelt down beside her and carefully lowered the frozen turkey into the water. Then they waited, side by side on their knees, gazing at the fat, plastic-wrapped bird like two besotted parents bathing a baby, for the bathtub to fill.

At one point Celia looked over at Roy and smiled. He felt an alarming quiver inside his chest, and it flashed through his mind that he was incredibly *happy*. About the happiest he could ever remember being, in fact. Didn't make sense, but there it was, no getting around it: it was Christmas Eve, he was down on his knees on a hard tile floor in a soap opera star's bathroom, baby-sitting a giant naked frozen bird, with a dangerous mission and the fate of millions of innocent people hanging over his head, and he, Roy Starr, was *happy*.

If that meant what he thought it did, what in the hell was he going to do?

"What did I tell you?" Celia stood back to survey the tree with what was admittedly a not very critical eye. *My first completely do-it-yourself Christmas tree.* She drew a breath and let it out carefully, so as not to disturb the big untidy lump of emotion that had been gathering in her throat all day. It had grown harder, as the evening advanced toward midnight and the dawning of Christmas Day, to keep it buried there, just beneath her surface veneer of holiday cheer. "Looks great, doesn't it?"

"Great?" Roy threw her a lopsided grin. "You just better hope nobody comes within twenty feet of it with anything resembling an ignition source. This thing's so dry it'd go up like a torch."

"Nobody's going to. Doc's not allowed to smoke in here. And we'll take it down right after Christmas—or anyway, before we leave to board Abby's boat, so we have nothing to worry about." She turned from the tree to rummage through the piles of boxes, bags and packaging materials that were scattered over every surface of the living room. "One last thing. Now where did I…okay, here it is." She pulled a box from the chaos, plucked away an errant strand of tinsel and for a moment just held it and gazed at the cellophane display window.

Mystifyingly, the knot in her throat seemed to grow even bigger, and her vision wavered. A memory floated into her mind: a towering Christmas tree, glittering with a thousand lights… snowflakes falling onto her upturned face as she laughed…

She drew a quick, sharp breath. "This goes on the top. Will you do it? I can't reach." She thrust the box at Roy. "It's not what I wanted," she said as he took it from her with a curious glance, then began to open it. "I wanted a star, like the one on the tree in Rockefeller Center, but this was all they had left." Because she felt shivery, she folded her arms on her chest.

"Nothin' wrong with this," Roy said as he drew the angel from its box.

She watched him separate it from its wrappings and give its wings a couple of straightening tugs, then step close to the tree, reach up and carefully place the stiff white folds of the angel's gown over the spindly twig at the tip-top of the tree. She watched him adjust it when it wanted to flop to one side, until he had it standing just…right.

She watched him with stinging eyes and aching throat, with a heaviness in her chest and a shivering in her skin…and it came to her as she watched him that what she wanted…desperately…was to be *held*.

"That should do it…" He'd turned from the tree to look at her. "Hey, what's wrong?"

"Nothing." She managed to produce a brilliant smile, gazing up at the angel, not at him. She didn't dare to look at him. "It looks pretty good, doesn't it?"

"Looks great." They stood together, studying the angel. She could feel him, feel the heat from his body, though they weren't touching.

Hold me, she thought. *Please hold me. It's Christmas.*

"Actually," he said, glancing over at her, "she looks kinda familiar."

She risked a glance back and found his smile had gone crooked. Bravely holding on to her own, she said, "Familiar?"

"Yeah—I thought I saw an angel, you know—when I was…out of it. Thought I musta died, but…turned out the angel was you."

"Oh." To her dismay it came out not as a word, but like a cry, high and breathless…a complete betrayal. Unable to withdraw it, she could only stare at him, standing utterly still, knowing her need for him was naked in her eyes…in her face.

He stood still, too, looking back at her, Christmas tree lights gleaming in his silver-touched hair and his smile fading slowly, like a mirage.

Hold me…please.

And then—she hadn't spoken it aloud, she was sure she hadn't— all at once he was. She hadn't moved, she was sure she hadn't, but somehow his arms were around her, and the fabric of his shirt was soft against her cheek, her face nested in the warm curve of his neck, the scent of his aftershave in her nostrils and her heartbeat knocking against his in crazy, out-of-sync rhythms. Her arms went around his waist, and his arms held her close…*closer*…and she felt warm and protected and completely safe.

They stood like that for…she didn't know how long. She felt his cheek resting on her head…just resting there, demanding nothing, giving only comfort, and she thought in mild surprise,

He's kind. Nothing like a pirate, really. A kind man. I wonder if he even knows how kind he is.

And then she thought, *I love him. Oh God, I wonder if he knows. He must know. No wonder he's being kind...*

Shaking, now, with chagrined laughter, she turned her face upward and murmured his name, meaning to release him gently from that obligation. But his answer was *her* name, spoken gruffly, raggedly as he lowered his mouth to meet hers.

Though even the kiss was gentle, at first... His lips touched hers sweetly, tentatively, with a first-kiss kind of innocence, as if neither of them had done such a thing before. But, like a spark dropped in dry tinder, it flared in the next instant into something neither tentative nor innocent.

She felt the blaze of heat inside him and drew a gasping breath, as if the shock wave of that heat had just hit her full in the face. Her mouth opened and he drove the kiss deep—straight to her heart, it seemed—while his hand cradled her head and he rocked her with the slow, sensuous motion of his tongue.

Celia, you're an idiot, she thought, before she gave up all thought. *This definitely isn't kindness!*

He pulled back, panting as if caught up in a terrible struggle, and she clutched his shirt in desperate handfuls.

"Please," she whispered, as shameless tears began to sting her eyes. "I know we said we wouldn't do this. But...just this once...just for tonight? It's *Christmas*."

She felt a brief sharp quiver go through his taut body, like the twanging of a bowstring. "Just for tonight," he growled. And in a whisper, just before his mouth found hers again: "Merry Christmas..."

His hands were gentle, pulling the bottom edges of her T-shirt from the waistband of her jogging pants, whispering over her skin to brush the sides of her breasts, holding her lightly as she leaned eagerly into his kiss. Her own hands were less gentle, too full of need to be gentle, as they dove beneath the waistband of his jeans, raked hungrily over his firm, warm flesh, fumbled with the buttons on his shirt. He drew her to him and as her nipples brushed...her soft breasts pillowed, then pressed against the hardness of him...the shock of it was so sweet, so exquisite, she whimpered and tears pooled in the corners of her closed eyelids.

She hardly felt it when he laid her down, sweeping and nudging aside boxes and wrappings to make a place for them on the couch. She barely noticed when he glided his hand over her taut, quivering belly, the pins-and-needles prickle of her scar when he touched it only one more small sensation in the dizzy, overwhelming circus of her senses. She didn't open her eyes when he laid his warm and supple length along her body, when his strong hands skimmed down her back and under her to lift her to him...when she felt the weight and press and sweet-hot sting of his body's entry into hers. She didn't open them even when he took her face between his big, warm hands and gently kissed her tear-damp lashes and whispered her name again...and again against her fevered skin.

She kept them closed because she didn't want to see his face...flawed and human and real. *Roy's face.* She kept them closed and filled her mind instead with the fantasy of him...the pirate, the billionaire, the secret agent...because that, after all, was all this was. *Fantasy.*

Like Christmas. Like TV movies and daytime dramas. Like all the other times she'd fallen in love with an image, a vision, a make-believe hero, her leading man. *Fantasy.*

This would end, she knew that, from all the times it had ended for her before. But while it lasted, it would be sweet and beautiful and, in its own way, real.

For her, because she was Celia Cross, it would have to be enough.

Chapter 15

Looking back on it, Roy couldn't recall a Christmas Day so full of emotional ups and downs. A real roller-coaster ride.

First, there was waking up and finding himself where he had no business being, with Celia in his bed, all tangled up in warm and sinful ways, with an unforgivable smile of well-being on his face and a faint queasiness of guilt lying ignored in his belly.

After that, his first thought—okay, maybe his second or third thought, probably because, after the murmured and kiss-interrupted good mornings and Merry Christmases, it was the first coherent word out of Celia's mouth—was *the turkey!*

They found it sitting in an inch or so of chilly water, maybe half-thawed.

"Don't panic," he ordered, after she gave him a stricken look, as if he'd let her down, somehow, and it was all his fault. "We've still got time."

He filled up the tub with fresh water and left her to shower and dress while he went downstairs to make coffee and start clearing away the debris in the living room. After he'd got most of the wrappings mashed into a plastic trash bag and the empty boxes stowed in the garage, and about half a bushel of pine needles swept up off the rug, he went and got the gold foil bag with the wind chime in it and put it under the tree.

He was standing there looking at it, thinking how lonely it seemed there all by itself after the mountains of presents he was used to seeing, when Celia came down the stairs. She was wearing red, some sort of bathrobe—that was all he knew to call it, though he imagined it probably had some other, fancier name—and her hair was tied up on top of her head with a red ribbon, with a sprig of some kind of greenery—holly?—stuck in it. She was carrying a box in her hands, wrapped in Christmas paper and ribbon, and she sort of checked when she saw him, as if she'd been hoping to sneak it under the tree when he wasn't looking.

Caught, she came to him instead, pink and excited as a child. She handed over the present, then stood on her tiptoes to kiss his cheek and whisper, "Merry Christmas," in his ear.

Touched and gravel-voiced, he said, "Hold on, I've got one for you, too," and swooped down and snatched up the gold bag.

Holding it in her hands, she stared at him, as stunned and open-mouthed as if Santa Claus himself had presented her with the gift. With a smile of pure delight and a breathy, "For *me?*" she clasped the gold foil bag to her chest. Then: "Open yours first," she ordered, clamping her teeth down on her lower lip to contain her excitement.

Quailing a little, recalling what he'd been told about her gift-giving tendencies, Roy shook his head. "Uh-uh—you first."

She didn't argue with him. Holding her breath, teeth clamped down on her lower lip, she opened the bag and peeked inside. The cry she gave when she pulled out the crystal heart about made *his* heart jump into his throat. She held it up, trailing all those little teardrops, then slowly turned, enraptured, as countless tiny rainbows splashed across the walls and the room filled with tinkling crystalline music. When she rotated back to him, he saw her eyes were bright with tears.

"How did you know?" she said in a wondering, catching voice. "When I was really little, I used to think sunbeams—you know, those little specs of dust in sunlight?—were fairies. This reminds me so much of that. Oh, I *love* it! Thank you!"

She sat on the couch and laid the wind chime carefully across the cushions beside her, then clapped her hands gleefully. "Now you."

Filled more with trepidation than anticipation, Roy tackled the gift-wrapped box. He untied the ribbon, peeled off the paper, took off the lid…and with hammering heart, lifted what was inside up from its nest of tissue paper. Then, for a moment, he simply sat and stared at it.

"It's your boat," Celia said, her voice sounding small, vulnerable and far away. "Is it…all right? Do you like it?"

"It's…" He couldn't look at her, so he went on gazing at the boat…the perfect miniature replica, obviously hand-made, of his boat, *The Gulf Starr.*

It had hit him so hard, so suddenly. He felt like he was holding his other life…his *real* life…in his hands. Except somehow, at some point, *this* life—the one with Celia—had become his reality. Now, *that* life—his boat, his charter business, his buddy and partner, Scott, even his family—all that seemed like fantasy to him, far-off and unreal. When had that happened?

He shot a blind look in her direction. "How did you…"

"I got a picture off your Web site. There's this old guy in Topanga Canyon—he makes all sorts of models, sailboats, mostly—I have one my parents gave me when I was small—but I gave him the picture and asked him if he'd make me one like it, and…" Hunched and breathless, she gave a shrug. "I hope he got it right."

He swiped a hand across his nose, then cleared his throat. "It's perfect. It's amazing. Thank you."

But he couldn't look at her, or take his eyes off the boat. He was still sitting there staring at it when he heard her get up and go in the kitchen to start Christmas dinner.

* * *

On the subject of which—Christmas dinner—Roy figured the less said, the better.

He tried his best to help her, he really did. But she kept chasing him off, evidently hell-bent on fixing him that Christmas dinner with all the trimmings he'd told her about and without making him peel, cut up, crack or chop stuff the way his momma did. The turkey went into the oven around noontime—Roy didn't know whether it ever had gotten defrosted all the way, and decided he didn't want to ask. By midafternoon the good smell of roasting turkey was beginning to override the odor of things burning, and Roy's hopes rose a little.

Doc wandered in around that time, bringing with him two bottles of wine and some red roses for Celia. She stopped what she was doing in the kitchen long enough to give him his gift, which turned out to be a box made out of ebony wood, carved and inlaid with gold, lapis and mother-of-pearl.

"It's the one from Mother and Daddy's movie *Pandora's Box*," she told him. "They had two of them made—I think the other one's in the Smithsonian."

Doc gave Roy a "What did I tell you?" wink.

After that, he and Doc retired to the den and the big-screen TV, and by the time Celia called them to the table, they'd both drunk enough wine that lumpy mashed potatoes, burned gravy, underdone turkey and various unidentifiable dishes probably wouldn't even register on their tastebuds.

Not that any of that mattered. As far as Roy was concerned, the vision he was going to carry with him for the rest of his life was Celia across the table from him, bathed in candlelight, flushed and sweaty in a food-spattered apron, with wisps of golden hair escaping from her red ribbon and a smudge of flour on her cheek, looking exhausted, radiant, *happy*…and more beautiful than he'd ever seen her look before. That image made everything else fade to insignificance.

That…and wondering how it was that the absolute worst

Christmas dinner he'd ever eaten in his life could also be the very best Christmas present he'd ever received.

The day after Christmas, Celia went for her morning jog, as usual. When she came back, she went straight to Roy's room to ask him for help hanging her new wind chime. Surely, she reasoned, a man raised in the rural South who captained his own fishing boat must possess the necessary masculine skills for such a task. And, somewhere in the house, she was sure, there must be at least some basic, rudimentary tools.

His bedroom door was pulled almost shut but not latched, the way it had been the night she'd almost gone to his bed. Remembering that night and all that had happened between them since, as she raised her hand to knock her heart had already quickened, though she sternly told it not to. *I can't think of him that way. Not now. Not until this is over.*

Her mind slammed shut on the tag-along question: *And then?*

With her hand uplifted, she took a steadying breath—and froze. Roy was talking on the phone. His voice was pitched low but sounded tense and angry, and she could hear him clearly when he spoke following a prolonged listening silence.

"I told you I drew the line at that. I told you I didn't want her anywhere near that boat. That was the deal." There was more silence. Then: "I know she has. I'm not arguing that. But she's still a civilian, and she's got no business being...*dammit,* Max, I don't want her in the way when this goes down...yeah, well...uh-huh..." His voice dropped to a furious mutter.

Celia realized she was still standing with her hand raised to knock on the door and that her whole body felt stiff and cold—literally frozen. From the other side of the door came a sharp explosive obscenity, then the thump of angry footsteps. And still she couldn't make herself move. Her face and neck muscles hurt.

The door swung open and Roy stood there, eyes black as midnight, hair wild, mouth set in a hard and angry line—once more a pirate, now poised on the gunwales of a ship, about to swoop down on the hapless crew.

Uttering the same sharp obscenity, this time softly and under his breath, he gripped the doorframe, making of himself a barrier against her. "I suppose you heard."

Every instinct she had wanted to cut and run. Every nerve, sinew and muscle in her body cramped in protest against the iron will that held her there to face him down in icy, trembling anger. "You asked Max to take me off the…the…" *Job? Mission? Operation?* That she didn't know what to call it, thus proving Roy's point—that she was, in fact, a civilian—infuriated her. "How *could* you?"

"Celia—"

"After I *told* you how I felt about it." *After I told you things…feelings I've never told anyone else before.* "You *knew* how much it meant to me."

"Dammit, that's got nothing—aw, *hell*. Look, if it's any consolation to you, *Max said no.…*"

The last part was shouted to her retreating back, as she finally found the strength to turn and walk stiffly and swiftly away and leave him there.

In the living room, she paused, breathing hard, and pivoting back and forth in indecision. *Upstairs to take a shower? Or back to the beach to run off some of this excess adrenaline?* Dammit, she didn't need exercise. She needed someone to talk to.

Out she went, across the deck, down her stairs and up Doc's. She was pounding with her fist on his sliding glass door before it occurred to her that, by Doc's reckoning, it was barely the crack of dawn. Too late to retreat; she could see him making his way toward her through the murky twilight inside the house like someone swimming through molasses.

He squinted blearily at her through the salt-crusted glass, then swept the door open and croaked, "Celia—oh, good God, don't tell me you've found another body."

"No—though I just may create one shortly." She pushed past him into the house.

"So, it's only angry she is, then," Doc muttered in a fake Irish accent as he pulled the door shut behind her. He shuffled over to a table covered with clutter, picked up a pack of cigarettes, shook one out, stuck it between his lips and lit it with an unsteady hand.

Celia paused in her pacing to glare at him. "Let me have one of those."

"I will do no such thing!" He looked at her as if she'd suggested he give crack to a kindergarten class. He inhaled deeply, sighed through a stream of smoke and, thus fortified, coughed and said, "Now, love…tell your Uncle Doc—what has our Roy done to put your back so far up?"

Celia told him. And was more than a little miffed when he merely shook his head and chuckled.

"And you haven't a clue, have you, why he would do such a thing?"

"No. I haven't. I don't understand. I thought I'd done a brilliant job, quite frankly. I thought—" *I thought we were good together.*

Doc shook his head and gave another sigh. "God, it is true what they say, isn't it? Love truly *is* blind."

Once again she paused to glare at him. "What do you mean?"

"My dear, the man is in love with you." She was shaking her head. "Yes, I'm afraid he is—completely besotted. He's only trying to do what strong men do when they love someone a great deal—he's trying to protect you, of course."

Celia whirled away from him and covered her face with her hands, desperate to hide her face from him because she'd somehow lost the ability to control it. Lost the ability to keep all the powerful and confusing things she was feeling from showing there. *Joy. Something overwhelming that felt like grief.*

He loved her. And she loved him. What a lovely fantasy it was…a beautiful story! It would make a terrific movie, wouldn't it? It would have a happy ending, of course—a "happily ever after" ending, as all good love stories do.

Except this wasn't a story, it was life. *Her* life. And nobody knew better than she did that things didn't always work out that way in life. This…whatever it was she and Roy were involved in together…would end. He'd go on to his next undercover operation, she'd go on to her next role, and no doubt fall in love with her next leading man.

But I don't want this to end. I don't want to move on! I want this…just this. I want him…Roy…forever.

She wanted very much to cry, but since she wouldn't do that—she'd die, first—she whirled back to Doc and said snappishly, "That's no excuse. All the more reason he should understand how I feel."

"Yes, he should," Doc said softly, "but as I said, love is blind." He smiled his ironic smile and lit another cigarette.

All things considered, during the next few days Roy decided it was just as well Celia wasn't speaking to him. Solved the problem of his wanting to take her to bed every time he got near her—or anyway, it prevented the *taking*. Definitely not the wanting.

At least, it made it a whole lot easier to keep his mind on what lay ahead of them.

And a whole lot harder to sleep at night.

During the day, he spent most of his time with Max, going over diagrams and blueprints, familiarizing himself with every inch of the yacht *Bibi Lilith*. Committing photos of known terrorists to memory, in case any of them turned up as members of the *Bibi Lilith*'s crew. Learning how to operate the various instruments they'd be taking on board the yacht with them.

"Speaking of which," he said to Max during one of their joint briefings, "how *are* we getting this stuff on board? I can't imagine they'll be searching everybody's luggage, but I'd hate to stake my life on it."

"Won't have to. We're having some special luggage put together for you—complete with secret compartments, well shielded…should stand up to all but the most sophisticated sweepers. That'll hold the laptop and other big stuff."

"Weapons?" Max looked at him. He could feel Celia's eyes

on him, too, and he knew she'd be remembering what he'd said to her. *We don't kill people.* He rubbed absently at his healing ribs and felt a chill go through him. "Just in case."

"Sure," Max said. "By all means. Okay. So, the small stuff, things you're gonna want to keep with you at all times—bugs, GPS tracking devices, chemical, biological and radiation sensors, things like that—they'll go in this." He held up a woman's leather handbag. "Celia, I'm assuming this'll be your responsibility…" He held it out to her with a smile.

Roy shook his head and held up a hand. "Uh-uh. She doesn't carry a pocketbook."

"I do now," Celia said as she took the purse, giving him an offended look before she began to inspect it inside and out with avid curiosity.

And a funny thing happened to Roy as he watched her, listening with somber attention to Max as he explained the various hidden compartments and bells and whistles in the custom-made bag. He felt most of his anger, and at least part of his fear, evaporate, and a more than grudging admiration for her come to take its place.

She means it, he thought. *This isn't a game to her, any more than it is to me. And she's good at it. Damn good.*

He was still afraid for her safety, of course. He was always gonna be that. Terrified. But at least he didn't have to be afraid of having her as his backup. Fact was, she was good. She'd be okay.

He just hoped he'd be able to say the same for himself.

Evidently, Max had the same doubts, because after the briefing, when Roy walked with him out to his car, he dragged off his sunglasses, gave him a piercing look and asked, with a little motion of his head back toward the house, "How you doing? You gonna be okay with this?"

Roy dug his hands into his pockets and dragged in a breath. "Oh, sure. Hell, yes."

Not looking much reassured by that response, Max said, "She's gonna be fine, you know. She'll do okay."

"I know." But he couldn't keep some of the worry he felt from showing; Max knew him too well.

With his car door open, Max hesitated, squinting against the lowering sun. "Look—all you need to do is find us something—you know that. Anything that'll give us a reason to move in. That's all. No unnecessary chances, nobody needs to get hurt."

"I know."

Max nodded, got into his car and slammed the door. Roy stood where he was, hands in his pockets, shoulders hunched, and watched him drive away.

Celia was on the upper starboard deck of the yacht *Bibi Lilith*, stretched out on one of the Balinese sunning beds—though "sunning" was hardly the right term, given that she was wearing slacks and a sweater, with a scarf wrapped around her head, a cashmere jacket buttoned to her chin and a lap robe covering her bottom half, from waist to ankles, against a biting December wind.

She was pretending to read, although a considerable amount of time had passed since she'd last turned a page of the book in her lap. Behind the cover of sunglasses, her eyes kept darting nervously toward the boat's stern. It was from there that Roy, according to their arrangement, was to come to join her, once Abby had finished showing him around the "backstairs" part of the yacht.

He and Celia had both been given a grand tour of the yacht's guest amenities shortly after boarding, of course. Then, using the pretext Celia had already planted for him—that he was planning to buy such a yacht for himself—Roy had asked to see the engine and control rooms, kitchens, crew's quarters, storage holds and the like. Abby had seemed delighted to show off his new toy. Even better, several of the other guests—all male—had asked to be included, as well, which nicely diverted any undue attention from Roy.

There was absolutely no reason for Celia to feel nervous and apprehensive because he was fifteen minutes late joining her. But she did. Tension skated over her skin, crawled through her scalp and gripped the back of her neck like teeth. She told herself he was in no danger—how could he be? It was broad daylight, they were on board the sleek and beautiful yacht *Bibi Lilith,* cruising toward Mexico on a sparkling sunny sea, and on board with them were fifty or so other people, nearly all of them world-famous for one reason or another. What could happen to them here?

But she felt the danger. Felt it all around her.

I'm afraid. I wish I weren't, but I am.

It was her damned imagination, she supposed. It insisted on showing her not a sunny December afternoon, but the dead of a moonless night and the yacht ploughing purposefully through a dark and lonely sea. And on board, one man, unarmed and all but naked, fighting to stay alive against impossible odds….

A powerful sense of awe and pride and love thumped her in the chest, and she thought: *I must not let him see I'm afraid. I can't…won't let him down…*

It was then, with those thoughts in her mind and awash in the attendant devastating emotions, that she looked up and saw their cause coming toward her…slim and elegant in blazer and slacks…sun glancing like sparks off the silver in his hair. Her breathing grew shallow and quick with desire…as it always did when she saw him dressed up in beautifully cut clothes. She thought: *He should have been a movie star. In Hollywood's golden age…my parents' time. He'd have been a natural.*

Oh, how she wished she could let him know how she felt. Wished she could let her desire for him show in her eyes…say flattering, seductive things to him with a smile on her lips and the promise of sex in her voice. If Doc was right about him being in love with her… Oh, but how could he be, when he only looked at her with coldness? With such an impassive expression and un-readable eyes?

And even if Doc *was* right…this wasn't the time or the place for it—for love or sex. Or promises.

"You're late," she said and casually turned a page.

"Some of the other members of the tour had questions," Roy

said. *Still mad,* he thought as he gazed down at tiny twin images of himself reflected in her sunglasses. *Just as well.*

And if it was just as well, why was it beginning to irritate him so much? What had he done that was so awful? Just tried to keep her out of a situation that could get her killed, was all, and this was the thanks he got? *Well, hell.*

A white-jacketed waiter came by, offering glasses of champagne on a tray. Roy shook his head, and Celia waved the waiter away with her most charming smile.

Roy waited until both the waiter and Celia's smile had gone, then said in an icy undertone, "You think you could try a little harder to pretend to be nice to me? I thought we're supposed to be this...loving couple. What the hell are these people gonna think?"

"They'll think we're having a lovers' quarrel, of course," Celia said without looking up from the book she was reading. "I suspect next week's tabloids will be full of the news of our impending breakup." She flashed the twin mirrors at him again. "The timing should be just about perfect, shouldn't it? Assuming this cruise goes the way we hope."

She closed the book, keeping her finger between the pages to mark her place. "Speaking of which...did you turn up anything?"

He let out a breath as he sat on the couch...or bed, or chaise longue, or whatever...next to hers. "Nothing. Far as I can tell with these things, the damn boat's clean."

He leaned over and opened the handbag that was sitting on the deck beside her bed, carefully unfastened the strap that had held the palm-size instrument in place above his wrist, hidden under the sleeve of his jacket, and returned it to its concealed compartment in the handbag. Then, for the benefit of anyone who might have been watching, he took out a tube of sunscreen.

"What's that for?" Celia asked, watching warily as he squeezed a small dollop of cream into the palm of his hand.

"Just in case we're being monitored. Take off your glasses." He waited, silent and dispassionate, for her to comply with his order, then dipped the tip of his index finger into the cream, leaned over and, ignoring her startled flinch, smeared it in a line down the ridge of her nose.

What the hell. He could deliver the cold shoulder as well as the next guy, if that was the way she wanted it.

Only trouble was, there wasn't any part of him, including his shoulders, feeling cold just then. His heart was an engine bent on pumping heat into the farthest reaches of his body; sweat beaded on his forehead, pooled under his arms and trickled down his ribs. His skin felt feverish, as if *he* were the one who'd been too long in the sun.

He kept his eyes focused on what his fingers were doing and tried not to let himself think about what *her* eyes might be telling him. He couldn't think of anything that could possibly be written in those incredible baby blues of hers that wasn't going to make him feel worse than he already did.

Slowly, he wiped the slippery sunscreen all over her nose, then smeared some onto her cheeks…smoothed out the watermark frown in the middle of her forehead…massaged what was left in his palm over her chin and throat. And while he was doing all that he was remembering the way he'd felt when she'd done almost the same thing to him, that day in her kitchen with Max looking on. He wondered whether she felt the same way he had then—angry, helpless, half-suffocated with arousal.

He could only hope so, dammit. Serve her right.

"Don't get burned," he said as he rose, rubbing his hands together.

She calmly lifted her sunglasses, slipped them on and opened her book. "I don't intend to," she replied softly.

Had to have the last word, did she? After the briefest of hesitations, he decided to let her have it.

As the day wore on and the *Bibi Lilith* churned steadily toward Mexican waters, Roy resigned himself to a return to the role he'd grown accustomed to playing during the past weeks: that of R. J. Cassidy, Canadian billionaire and consort of Hollywood royal, Celia Cross. Whether in the lounge, the dining salon, or gathered around the hot tub on the yacht's stern deck, his place was on the fringes of the crowd, where he lounged casually, sipped Mexican beer and watched Celia charm and entrance…keeping his own expression indulgent, perhaps just a bit sardonic.

Always when he did that, while he watched her and marveled at her beauty, her charm, her grace, he felt a sadness come over him and heaviness settle around his heart. How perfectly she fits that world, he thought. How easily she blends into it, how comfortable she is with all those wealthy, talented, famous and beautiful people.

And why not? They were her people. It was her world; she was born into it, had never known any other. She belonged to it.

He didn't. And never would. It was that simple.

At that moment, as if she'd felt his eyes, or maybe the intensity of his thoughts, in the midst of a laughing conversation, Celia happened to look up and lock eyes with him across the crowded, noisy lounge. As her smile slowly faded, Roy lifted his beer bottle toward her in an ironic little salute.

He would have drained the rest of it then, but his throat ached too much to swallow.

Chapter 16

The next time Celia looked up, Roy had gone.

Disappointment slammed into her, and for the first time she understood what it meant to feel "crushed." She felt flat and deflated, like a beach ball run over by a truck, all the air and bounce and joy gone out of her.

As soon as she reasonably could, she excused herself and, carrying her champagne glass and remembering at the last moment to take her new and unfamiliar handbag with her, slipped out of the lounge and went to look for him. Music followed her as she went from deck to deck, all brightly lit and party-festive, and she raised her glass and smiled at the people she met, standing, strolling or sitting in pairs or small groups, murmuring and laughing together.

She'd never felt so isolated...so alienated. So lonely.

Roy, where are you? I miss you. I need you.

Unable to bear the thought of rejoining the noisy crowd in the lounge, she decided to go back to her stateroom. Then her stomach clenched, and she thought, *No, not mine. Ours.* And how, she wondered, are we going to share a room tonight? *A bed?*

Pain caught at her throat and shuddered through her chest. Pain and regret and longing. *This could have been so different... so wonderful. It should be wonderful, shouldn't it? Love? Why does it have to hurt so much?*

She inserted her card key into its slot and opened the door—and checked, cold and tingling, as if she'd touched live electric wires. Roy was standing in front of the dressing table, struggling with his ascot. His eyes, blue and glaring, glanced off the mirror and collided with hers.

For a long moment, neither of them said a word. Then Celia was floating toward him, unaware of heartbeat or breath, the carpeted floor unfelt beneath her feet.

"Oh, for heaven's sake. Here, let me help you with that," she said. Her voice sounded sharp and bright in her ears, like the tinkle of wind chimes. She lifted her hands to the front of his shirt.

He made a sharp hissing sound, and his hands closed around her wrists. He stared down at her and his eyes seemed to smolder behind the blue contacts. "Don't need your help."

She stared back, unflinching. "Yes, you do."

It was a standoff that could only end one way, given the circumstances. The moment and the tension stretched until they couldn't anymore, until, with a harsh sound that was either anguish or anger—perhaps both—Roy lowered his mouth to hers.

There was violence and frustration, hunger and despair in the way he kissed her...in the way he crushed her to him...in the way she kissed him back—her hands clawed at his shoulders and clung to the back of his neck. Mouths opened...devoured. Teeth nipped and clashed...tongues dueled rather than mated. Breaths came in pants and whimpers, a primitive combat in which no words were spoken.

Undressing was a battle fought without regard for collateral damage, either to flesh or fabric. Fingers raked, buttons popped, seams ripped and in the end, the tattered remnants of the evening's costumes lay strewn across the field of conflict like so many casualties of war. And even when they were both naked, the struggle continued. Hair was gathered and clutched in greedy handfuls. Teeth bruised and nails raked in ways that would leave marks for days to come but in those frantic moments went unnoticed.

He pushed her or she pulled him—impossible to tell—so that she tumbled backward onto the bed and he followed her down, and they wound up as one, already intertwined and straining to somehow get closer to each other yet, to crawl inside each other's skin, if that were only possible. Panting, she made a place for him and her legs wrapped around him. She cried out as he plunged into her; her body arched and opened to him, urging him deeper…deeper. Clutching his shoulders with all her strength, she lifted herself to meet his mouth with a mindless, demanding hunger.

She had no awareness, no thought in her mind; she existed in a black void of need, of instinct that predated thought and overrode awareness. Wars could have raged all around her and she wouldn't have cared; she cared only for the war within.

And war it was, although she couldn't have defined the causes or combatants if her life had depended on it. She knew only that it was violent and devastating and terrible; when the explosions had ceased, she lay for a time, as survivors of wars do, in dazed stillness, before realization finally hit her and she covered her face with her hands and wept.

As she sobbed, she felt Roy's arms folding warmly and gently around her, a hand stroking her hair, lips brushing wordless whispers across her forehead. She turned her face into the warm darkness below his ear and, shuddering, curled herself toward his hard, sinewy body, wishing she could somehow melt into it and simply…vanish. Never in her life had she felt so vulnerable…so utterly and completely exposed.

After a while, when her shaking and sobbing had quieted somewhat, she felt the chest beneath her cheek exhale a long, slow breath. "What a pair we are, eh?" Roy said in R. J. Cassidy's hoarse whisper. She felt his chin bump her temple as he shook his head, then heard, in pure Georgian: "When it comes to you, I haven't got a lick o' willpower, and that's the God's honest truth."

She lay quiet as understanding of what he'd just done came inside her like a warm and lovely fragrance. He'd known about her vulnerability. He'd known and had purposefully taken all responsibility for what had just happened onto himself. The sweetness of that was almost as devastating, in its way, as the violence that had come before, and new tears pooled warmly beneath her lashes as she said softly, "What am I gonna do with you?"

His lips touched her temple, along with a chuckle that was barely audible. Even so, she heard the pain in it and lifted her head to find his mouth with a soft kiss of acknowledgment and gratitude. Then he folded her once more into his arms and simply held her, stroking her…petting her, neither of them saying anything.

After a long while, though no words had passed between them, she turned her face up to his and he found her mouth and began to kiss her again, gently this time. Then, slowly, he deepened the kiss, and made love to her for a long, leisurely time, every touch unhurried and tender, sensual and erotic, until every cell in her body felt excited, exhilarated and alive, thankful that the darkness and devastation that had gone before had faded to an already half-forgotten memory.

Celia woke, disoriented, in semidarkness. The muscular chest that had been her pillow was heaving beneath her cheek, the once slow and steady heartbeat now quick and hard.

"What izzit?" she murmured sleepily as Roy eased her to one side and sat up.

"That's what I'm tryin' to figure out. Can't you feel that? We've stopped." He was on his feet, rummaging through the articles of clothing on the floor. He picked up something unidentifiable, stared at it, then tossed it aside and reached for the small overnighter that, still unpacked, held most of his clothes.

She watched him for a moment, propped on one elbow, then threw back the covers. Already half-dressed, he paused to throw her a look. "Where you going? Stay put. I'm just gonna go see what's goin' on."

Celia rose to her feet, folded her arms on her chest and gave him a long, hard look. He looked back at her, opened his mouth, then closed it again. His shoulders sagged in surrender. "Okay, fine. Just…hurry it up."

He dragged a hand through his hair and turned, preparing, Celia could tell, to pace with typical masculine impatience. She opened the closet—she'd unpacked *her* clothes—took out a dressing gown, slipped it on and was beside him, still belting it around her waist, before he'd completed a single circuit of the room. He said, *"Huh,"* and opened the door to allow her to pre-cede him, which she did, regal as a duchess, after giving him a serene smile she hoped would hide the fact that she felt almost light-headed with excitement.

"It's got to be on the other side," Roy whispered as they hur-ried down the dimly lit passageway toward the main salon. From there, through the bank of windows that curved around the bow, they should be able to see most of the way along both sides of the yacht, though not, probably, all the way to the stern.

The salon was deserted, though, as elsewhere on the boat, lights had been left burning. Heart hammering, Celia paused to let Roy take the lead. She was close behind him as he stepped up to the windows, staying to one side behind the bank of open draperies.

"It's a ship," he whispered, shifting a little so she could look past him. "We've docked with it…they're off-loading…some-thing. Looks like we're taking on cargo of some kind…"

Celia didn't reply. Even with Roy's warmth beside her she felt chilled as she watched the oceangoing ship's huge dark shape ris-ing and falling slowly only a few yards away, blotting out the stars…the flickering lights and shifting shadows going about their silent business.

"May I help you?"

The voice was quiet, courteous. Nevertheless, it sent a shock wave of adrenaline coursing through Celia's body, and, she suspected, judging from the way the hand holding tightly to hers jerked at the sound, through Roy's, too. Turning, she saw a man she recognized—one of Abby's bodyguards—dressed now in casual slacks and a dark pullover. The salon's warm, golden lamplight gleamed in his black hair.

"Uh, yeah, you could—" Roy began in a rasping voice, but Celia squeezed his hand hard, and her own voice, breathless and a little frightened, washed over his.

"Oh—yes! Please tell us—what's going on? We—I couldn't sleep, and I felt that we weren't moving, and I thought…what's happened? Is something wrong?"

The man's teeth gleamed in the light. "Oh, no…nothing is wrong, I assure you. Far from it. We are simply taking on a few additional supplies. Nothing for you to be concerned about."

"Supplies? What kind of supplies?" This, thankfully, was from a newcomer, as some of the other passengers had begun to wander into the salon, looking sleepy, disgruntled and curious, and not nearly as glamorous as they had the night before.

The spokesman glanced around at them, then gave a little bow and a shrug of resignation. "Ah. Prince Abdul will be disappointed. He had hoped to make this a big surprise. But…I suppose I must explain—perhaps you would keep it a secret from the other guests?"

"Oh, of course," Celia breathed. Beside her, Roy's body seemed to hum with tension.

The spokesman looked around, leaned forward and lowered his quiet but strangely staccato voice still further. "We have just taken on a very large selection of fireworks."

"Fireworks!" someone exclaimed.

"Yes, yes—fireworks. For the New Year's celebration. As I am sure you are aware, such fireworks are illegal in California.

Which is why we are at the moment in the waters of Mexico." The man's teeth gleamed as he smiled.

"Ooh, how exciting—I can't wait for tonight," Celia gushed, giving a theatrical shiver. She threw a glance in Roy's direction. "We won't tell a soul—will we, darling?" She put out her hand and lightly touched the spokesman's sleeve—and felt Roy give a violent jerk behind her. Breathless, her heart hammering, she ploughed on. "Thank you so much—I think I'll be able to sleep now, don't you, R.J.? 'Night, everyone…" Towing Roy behind her, she waltzed out of the salon.

Once in the passageway, she had to fight the urge to break into a run. The shakes hit her about the time they reached their stateroom door, and she handed the key card over to Roy and let him fit it into the slot.

"Fireworks!" she exploded softly as the door closed behind them. She turned to him, out of breath. "Do you believe him?"

He didn't answer immediately, bending over instead to snatch up the jacket he'd been wearing the night before and toss it onto a chair. When he rounded on her, his smile was painful to see. "Right now, 'bout the only thing I know for sure is that's the guy who shot me, and every time I get that close to him I get a powerful urge to kill him with my bare hands." He dragged a hand over his hair and the awful smile disappeared.

He began to pace, a thoughtful frown creasing his brow. "Fireworks? Could be… Most likely is, in fact. Question is whether that's *all* that's in those crates. And *that* is something I'm gonna have to find out." He threw her a distracted glance. "Where's your pocketbook? I'm gonna need those sensors. I'm figuring, once people start getting up, maybe while they're serving breakfast… There's enough confusion, comin' and goin', I should be able to slip down— *What?*" He halted, having just noticed she was shaking her head.

"No," Celia said, folding her arms on her chest as she faced him, bracing for the objections she knew were coming. "Not you—it'll be a lot less suspicious if I do it. I'm a woman—you *know* how we women are about getting lost." She paused to roll her eyes. *As if.* "Besides—I'm an actress. I can play the ditzy blonde in my sleep. I know how to take readings with those sensors—Max showed us both, remember? I'm the logical one to go. If they find me wandering around down in the hold, they'll more than likely pat me on the head and send me on my way. You—all I can say is, remember what happened to you the last time you were caught doing that? I don't even want—"

"You're right."

"—to think what they might…what did you say?"

He took a deep breath. "I said, you're right. God…I can't believe I'm saying this, but…like you said, you've got the best chance to do it without raising suspicions. So…you're the one who should go."

Shock, love and happiness rushed through her like a gale-force wind, literally taking her breath away. Her voice was faint and airless as she asked, "You mean it?" He nodded, eyes steady and grave. She gazed at him for a long time, wondering whether anything in her life had ever meant as much to her as the fact that he trusted her to do this thing…this thing her life and his and millions more might depend on. Then she stood on her tiptoes and pressed her soft mouth against his grim one.

"Thank you," she whispered.

Roy was fairly certain nothing he'd ever done in his life—not counting surviving being shot and thrown into a dark ocean, of course—had been as hard as the hour he spent later that morning pacing in the confines of his stateroom, waiting for Celia to return from her mission.

He'd never been much of a worrier before. He'd been accused of being happy-go-lucky, but that didn't seem quite the right way to describe his outlook on life, given the nature of his job and the inherent dangers and life-and-death choices involved. He'd just never wasted much time calculating odds and worrying about outcomes, put it that way. So maybe *que sera, sera* would have summed it up better. What happened, happened. When his number came up, he figured there wasn't much he could do about it, no sense worrying about it ahead of time, right? Until it did, he intended to keep on making the best decisions he could, given the information available to him at the time, which was all anybody could do.

But now, here he was, all of a sudden pacing up and down in a box-size room, imagining every possible complication and every bad outcome in the book, and feeling helpless and frustrated because none of it was under his control. *Worrying.*

It was what came of working with a partner, he supposed. Worse, a partner he cared about—*a lot.* He wasn't used to it. He'd always worked solo before. Kind of a lone wolf. Responsible to and for nobody but himself—and the mission, of course. That was the way he liked it.

He wished he could have made himself believe it was Celia's civilian status, the fact that she was inexperienced and mostly untrained that had him so edgy. But he wasn't in the habit of telling himself lies. He'd seen her in action enough these past few weeks that he'd come to have a healthy respect for her abilities. The truth was he knew he'd have worried about her even if she'd had the complete course of training all federal agents went through at Quantico.

And where in the hell had *that* notion come from?

He wasn't going to have a chance to ponder the answer to that question, though, because right about then he heard the scrape of a key card in the lock. His heart jumped into his throat as Celia came through the door, looking calm and cool and absolutely normal, except for a little bit of pink in her cheeks and a sparkle in her eyes. As if she were having *fun,* he thought. *The time of her life, dammit.*

"Well?" he growled, making an impatient "give it here" gesture toward the pocketbook she had looped over her shoulder.

"It went just like I told you it would," she said as she slipped it off and handed it over, a triumphant smile creeping across her face. "They patted me on my head and sent me on my way. But I got close enough to the storage compartments, I think." She bit down on her lower lip to contain the smile. "I told them I wanted to see the kitchen. Because I'm such an enthusiastic cook, you see." Laughter spurted from her and she stifled it with her hand, as if she were ashamed of it.

The specially prepared suitcase lay on the bed. Working quickly and in silence, Roy opened the secret compartment and powered up the instruments hidden inside. He opened the handbag and carefully removed the sensitive monitoring devices from their hiding place. Silent, now, too, Celia watched over his shoulder as he bent over the suitcase, working his way through procedures practiced a hundred times. Nothing moved except his hands and the pulsing of his heart sending blood through his veins. He didn't breathe…didn't think Celia did, either. Sweat beaded his forehead and trickled down his ribs. Tension sang in his ears, a high-pitched, nerve-wracking whine, like mosquitoes.

A few minutes later, he straightened and rubbed at his eyes with the fingers and thumb of one hand…maybe trying to erase the images that had been recorded there. He felt cold…cold all over. And sick. And scared.

He uttered a single syllable, blunt and sibilant and crude.

He flicked a glance at Celia and saw she'd gone deathly pale. He wondered if he looked the same.

"Radiation?" she whispered.

He nodded. Cleared his throat. Forced words through the block of ice in his chest. "Could be just radioactive materials, I guess, but given all the other factors—the chatter…the timing—I'm thinking it's a dirty bomb. They brought it in with the fireworks, and they mean to set it off the same way. At midnight tonight. Happy New Year."

"Dear God."

"Yeah. Depending on how big it is, it's almost a certainty they'd wipe out this boat and everybody on it, and probably a good bit of Catalina along with it. That by itself would make a helluva splash, but that's not what they're after. It's the radiation cloud. With the onshore breeze…"

"I can't believe Abby would do this," Celia said, hugging herself, her voice tight and furious. "He *loves*—L.A.—Hollywood—the whole lifestyle. These people are his *friends*."

"He might not know about it," Roy said grimly. "Maybe he's just the sacrificial lamb. From what I hear, he's not exactly a role model in the radical fundamentalist world. Maybe they mean to take him out—punish him for his decadent lifestyle—at the same time they make their big statement. Who knows?"

While he talked, he took a laptop computer out of the suitcase and carried it to the small writing desk that was part of the room's amenities. He'd recovered his equilibrium, a little. The shock was fading. His brain was beginning to function again. "Whatever they mean to do," he went on as he connected the computer to the yacht's power and fired it up, "our job is to keep 'em from doing it. Now we've got the evidence we need…just have to get this to…" He broke off, stared at the computer screen, tapped some keys, waited a moment, then uttered the same succinct and violent syllable.

"What?" Celia was beside him in an instant, breathless with dread.

He stared at her, paralyzing horror and helplessness creeping around his heart. "They've pulled the plug."

"I don't understand."

"We're in the middle of the flamin' ocean. Our only means of communication is through the yacht's satellite hookup…right? Guess they're not taking any chances on lettin' word of their little party get out, because they've cut it off. Shut it down. We're dark," he said grimly, beginning to pace again. "Incommunicado. Short of puttin' a message in a bottle and pitchin' it overboard, we've got no way to call in the cavalry."

"A message in a bottle?" Celia was gazing past him, tapping her lips with a rose-tinted fingernail. "That could work."

He stared at her openmouthed for several seconds, then snapped, "Come on, this is no joke."

"No, wait—" She clutched his arm. "I'm serious. We've got the GPS thingies, right? I bet they're small enough to fit into a champagne bottle. All we'd have to do is put in a note, cork it, and—"

"And these guys, who are paranoid enough they've shut down their own satellite communications, are just gonna stand there and let us throw it overboard?"

"They will if we stage it right," Celia said, teeth pressing on her lower lip to subdue her smile. "Leave that to me. I told you, didn't I, I've always wanted to write scripts?"

Powerful emotions filled his chest as he gazed at her, scowling—as if that would hide them. "I don't know whether you're a lunatic or a genius, you know that?" he said huskily.

"Neither one, actually," she said, pink and breathless with something that looked impossibly like happiness. "It's just…I told you—I have this imagination…"

An hour or so later, Celia and Roy joined the sunbathers drinking champagne and lounging around the spa on the stern deck. She carried a corked champagne bottle in one hand and a half-filled glass in the other; while in no way sloppy or obnoxious about it, as she greeted friends and acquaintances among the gathering it was obvious she'd already had quite a bit to drink.

When she reached the farthest aft part of the deck, she turned and propped her elbows on the railing, leaned back and shook her head so that the wind caught her hair. She lifted the glass and drained it, then held it out to R. J. Cassidy, who was, as always, patient and attentive at her side.

"Darlin'," she cried gaily, waggling the champagne bottle at him, "I seem to be empty. Pour me some more, will you please?"

In a raspy voice that nevertheless carried to the nearest interested parties, R.J. responded, "I…think you've had about enough, don't you? Here—why don't you let me have that…"

As he held out his hand to take the bottle from her, Celia opened her mouth in outrage and gasped, "I have not. No—don't you dare—" She snatched the bottle away from him and leaned backward over the railing, holding it high over her head, as if trying to keep it out of his reach.

Many interested eyes watched as his fingers closed around her wrist. Several people, including Celia, gasped as the bottle slipped from her hand and fell into the foaming wake. She whirled and stared at the bottle, now retreating rapidly behind them, then drew herself up like a duchess and said icily, "Well. I hope you're satisfied."

No one but R. J. Cassidy would have seen the glint of excitement and triumph in her eyes.

"We don't even know if they got the damn message," Roy growled later that evening, as Celia tugged and fussed with the collar and lapels of his white dinner jacket. His shirt collar was open. He'd told her if this was to be his last night on earth, he was damned if he was going out wearing a bow tie.

"We don't know they didn't... *There*—that's better." She stood back and regarded him with her head tilted to one side. "You look nice," she said softly, her chest too full of emotion for breath.

"Thanks. So do you."

She knew she did, of course, in the ruby-red gown she'd had copied from an old Rita Hayworth film and with her hair loose on her shoulders and diamonds and garnets at her ears and throat. But his eyes, glittering blue in the contact lenses, weren't looking at her. Instead, they scanned the horizon, where the lights of Avalon Harbor twinkled festively in the distance. Looking, she thought, for some sign of the Special Forces teams...the cavalry that even she knew might never come.

They were on one of the portside decks, a private spot they'd managed to find since neither of them felt much like joining the party that was in full swing in the lounge. And staying in their stateroom had felt too much like being trapped...

Roy flicked a restless glance at her. "I can think of a million things that could have gone wrong."

"Sounds like I'm not the only one with an imagination," Celia said lightly, and pain reminded her to take a breath.

"Celia—listen to me." He caught her wrists and pulled them against his chest, demanding her attention. As if his voice wouldn't have been enough…it sounded like tearing cloth. "If they don't show up soon, I'm going in." She was already shaking her head violently, whispering wordless rejections, but he held her still and overrode them. "Yes…I have to. You know I do. I can't let this happen."

"There're so many of them." Her voice broke. "You're only one man. How can you possibly—"

"I'll find a way. They'll have the fireworks on the stern deck. Stands to reason the bomb'll be there, too. All I have to do is figure out which one it is—shouldn't be too hard—get to it and heave it overboard. Piece o'cake."

"It's not. It's suicide. Roy—" She hadn't meant to cry. He'd be upset if she cried. And he was—she could feel him quivering with held-in emotions when he pulled her against him, murmuring soothing things in a broken voice.

She pushed him away and dashed a hand across her cheeks. "Roy, you can't die now. You can't. I love you. And I know what you're thinking, but this is *not* my imagination. I *love* you, dammit. I think I was meant to love you. I think…" She paused, touched her nose, swallowed and continued, speaking rapidly so he couldn't interrupt her and she could get it all said before it was too late.

"Remember when I told you I always wondered why, when the accident happened, I was allowed to live? I thought there must be some reason…some purpose. I thought first it was because I was supposed to find you and save your life. Then I thought it was because of this mission—because only I could get you on Abby's boat. But…I think it's bigger than that. And way more simple." She was crying in earnest, now, harder than she'd ever cried in her life before, all the anguish and pain of a lifetime saved up for this. "I think," she sobbed, "I was simply meant to *live*. To live the best life I can. To find someone to love, and to be *happy*. Well, I found that someone, dammit. I found you. Literally. I found *you*. I love *you*. If you die, it will all have been for nothing—the accident, her dying. Because how am I supposed to live my life and be happy if you're not here?"

"Ah, God. Celia." He kissed her tear-drenched mouth, then clasped her tightly to him. "Love…my love…it doesn't matter. It doesn't. I have no choice. You know that."

Suddenly, there in the warm protective circle of his arms, she felt a great stillness come over her. A kind of peace. And she nodded and whispered brokenly, "I know."

They were standing like that, holding each other, when it occurred to both of them at about the same moment that the thumping sound they were hearing wasn't heartbeats. Drawing apart and lifting their eyes heavenward, they watched the Apache helicopters swoop in out of the darkness. Only when the dark shapes began dropping into the water and swarming up over the sides of the yacht *Bibi Lilith* did Roy finally pull Celia to the deck and cover her body with his.

Early in the evening of the first day of the new year, Celia went for a walk on the beach. She was alone; Roy had stayed behind with Max, the first of what would undoubtedly be many briefings. She'd turned back toward home, because the sun had slipped behind an angry-looking bank of clouds and a wind had sprung up, carrying the promise of storms. And she looked ahead and there he was, coming toward her along the water's edge.

She checked, her heart lifting frighteningly under her ribs. As she went to meet him she felt it thumping madly in her chest and her belly quivering with nervous anticipation, like the worst case of stagefright she'd ever known. She'd said so much, there on the boat when she'd thought she would lose him forever. And he'd said so little. There'd been no time, before all hell had broken loose, or since then, either.

Wordlessly now, he took her hand, turned, and they walked on together.

"Did Max leave?" she asked, her voice showing no signs of the turmoil inside.

He nodded. "Lotta loose ends to tie up, but he wanted us out of the way when it all hits the media. They'll find us anyway, I'm sure. You, anyway. You don't mind, do you?"

She shook her head. Watching her bare feet in the sand, she said, "What about Abby?"

"He's claiming he didn't know anything. His crew's been…detained—they'll be sent to Gitmo for interrogation. The yacht's been impounded—CSI's going over it with a fine-tooth comb as we speak. The public's not being told what the nature of the threat was. Which is probably for the best."

"So," Celia said after drawing a careful breath and lifting her face to the wind, "I guess we done good, huh?"

She heard his exhalation…a soft chuckle. "Yeah, we did."

"We made a pretty good team, didn't we?" She felt him look over at her. *Oh please,* she thought. *Please don't make me beg for this.* But he didn't say anything, so she went on. "Our cover didn't even get blown." She paused, but he still didn't say anything. "Just think what we could accomplish if we—"

That did it. "Don't even *think* about it," he growled. "I mean it. There's no way in hell I'm doing this again."

Fear and hope were warring furiously inside her, but somehow she managed to keep her voice light. "But why? When we work so well together."

"I can't, that's all. It's just too damn hard, workin' with someone I—"

"Someone you…" she paused and turned, forcing him to stop, too, as she squeezed his hand, gathered all her courage and said it for him: "*Love?*"

He gripped hers tightly while he glared at her. Then he shifted that fierce gaze to the horizon, drew a ragged breath and on its exhalation said, "Yeah. That."

She went light-headed with happiness; her knees all but buckled. "Well," Celia said, after a long, sweet moment, "I already talked to Max about it. He thinks it's a great idea. He's going to run it by the director."

"You *what?*" His voice soared upward an octave. "Are you *nuts?* There's no way you're doing this. No way. Out of the question."

Up ahead on his deck, she could see Doc standing, watching them. She lifted her arm and gave him a smile and a wave as she said sweetly, "Well…it's a good thing it's not up to you, isn't it? It's up to me—and Max, of course. And the director. Naturally. I'd have to go to Quantico for training. And it doesn't look like I'll be playing Nurse Suzanne any longer.

"You know…" she paused to give him a radiant smile, her heart quivering with delight and overwhelming love at the look on his face "…there really isn't that much difference between acting and undercover work. That scene on the deck, when we dropped the bottle overboard—you were quite good, you know. I think maybe you're a natural."

Dazed, Roy could only stare at her. It never occurred to him in that moment that the woman smiling up at him was Celia Cross, TV star, Hollywood princess and one of the most beautiful women he'd ever seen, or even that she'd saved his life once. The face he saw before him now and would forever after was the one imprinted on the part of him referred to, poetically if erroneously, as the heart. That part of him—his heart—didn't register homely or beautiful, young or old. His heart knew only one thing: This was the face of the woman he loved more than life itself.

And if that's true, the reasoning part of him asked, how can I even consider a life that doesn't include her in it?

How that might work he didn't quite know, but he couldn't see the white picket fence working for either one of them.

"Did you know," he said in a wondering tone, "that you're an amazing woman?"

"Really?" She lifted her face to his. "I thought I was exasperatin'."

"That, too," he murmured as he kissed her.

Whatever a future with Celia might hold, he knew for sure it wasn't ever going to be dull.

* * * * *

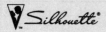

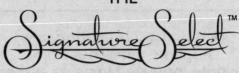
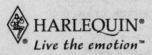

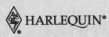

If you enjoyed what you just read,
then we've got an offer you can't resist!

Take 2 bestselling
love stories FREE!

Plus get a FREE surprise gift!

SPOTLIGHT

"Debra Webb's fast-paced thriller will make you shiver in passion and fear...."—*Romantic Times*

Dying To Play

Debra Webb

When FBI agent Trace Callahan arrives in Atlanta to investigate a baffling series of multiple homicides, deputy chief of detectives Elaine Jentzen isn't prepared for the immediate attraction between them. And as they hunt to find the killer known as the Gamekeeper, it seems that Trace is singled out as his next victim...unless Elaine can stop the Gamekeeper before it's too late.

Available January 2005.

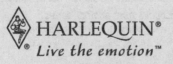

HARLEQUIN®
Live the emotion™

Exclusive Bonus Features:
Author Interview
Sneak Preview...
and more!

INTIMATE MOMENTS™

and award-winning author
VIRGINIA KANTRA
present
STOLEN MEMORY
(IM #1347)

The next book in her exciting miniseries

TROUBLE IN EDEN

**Small town, big secrets—
and hearts on the line!**

Dedicated cop Laura Baker is used to having all the answers. But when reclusive inventor Simon Ford wakes up on the floor of his lab with a case of amnesia and a missing fortune in rubies, all Laura has are questions. As her investigation heats up, so does her attraction to the aloof millionaire. Can she find the missing jewels…before she loses her heart?

*Available February 2005
at your favorite retail outlet.*

And look for the other electrifying titles in the TROUBLE IN EDEN miniseries available from Silhouette Intimate Moments:
**All a Man Can Do (IM #1180), All a Man Can Ask (IM #1197),
All a Man Can Be (IM #1215)**

COMING NEXT MONTH